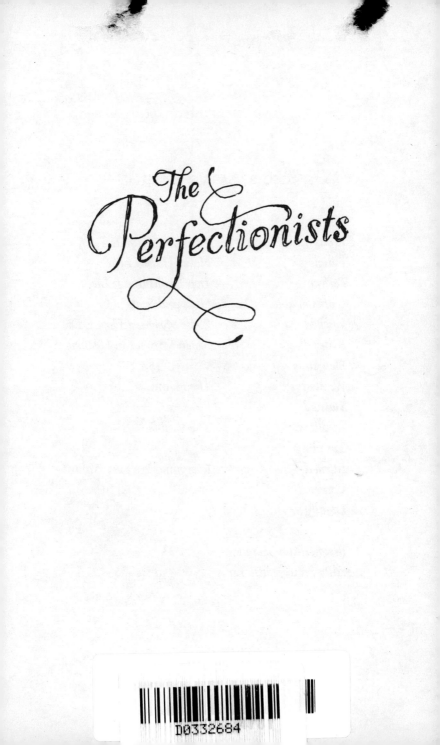

The Perfectionists

ALSO BY SARA SHEPARD

Pretty Little Liars	*The Lying Game*
Flawless	*Never Have I Ever*
Perfect	*Two Truths and a Lie*
Unbelievable	*Hide and Seek*
Wicked	*Cross My Heart, Hope to Die*
Killer	*Seven Minutes in Heaven*
Heartless	
Wanted	*The Heiresses*
Twisted	
Ruthless	*The Visibles*
Stunning	
Burned	*Everything We Ever Wanted*
Crushed	
Deadly	

Pretty Little Secrets
Ali's Pretty Little Lies

SARA SHEPARD

HOT
KEY
BOOKS

First published in Great Britain in 2014 by Hot Key Books
Northburgh House, 10 Northburgh Street, London EC1V 0AT

alloy**entertainment**

A CIP catalogue record for this book is available from the British Library.

ISBN: 978-1-4714-0434-4

1

This book is typeset in 10.5 Berling LT Std using Atomik ePublisher

Printed and bound by Clays Ltd, St Ives Plc

In the midst of life, we are in death.

– AGATHA CHRISTIE, *And Then There Were None*

PROLOGUE

In many ways, Beacon Heights, Washington, looks like any affluent suburb: porch swings creak gently in the evening breeze, the lawns are green and well kept, and all the neighbors know one another. But this satellite of Seattle is anything but average. In Beacon, it's not enough to be good; you have to be the *best*.

With perfection comes pressure. Students here are some of the best in the country, and sometimes, they have to let off a little steam. What five girls don't know, though, is that steam can scald just as badly as an open flame.

And someone's about to get burned.

On Friday night, just as the sun was setting, cars began to pull up to Nolan Hotchkiss's huge, faux-Italian villa on a peninsula overlooking Lake Washington. The house had wrought iron gates, a circular driveway with a marble fountain, multiple balconies, and a three-tiered, crystal chandelier visible through the front two-story window. All the lights were on, loud bass thumped from inside, a cheer rose up from the backyard. Kids with liquor spirited from their parents' cabinets or bottles of wine shoved into their purses sauntered up to the front steps and walked right inside. No need to ring the bell – Mr. and Mrs. Hotchkiss weren't home.

Too bad. They were missing the biggest party of the year.

Caitlin Martell-Lewis, dressed in her best pair of straight-leg jeans, a green polo that brought out the amber flecks in her eyes, and TOMS houndstooth sneakers, climbed out of an Escalade with her boyfriend, Josh Friday, and his soccer friends Asher Collins and Timothy Burgess. Josh, whose breath already smelled yeasty from the beer he'd drunk at the pre-game party, shaded his brown eyes and gaped at the mansion. 'This place is freaking sick.'

Ursula Winters, who desperately wanted to be Timothy's girlfriend – she was also Caitlin's biggest soccer rival – stepped out of the backseat and adjusted her oversize, dolman-sleeve shirt. 'The kid has it all.'

'Except a soul,' Caitlin muttered, limping up the lawn on her still-sore-from-a-soccer-injury ankle. Silence fell over the group as they stepped inside the grand foyer, with its checkerboard floor and a sweeping double staircase. Josh cast her a sideways glance. 'What? I was kidding,' Caitlin said with a laugh.

Because if you spoke out against Nolan – if you so much as boycotted his party – you'd be off the Beacon Heights High A-list. But Nolan had as many enemies as friends, and Caitlin hated him most of all. Her heart pounded, thinking about the secret thing she was about to do. She wondered whether the others were there yet.

* * *

The den was filled with candles and fat red cushions. Julie Redding held court in the middle of the room. Her auburn hair hung straight and shiny down her back. She wore a strapless Kate Spade dress and bone-colored high heels that showed off her long, lithe legs. One after another, classmates walked up to her and complimented her outfit, her white teeth, her amazing jewelry, that funny thing she'd said in English the other day. It was par for the course, naturally – everyone *always* loved Julie. She was the most popular girl in school.

Then Ashley Ferguson, a junior who'd just dyed her hair the same auburn shade as Julie's, stopped and gave a reverent smile. 'You look amazing,' she gushed, same as the others.

'Thank you,' Julie said modestly.

'Where'd you get the dress?' Ashley asked.

Julie's friend Nyssa Frankel inserted herself between the two. 'Why, Ashley?' she snapped. 'Are you going to buy the exact same one?'

Julie laughed as Nyssa and Natalie Houma, Julie's other best friend, high-fived. Ashley set her jaw and stomped away. Julie bit her lip, wondering if she'd been too mean. There was only one person she wanted to be mean to deliberately tonight. And that was Nolan.

Meanwhile, Ava Jalali stood with her boyfriend, Alex Cohen, in the Hotchkisses' reclaimed oak and marble kitchen, nibbling on a carrot stick. She eyed a tower of cupcakes next to the veggie tray longingly. 'Remind me why I decided to do a cleanse again?'

'Because you're insane?' Alex raised his eyebrows mischievously.

Ava gave him an *uh-duh* look and pushed her smooth, straight, perfect dark hair out of her eyes. She was the type of girl who hated even looking at cross sections of the human body in biology class; she couldn't stand the idea that *she* was that ugly and messy inside.

Alex swiped his thumb on the icing and brought his hand toward Ava's face. 'Yummy . . .'

Ava drew back. 'Get that away!' But then she giggled. Alex had moved here in ninth grade. He wasn't as popular or as rich as some of the other guys here, but he always made her laugh. But then the sight of someone in the doorway wiped the smile off her face. Nolan Hotchkiss, the party's host, stared at her with an almost territorial grin.

He deserves what he's going to get, she thought darkly.

In the backyard – which had high, swooping arcades that connected one patio to another; huge potted plants; and a long slate walkway that practically ended in the water – Mackenzie Wright rolled up her jeans, removed her toe rings, and plunked her feet into the infinity-edge pool. A lot of people were swimming, including her best friend, Claire Coldwell, and Claire's boyfriend, Blake Strustek.

Blake spun Claire around and laced his fingers through hers. 'Hey, watch the digits,' Claire warned. 'They're my ticket to Juilliard.'

Blake glanced at Mac and rolled his eyes. Mac looked away, almost as if she didn't like Blake at all.

Or perhaps because she liked him *too* much.

Then the patio door opened, and Nolan Hotchkiss, the man

6

of the hour, sauntered onto the lawn with a smug, *I'm-the-lord-of-this-party* look on his face. He strolled to two boys and bumped fists. After a beat, they glanced Mac's way and started whispering.

Mac sucked in her stomach, feeling their gazes canvass her snub nose, her glasses with their dark hipster frames, and her large, chunky knit scarf. She knew what they were talking about. Her hatred for Nolan flared up all over again.

Beep.

Her phone, which sat next to her on the tiled ground, lit up. Mac glanced at the text from her new friend Caitlin Martell-Lewis.

It's time.

Julie and Ava received the same missives. Like robots, they all stood, excused themselves, and walked to the rendezvous point. Empty cups lay on the ground in the hall. There was a cupcake smashed on the kitchen wall, and the den smelled distinctly of pot. The girls convened by the stairs and exchanged long, nervous glances.

Caitlin cleared her throat. 'So.'

Ava pursed her full lips and glanced at her reflection in the oversize mirror. Caitlin rolled back her shoulders and felt for something in her purse. It rattled slightly. Mac checked her own bag to make sure the camera she'd swiped from her mom's desk was still inside.

Then Julie's gaze fixed on a figure hovering in the doorway. It was Parker Duvall, her best friend in the world. She'd *come*, just as Julie hoped she would. As usual, Parker wore a short denim skirt, black lace tights, and an oversize black sweatshirt.

When she saw Julie, she poked her face out from the hood, a wide grin spreading across her cheeks and illuminating her scars. Julie tried not to gasp, but it was so rare that Parker allowed anyone to see her face. Parker rushed up to the girls, pulling the hoodie around her face once more.

All five of them glanced around to see if anyone was watching. 'I can't believe we're doing this,' Mackenzie admitted.

Caitlin's eyebrows made a V. 'You're not backing out, are you?'

Mac shook her head quickly. 'Of course not.'

'Good.' Caitlin glanced at the others. 'Are we all still in?'

Parker nodded. After a moment, Julie said yes, too. And Ava, who was touching up her lip gloss, gave a single, decisive nod.

Their gazes turned to Nolan as he wove through the living room. He greeted kids heartily. Slapped friends on the back. Shot a winning smile to a girl who looked like a freshman, and the girl's eyes widened with shock. Whispered something to a different girl, and her face fell just as quickly.

That was the kind of power Nolan Hotchkiss had over people. He was *the* most popular guy at school – handsome, athletic, charming, the head of every committee and club he joined. His family was the wealthiest, too – you couldn't go a mile without seeing the name *Hotchkiss* on one of the new developments popping up or turn a page in the newspaper without seeing Nolan's state senator mother cutting a ribbon at a new bakery, day care facility, community park, or library. More than that, there was something about him that basically . . . *hypnotized* you. One look, one suggestion, one command, one snarky remark, one blow-off, one public embarrassment, and you were under his thumb for life. Nolan controlled Beacon, whether you liked it or not. But what's that saying? 'Absolute power corrupts absolutely.' And for all the people who worshipped Nolan, there were those couldn't stand him, too. Who wanted him . . . *gone*, in fact.

The girls looked at one another and smiled. 'All right, then,' Ava said, stepping out into the crowd, toward Nolan. 'Let's do this.'

Like any good party, the bash at the Hotchkiss house lingered into the wee hours of the morning. Leave it to Nolan to have an in with the cops, because no one raided the place for booze or even told them to cut the noise. Shortly after midnight, some party pics were posted online: two girls kissing in the powder room; the school's biggest prude doing a body shot off the star running back's chest; one of the stoners grinning sloppily, holding several cupcakes aloft; and the party's host passed out on a Lovesac beanbag upstairs with something Sharpied on his face. Partying hard was Nolan's specialty, after all.

Revelers passed out on the outdoor couch, on the hammock that hung between two big birch trees at the back of the property, and in zigzag shapes on the floor. For several hours, the house was still, the cupcake icing slowly hardening, a tipped-over bottle of wine pooling in the sink, a raccoon digging through some of the trash bags that had been left out in the backyard. Not everyone awoke when the boy screamed. Not even when that same someone – a junior named Miro – ran down the stairs and screamed what had happened to the 911 dispatcher did all the kids stir.

9

It was only when the ambulances screeched into the driveway, sirens blaring, lights flashing, walkie-talkies crackling, did all eyes open. The first thing everyone saw were EMT workers in their reflective jackets busting inside. Miro pointed them to the upper floor. There were boots on the stairs, and then . . . those same EMT people carrying someone back down. Someone who had Sharpie marker on his face. Someone who was limp and gray.

The EMT worker spoke into his radio. 'We have an eighteen-year-old male DOA.'

Was that Nolan? everyone would whisper in horror as they staggered out of the house, horrifically hungover. *And . . . DOA? Dead on arrival?*

By Saturday afternoon, the news was everywhere. The Hotchkiss parents returned from their business meeting in Los Angeles that evening to do damage control, but it was too late – the whole town knew that Nolan Hotchkiss had dropped dead at his party, probably from too much fun.

Darker rumors posited that perhaps he'd *meant* to do it. Beacon was notoriously hard on its offspring, after all, and maybe even golden boy Nolan Hotchkiss had felt the heat.

When Julie woke up Saturday morning and heard the news, her throat closed. Ava picked up the phone three times before talking herself down. Mac stared into space for a long, long time, then burst into hot, quiet tears. And Caitlin, who'd wanted Nolan dead for so long, couldn't help but feel sorry for his family, even though he had destroyed hers. And Parker? She went to the dock and stared at the water, her face hidden under

10

her hoodie. Her head pounded with an oncoming migraine.

They called one another and spoke in heated whispers. They felt terrible, but they were smart girls. Logical girls. Nolan Hotchkiss was gone; the dictator of Beacon Heights High was no more. That meant no more tears. No more bullying. No more living in fear that he'd expose everyone's awful secrets – somehow, he'd known so many. And anyway, not a single person had seen them go upstairs with Nolan that night – they'd made sure of it. No one would ever connect them to him.

The problem, though, was that someone had seen. Someone knew what they'd done that night, and so much more.

And someone was going to make them pay.

FIVE DAYS LATER

CHAPTER ONE

On a sunny Thursday morning, Parker Duvall fought her way through the crowded halls of Beacon Heights High, a school that handed out MacBooks like they were, well, apples, and boasted the highest average SAT scores in all of Washington State. Overhead, a maroon-and-white banner read CONGRATULATIONS, BEACON HIGH! VOTED BEST HIGH SCHOOL IN THE PACIFIC NORTHWEST FOR THE FIFTH YEAR IN A ROW BY US NEWS & WORLD REPORT! GO SWORDFISH!

Get over yourselves, Parker wanted to shout – though she didn't, because that would seem crazy, even for her. She looked around the corridor. A gaggle of girls in their tennis skirts congregated around a locker mirror, diligently applying lip gloss to their already impeccably made-up faces. A few feet away, a guy in a button-down shirt handed out flyers for the student government elections, his smile blindingly white. Two girls came out of the auditorium and brushed past Parker, one of them saying, 'I really hope you get the part if I don't. You're just *so* talented!'

Parker rolled her eyes. *Don't you realize none of this matters?* Everyone was striving for something or clawing their way to the top . . . and for what? A better chance at the perfect scholarship?

A better opportunity to score that perfect internship? Perfect, perfect, perfect, brag, brag, brag. Of course, Parker used to be like that. Not long ago, Parker had been popular, smart, and driven. She had a zillion friends on Facebook and Instagram. She made up complicated polls that everyone participated in, and if she showed up at a party, she *made* the event. She was invited to everything, asked to be part of every club. Guys would escort her to class and beg her for dates.

But then *It* happened, and the Parker who rose from the ashes a year ago wore the same hoodie every day to hide the scars that marred her once beautiful face. She never went to parties. She hadn't looked at Facebook in months, couldn't imagine dating, had no interest in clubs. Not a single soul glanced at her as she stomped down the hall. If she *did* get a look, it was one of apprehension and caution. *Don't talk to her. She's damaged. She's what could happen if you aren't perfect.*

She was about to walk into the film studies classroom when someone caught her arm. 'Parker. Did you forget?'

Her best – and only – friend, Julie Redding, stood behind her. She looked perfectly polished in a crisp white blouse, her reddish-brown hair gleaming and her eyes round with worry.

'Forget what?' Parker grumbled, pulling her hoodie tighter over her face.

'The assembly today. It's mandatory.'

Parker stared at her friend. Like she cared about mandatory *anything.*

'Come on.' Julie led her down the hall, and Parker reluctantly followed. 'So where have you been, anyway?' Julie whispered. 'I've been texting you for two days. Were you sick?'

16

Parker scoffed. 'Sick of life.' She'd bagged class for most of this week. She simply hadn't felt like going. What she'd *done* with her time, she couldn't quite recall – her short-term memory was a tricky thing these days. 'It's contagious, so you might want to keep your distance.'

Julie wrinkled her nose. 'And were you smoking again? You smell disgusting.'

Parker rolled her eyes. Her friend was in what Parker had always called Mama Bear Mode, fierce and protective. Parker had to keep remembering that it was endearing, especially because no one else cared whether she lived or died. Julie was the only remaining vestige of Parker's old life, and now that Parker was shrouded in shadow, Julie was Beacon's new It Girl. Not that Parker begrudged her the title. Julie had her own demons to battle; she just wore her scars on the inside.

They swept down the hall, passing by Randy, the hippie janitor, who was working his hardest to keep the school squeaky-clean at all times. The auditorium was ahead, and Julie pushed open the heavy wooden door. The large room was filled with kids, yet it felt eerily quiet. A lot of people were sniffling. More shook their heads. A knot of girls hugged. As soon as Parker saw the big picture of Nolan on the stage, her blood pressure dropped. The letters *RIP* were spelled out in flowers beneath his photo.

She looked at Julie, feeling tricked. She'd hoped the Nolan memorial had already happened on one of the days she'd ditched. 'I'm outta here,' she whispered, backing up.

Julie grabbed her arm. 'Please,' she insisted. 'If you don't stay . . . well, *you* know. It might look strange.'

Parker bit her lip. It was true. After what happened at Nolan's party, they couldn't afford to call attention to themselves.

She gazed out into the seats. Mackenzie Wright and Caitlin Martell-Lewis sat a few rows ahead. Ava Jalali was on the other side of the aisle, sitting stiffly next to her boyfriend. They looked over and exchanged looks with Julie and Parker. Although they were all trying to hold it together, everyone looked spooked. It was strange. Parker still barely knew them, yet she felt connected to them for life.

How would you do it? If you were going to kill him, I mean?

Parker flinched. Ava's words from that day in film studies floated up so naturally in her mind that it was as if Ava were right beside her, whispering in her ear. She looked at the stage again. Mr. Obata, the principal, was flipping through some slides for the presentation he was about to give. Some were pictures of Nolan through the years – winning the lacrosse state championship, being crowned homecoming king, holding court in the cafeteria. Parker was even in a few of them, from back when she and Nolan had been friends. Other slides were generic images of prescription pills. So this was also going to have an antidrug message, since all the rumors said he'd accidentally overdosed on OxyContin, his drug of choice.

And then came the kicker: the image of Nolan that Mackenzie had posted online shortly after the party, the one with the writing on his face. The picture was mostly blurred out, but the comments below – a long paragraph telling the world how horrible Nolan was – were not. So it was going to be a bullying assembly, too.

Irony of ironies, considering Nolan had been the biggest bully of all.

Parker's memory began to spin with thoughts of Nolan. Climbing in the car with him. Laughing at his dirty jokes. Driving fast along the coastal road to chase away the fear. The shiny feeling from drinking almost a whole bottle of vodka between the two of them. And then, that last night, when he slipped OxyContin into her drink without telling her. Afterward he'd said, *Isn't it amazing? No charge. My gift to you.*

They'd been friends for years, but after that night, he never spoke to her again. He pretended as if she didn't exist. And meanwhile, *it was all his fault*. If he hadn't given her those pills, things would be different now. She would be her old self. Undamaged. Beautiful, full of life. Present. *Perfect*.

He deserves it, she remembered saying mere days ago. *Everyone hates him. They're all just too scared to admit it. We'd be heroes.*

All at once, the world swirled unsteadily. A white-hot spike of pain shot through Parker's forehead, streaking like lightning across her vision. When she tried to move, her muscles cramped. Her eyes fluttered shut.

Julie nudged her forward. 'Come on,' she whispered. 'We have to sit down. We have to act *normal.*'

Another wave of pain hit Parker's head. Her knees buckled. She'd gotten enough migraines after her accident that she knew this was the start of another. But she couldn't have it here. Not in the auditorium in front of all these people.

A weak groan emerged from her lips. Through blurred vision, she could just make out the sudden concern in Julie's face. 'Oh my god,' Julie said, immediately seeming to recognize what was going on. 'I didn't realize. Come on.'

Julie pulled her up and led her out of the auditorium and to the box office alcove above. The air smelled like lemon cleaner, and dust motes swirled in the air. Posters for upcoming events papered the ticketing window – a flyer for *Guys and Dolls*, another for the upcoming Honors Orchestra Fall Concert. There was even an old playbill with Parker on it, from when she played Juliet sophomore year.

Julie sat Parker down. 'Breathe,' she said softly. 'It's a bad one, isn't it?'

'I'm fine,' Parker managed to say, her fists clenched in her blond hair. She blinked a few times, her vision clearing. The pain subsided to a dull ache, but her mind felt scattered.

'Are you *sure*?' Julie asked, kneeling next to her. 'Do you want me to get the nurse?'

'No,' Parker croaked. She took a shuddering breath. 'I'm okay. It's just a headache.'

Julie set her jaw, reached into her purse, and pulled out the bottle of aspirin she carried around for just this occasion. She handed two pills to Parker, and Parker swallowed them dry, feeling the rough tablets grate against the sides of her throat.

Julie waited until Parker had choked down the pills, then breathed in. 'Have you thought more about . . . talking to a therapist?'

Parker recoiled. 'Not this again.'

'I'm serious.' Julie's eyes were pleading. 'Parker, your headaches are getting worse, and the stress doesn't help. And with this Nolan thing . . . well, I'm just worried about you.'

'No therapist.' Parker crossed her arms over her chest. She pictured baring her soul to a complete stranger while he stared at her and asked, 'Well, how do you feel about that?' As if he really cared.

'I spoke to someone recently . . . about my mom.' Julie lowered her eyes.

Parker whipped her head up. 'What? When?'

'Last week. I was going to mention it, but then everything happened, and . . .' She trailed off.

Parker held her best friend's gaze. Julie looked so hopeful. Parker knew this was hard on her best friend, that she was different now in the After part of her life than she'd been Before. And Julie was all she had left. She didn't want to let her down.

'Fine,' she grumbled. 'But don't be upset if I bail after ten minutes.'

'Deal.' Julie's shoulders visibly relaxed. She gave Parker an earnest, grateful smile. 'But you won't. I think he could really help you.'

Parker had already stood up and headed for the door. She suddenly, desperately needed a cigarette.

She walked across the parking lot to a place she called the Grove, a copse of trees she and Nolan had discovered sophomore year and made their smoking hangout. It always smelled like fresh rain and sap. Here, Parker could be herself under the cover of the leaves – angry Parker, crazy Parker, or tormented and damaged Parker. It didn't matter. No one ever came here.

She dug for a smoke and lit up eagerly. As the nicotine hit her bloodstream, another memory of Nolan hit her. Just when he was getting woozy that night at his party, he'd looked at her, *really* looked at her, for the first time since her accident. And all he'd said was, *I always knew you were a crazy bitch*.

Parker forced her eyes back open. *No*, she told herself. She would *not* fall down that hole. She would *not* relive last week. She would move forward and forget *everything*.

'Hey there.'

She looked up. Her film studies teacher, Mr. Granger, stood at the edge of the trees. Granger was one of those cool, good-looking, young teachers who always knew about current music, looked the other way when kids texted in class, and talked about his semester abroad in Paris, when he'd drunk absinthe and made out with a burlesque dancer. He'd started a photography club, where kids developed black-and-white photos the old-fashioned way, and nearly the entire female student population had signed up.

Anger pricked Parker's skin. He wasn't supposed to know about this place. And she was angry at him for other reasons, too. He'd been the one who made them watch that damned film. He'd been the one to sort them into groups after. He'd been the one to ask, *Is murder justified so long as the person really, truly deserved it?*

Now Granger came closer, pulling a cigarette out of his pocket himself, which surprised her. 'I didn't take you for a smoker,' he said quietly, lighting up.

Parker took a drag. She didn't know whether he was kidding – she looked *exactly* like a smoker.

'I have to go,' she said gruffly, throwing the butt onto the grass and twisting it out with her shoe. Even the Grove was ruined today. And when she walked back into school, she felt yet another stabbing migraine coming on.

Maybe, she suddenly thought, going to a therapist would be helpful after all. Maybe he would help her black out all those memories. Maybe he'd do some sort of hypnosis thing until she no longer had any feelings at all. Maybe he could fix her.

Or maybe, a small voice in the back of her head said, what she did to Nolan proved that she really *was* broken beyond repair.

CHAPTER TWO

Caitlin Martell-Lewis shifted from foot to foot on the Beacon Heights soccer field. The manicured lawn looked vivid green against the woolly gray afternoon clouds that hung low in the sky. It felt as if the gentle autumn warmth had been sucked out of the air overnight, leaving a moist chill that cut through her warm-up pants. Caitlin breathed in the scent of freshly cut grass and impending rain. The smells of soccer.

'All right – we're going to have to go heavy on the offense.' Caitlin rubbed her hands together as her team-mates listened. 'Megan and Gina, you two take the midfield. Shannon, Sujatha, Katie, and Dora, you're defense. You guys are going to have to stay on your toes. The rest of us are on forward.'

'We're going to crush those boys.' Katie O'Malley glared at the opposing team: Beacon's varsity boys' soccer squad. Today was the annual girls-boys play-off.

The boys' coach, Coach Marcus, and the girls' coach, Coach Leah – who were, incidentally, married to each other – paced the sidelines in identical maroon-and-white soccer anoraks. Caitlin glanced at her coach briefly, then looked back at her team. 'Viking, you've got our goal, right? Don't let those bastards score.'

'I've got this,' Vanessa Larson said. At almost six feet two and stunningly beautiful with her long red hair and chiseled cheekbones, Vanessa the Viking was also Caitlin's best friend on the team.

Then Ursula Winters, who normally played center mid but had taken over as striker when Caitlin was injured, looked at Caitlin harshly. 'Are you sure your ankle's healed? You don't want to hurt it more by coming back too early.'

Caitlin frowned. 'I'm fine,' she insisted. Of course Ursula didn't want Caitlin to play – she wanted to take her place. But Caitlin *was* fine . . . mostly. She had a high ankle sprain, but she'd powered through it with physical therapy and the occasional hit of OxyContin – the same drug, actually, that Nolan allegedly OD'd on. And now here she was, back on the field after just three weeks. She had to prove to the coach that she was ready for the big play-off game in two weeks. Winning that was her ticket to an athletic scholarship at the University of Washington, something she'd been working toward her whole life.

Suddenly, Caitlin felt two strong arms wrap around her shoulders. 'Gotcha,' her boyfriend, Josh Friday, murmured in her ear.

'Get off me,' Caitlin mumbled good-naturedly, elbowing him. 'I'm trying to focus.'

Josh snickered. 'You're cute when you're in game mode.' He bumped fists with two of his buddies, Guy Kenwood and Timothy Burgess, who'd also wandered over.

'Ha-ha,' Caitlin said with a laugh, trying not to be irritated that Josh wasn't taking this game seriously. 'It'll be less cute when we kick your butts.'

She and Josh had been together forever. Their parents had been best friends since college – they'd been in each other's weddings and had moved to Beacon Heights at the same time. Sibyl and Mary Ann, Caitlin's two moms, had adopted Caitlin from Korea the same year Josh was born – and then when they went back to Seoul a few years later to adopt Caitlin's brother, Taylor, they left Caitlin with the Friday family for two months. There were framed photos in both houses of Caitlin and Josh holding hands on a playground, or red-faced and crying in a mall Santa's lap. There'd been a few of them sharing a bathtub as toddlers, too, but those had been banned by both Josh and Caitlin on the grounds that they were weird and creepy.

Over the years, the Martell-Lewises and the Fridays did joint vacations and holidays, held weekly board game nights, had standing Saturday-night barbecues, and were always on the sidelines at Caitlin's and Josh's games. And now Caitlin and Josh were both being courted by UDub's respective soccer coaches . . . which meant the Martell-Lewis/Friday lovefest could continue into college. And then, if everything went according to plan, they would graduate, get married, and have Martell-Lewis-Friday babies.

And that plan was more important than ever now. Josh and soccer were her only two constants, the only things holding her together when it felt like her world was falling apart. With Taylor gone, her whole family had shifted. She was suddenly an only child, and the family her parents had worked so hard to create was crumbling. Her moms kept it together in front of her, but she often heard Sibyl crying quietly in their room. Mary Ann stared out the window as she did the dishes, as if she looked long enough, she would finally see Taylor coming in for dessert. The only times her moms seemed like themselves were at dinner with the Fridays or cheering for Caitlin on the soccer field.

Shannon, who played left defense, cleared her throat, breaking Caitlin from her thoughts. 'So how weird was that memorial today?' she asked in a low voice, looking at the girls' team and all the boys who'd wandered over. 'I guess I haven't been to too many things for people our own age.' Then she paled and looked at Caitlin. 'I'm sorry, Caitlin. I didn't mean –'

Caitlin looked down. She wasn't about to have a conversation about her brother right now.

Sujatha, a lean Indian girl who ran faster than anyone on the team, placed her hands on her thin hips. 'Do you really think he committed suicide?'

'No way,' Asher Collins, the boys' goalie, interjected. 'That guy was too vain to kill himself.'

Marnie Wilson, who had an on-again, off-again thing with Asher, glared at him. 'It's not nice to talk like that about someone who's dead.'

'Not if he's an asshole,' Ursula piped up. Then she stared straight at Caitlin. 'Right?'

Caitlin's cheeks reddened. She'd heard something about Nolan jilting Ursula last year – then again, he'd jilted everyone. But it wasn't a rumor how much *Caitlin* hated Nolan. She cleared her throat, looking to Josh for help, but he was busy mock-wrestling Timothy.

'I wonder what it's like to take *that* much Oxy,' Ursula went on.

26

Shannon frowned. 'How much did he take, anyway?'

'Enough to kill him, I guess,' Ursula said, still staring at Caitlin.

Suddenly, Caitlin heard a voice – her voice – from that day in film studies a few weeks before. *You know how I'd do it? Oxy. Everyone knows it's his drug of choice.*

She blinked the memory away.

Ursula shrugged. 'Do you think they're doing an autopsy? Have you ever seen those shows on TV where they do that? They're so gross. The coroner, like, cracks open the ribs with pliers and *weighs* the heart on a fruit scale.'

'Enough!' Caitlin said loudly. 'Can we please focus?'

Everyone fell silent.

No one knew what went down between her and Nolan the night he died, but they all knew perfectly well that her brother had an autopsy performed on him only six months before – and that her brother was dead because of Nolan Hotchkiss.

Josh coughed uncomfortably, then grabbed Asher's arm and guided him away. 'Let's talk strategy. See you guys.'

The whistle blew. Caitlin faced her team, looking at all of them except Ursula. 'Take your places,' she roared, her voice still a little shaky. 'Let's kick some balls, ladies.'

They broke and moved into formation across from the boys. Caitlin felt anxious and unfocused, her body full of pent-up anger. When Coach Marcus blew the whistle for kickoff, she shot forward, her speed surprising even herself.

The world beyond the field became a blur. Caitlin charged forward to take the ball, her cleats tearing into the field as she passed to Gina Pedalino. The boys on the other side looked momentarily dazed – Gabe Martinez, the boys' best forward, hadn't even moved by the time the ball was halfway to the goal. Caitlin smirked. *That's right, idiots*, she thought. *Girls can play better than you think.*

She raced up the field. The ball flew between her team-mates' feet, passing back and forth through the defenders. For a split second, Rocky Davidson intercepted her, but Gina flew past him, stealing the ball right back. Fat raindrops were starting to fall, their rhythm slow at first and then picking up speed. Caitlin felt her blood singing in her veins, pumping with excitement and the thrill of the game.

Suddenly, the ball was hers, and she took off along the sideline, pounding straight toward the boys' goal. Behind her she could hear grunts of exertion as her teammates kept the defense off her tail. Her heart soared. But then a blur of maroon and white shot in front of her. *Ursula.* She stole the ball from Caitlin and ran toward the goal.

'What the hell are you doing?' Caitlin screeched. 'We're on the same team!'

But Ursula just jostled her with her shoulder. Anger boiled in Caitlin's chest. It was bad enough when someone stole a ball, let alone someone from her own *team*.

A scream spewed out of Caitlin from somewhere deep and frustrated, and she stuck out her foot to trip her teammate.

'Oof!' Ursula shrieked, going down hard to the turf, her limbs flailing.

The whistle tweeted. 'Caitlin!' Coach Leah roared behind her.

Her husband ran up as well. 'Yellow card!' he bellowed, standing over Ursula. 'Are you all right?'

Ursula was breathing heavily and dusting grass off her knees. 'That *hurt*,' she whined.

Coach Leah narrowed her eyes at Caitlin. 'What's going on with you? This is just a *practice*. I understand your need to be competitive, but there's no excuse for hurting someone. Hit the showers.'

'What?' Caitlin cried, her jaw dropping open. 'Did you not see her steal the ball?'

'I mean it.' Coach pointed at the school. 'Go.'

Everyone was gawking. A couple of guys nudged each other. Josh looked at her questioningly. Caitlin exhaled loudly. 'Whatever,' she said, waving a hand and stomping off the field. Behind her, the whistle blew again. Ursula, perfectly recovered, took Caitlin's place as striker.

Caitlin stormed along the edge of the school, glaring at her reflection in the long windows that faced the fields; inside was the computer center, a massive space filled with state-of-the-art machinery. The place where her brother used to hang out all the time.

Unbidden, an image of him streaked through her mind. Taylor, short and scrawny even for a freshman, his glasses too big for his face, the hems of his too-long pants dragging on the ground. He'd been a happy kid – always crouched over his Nintendo DS or reading some enormous fantasy novel. But then he'd gotten to high school. It was one thing for Caitlin, a cute, athletic girl, to have two adoptive moms. But it was entirely another thing for her dorky brother, a skinny Korean kid with no interest in sports or booze or popularity – the social currency of Beacon High. Nolan and his friends had eaten Taylor alive.

'Babe?'

She turned around. Josh had jogged after her, his short dark hair slick from the rain. 'Hey,' he said cautiously, as if she were a potentially dangerous animal. 'Are you okay? What happened back there?'

Caitlin just shrugged. 'I'm fine.' She hiked her gear bag higher and pulled her keys out of a small pocket in the front. 'I shouldn't let Ursula get to me.' She waved him toward the field. 'You should go back. Keep playing. Every practice is an important stepping-stone to UDub, you know?'

But Josh kept pace. 'You heading home?'

Caitlin licked her lips. 'I'm going to the cemetery,' she said, deciding it in that very moment. 'I want to see Taylor.'

She couldn't say for sure, but it seemed as if Josh's face fell for the briefest second. But then he stepped forward, like the good boyfriend he was. 'I'll drive you.'

Twenty minutes later, Josh and Caitlin parked in the lot at the McAllister Cemetery. As final resting places went, it wasn't a bad one, with a view of the lake; a lot of old, beautiful trees; and quaint little garden paths.

But as Caitlin undid her seat belt and climbed out of the car, Josh stared at his phone. 'Shit. I think the UDub recruiter is calling me.'

Caitlin frowned. 'Your phone's not ringing.'

Josh was holding his phone in a way that she couldn't see the screen. 'I have it on silent. I gotta take this. You go.'

He put the phone to his ear and said hello. Caitlin watched him for a moment, not sure if he'd actually received a call or not. But would Josh actually fake a phone call to get out of going to the cemetery with her?

30

He *did* hate it, though. He'd come only once since Taylor died. Anytime after that, he said he was busy . . . or that the flowers aggravated his allergies . . . or that it was too rainy . . . or any other excuse he could think of. Caitlin thought again of the brief flash of – what was that? Annoyance? – that had passed across Josh's face at the soccer field when she mentioned Taylor's name. He had that reaction a lot, if Caitlin was honest with herself. But she couldn't figure out how to ask him what he was feeling – they didn't have that sort of relationship. Before Taylor died, they hadn't needed to. But now she wished she could talk to him about it. Even just a *little*.

Josh said a few more things into the phone, and finally, Caitlin slapped her arms to her sides and crossed the parking lot without him. She could do the walk to her brother's grave blindfolded: twenty paces from the car, left for thirty-three paces, and then down a little aisle next to a gravestone with a statue of a German shepherd on top of it. Tommy Maroney, who died at an appropriate age eighty-five, had raised German shepherd champions.

And there it was: TAYLOR ANTHONY MARTELL-LEWIS. He died two days after his fifteenth birthday.

'Hey,' she said softly, pausing to kick off a few dried leaves from the grave. 'Sorry it's been a couple weeks. I've been busy. And this crazy ankle kept me off my feet.' She held up her leg for him to see.

A gust of wind kicked up, blowing her hair into her face. Caitlin took a breath. 'So I guess you heard?' she said softly. 'I mean, who knows? Maybe you've . . . *seen* Nolan, wherever you are now. Although I seriously hope not.' She stared at

31

her fingers. 'Look, I don't know what you can see up there, wherever you are, and maybe you saw me . . . with him . . . that night. But I did it for you. He couldn't get away with it.'

She paused, just like she always did, pretending that Taylor, who was always so thoughtful and introspective, was taking a moment to let this sink in. Then she cleared her throat again. 'I don't feel bad for what happened, though. And I don't agree with what Mom said. It wasn't enough for Nolan to live with what happened. He needed to pay.'

If he could still speak, Caitlin was sure Taylor would second her opinion that what happened to Nolan was karma. When she came home from practice one day to find a suicide note on Taylor's bedroom door, she'd been blindsided. Later that same night, Caitlin had gone into his room, which still smelled like him, and found a journal sitting in plain view on the bed: *Reasons Death Is Better Than School*, it was called. She'd opened to the first page. *September 17: Someone put a bag of dog poop in my locker. Have a feeling it was N. September 30: N and his buddies stole my clothes during gym and stuffed them in the toilet. I smelled like bleach all afternoon. October 8: Girls laughing at me in bio today. Turns out someone wrote a letter to Casey Ryan, the hottest girl in my class, and signed my name on it.*

The worst part of it was that Caitlin hadn't even *seen* it happening . . . and they went to the *same school*. She'd been too busy with soccer and Josh to worry. Taylor never came to her, either. He never complained during family dinners or on weekends. He just . . . *endured* it, until he broke.

Hot tears pricked her eyes. 'I'm so sorry,' she choked out, staring at her brother's grave, the guilt washing over her anew.

'I wish I'd known. I wish I hadn't been so selfish.'

'Cate?'

Caitlin jumped and looked over. A tall guy in rumpled skinny jeans and a gray T-shirt was walking toward her. For a moment, she thought he was Josh, but then she realized he was Jeremy Friday – Josh's younger brother.

'H-hey,' she said. 'W-what are you doing here?'

Jeremy gave her a sad smile. 'Probably the same thing you are.'

Caitlin blinked. Right. Jeremy and Taylor had been friends. Whenever the families had dinner together, they'd disappear and play video games for hours.

Jeremy crouched down next to Taylor's headstone and positioned a tiny figurine on the top. 'There you go, buddy,' he said softly. He moved to the back of the headstone and plucked several more figures from the ground. Though they were faded and muddy, he propped them back up next to the new one. Caitlin had always wondered who brought those figurines.

'Is that a character from *Dragon Ball Z?*' she said.

Jeremy glanced at her. 'How did you know that?'

She felt her cheeks redden. 'I might have watched an episode or fifty with Taylor. Just to keep him company or whatever.'

'Not because you actually *liked* it,' Jeremy joked, a smile on his face. 'You know, it's okay to say you like anime. The stories are amazing. Way better than American cartoons.'

'Agreed,' Caitlin admitted, remembering how much she used to enjoy watching the episodes with her brother. They'd settled on the couch together, sharing a bowl of Parmesan-and-pepper-covered popcorn and discussing what crazy machine they'd have the inventor character Bulma build for them. 'Do you still watch it?' she asked.

'Sure, though it's only available online or on DVD these days,' Jeremy said. He peeked at her. 'If you're ever in the mood, I'm game.'

Caitlin's face reddened again. 'Oh, no. That's okay.'

Jeremy looked at her evenly. 'I get it. It's not really Josh's thing.'

Caitlin lowered her head. She wanted to tell him she didn't do everything with Josh, but that wasn't really true.

She peeked at Jeremy again. His features looked a lot like Josh's – they both had the same honey-brown eyes, the same high cheekbones, but Jeremy's face was sharper, his chin and nose more pointed. The two of them were so different, Josh sporty and Mr. Popular, Jeremy a lot like Taylor – quiet, introspective, more into books than sports. Whenever she was at the Fridays, he would sit at the end of the dinner table reading while Josh and his buddies played *Madden*.

It was strange. When they'd been kids, Caitlin and Jeremy had shared a tent on camping vacations and spent hours together in the back of the car playing I Spy. Now they were almost strangers.

She cleared her throat and looked at the action figures, then at Jeremy. 'You come here a lot, huh?'

Jeremy nodded. 'I try to come every week.'

Caitlin felt more tears rush to her eyes. 'You do?'

'Of course I do,' Jeremy said, pushing his hands in his pockets. 'I miss him.' Then he squinted at her. 'Aren't you supposed to be at soccer right now?'

34

Caitlin lowered her shoulders. 'I pissed off the coach.' She looked at her brother's grave again. 'And then I just needed to talk to him.'

'I know the feeling,' Jeremy said softly.

She swallowed hard. 'Sometimes I'm not sure I'll *ever* get over it, you know.'

Jeremy squinted. 'Maybe you don't have to. And maybe that's okay.'

It was the most perfect thing he could have said to her. It was what she always wanted *Josh* to say. 'Thank you,' she said softly.

Jeremy looked surprised. 'For what?'

Caitlin shrugged. 'For coming here. For saying hi to Taylor. For *understanding*.'

'Well. You're welcome.' Jeremy stood up and brushed off his pants. 'I should probably go.'

Caitlin nodded, and before she could overthink it, she threw her arms around Jeremy and hugged him. After a moment, he hugged her back. And as she stood there, warm in his embrace, she realized that it was the first time since her brother died that she didn't feel so terribly alone.

CHAPTER THREE

Early Thursday evening, Mackenzie Wright, dressed in a patchwork skirt with her long, unruly blond hair clipped back from her face, sat in the passenger seat of her best friend Claire Coldwell's car, humming along to Dvořák's *New World Symphony*. Mrs. Rabinowitz, their honors symphony conductor, insisted they live, breathe, and sleep the piece until their upcoming concert. Mackenzie absentmindedly moved her fingers along with the melody, as if her cello were right there in front of her rather than tucked in the hatchback of Claire's blue Ford Escape.

'Hello? Earth to Mackenzie.' Claire waved a hand in front of Mackenzie's glasses.

Mackenzie snapped to focus, realizing that Claire had been talking to her. 'Oh, sorry. I'm kind of out of it today.'

Claire glanced at Mac sympathetically, her perfectly pink lips pressed together. 'Me too,' she confided. 'That assembly about Nolan was so awful. I can't get over that he's just . . . *gone.*'

Mackenzie glanced out the window, staring at the too-green front lawns of the passing houses. Nolan might be gone, but there were reminders of him *everywhere* – photos of him on the walls, news programs about his 'accidental overdose,' the morning announcements saying that his funeral was on Sunday, just three days from now. And that assembly, *ugh*. The principal had shown the pictures of Nolan's marked-up face that *Mac* herself had posted anonymously from an Internet café. Leave it to Beacon High, pressure cooker of all pressure cookers, to even make a memorial assembly intense.

But most intense were Mackenzie's own memories of that night. 'Can we change the subject?' she mumbled.

'Sure. Have you heard back about your audition schedule yet?' Claire said.

The word *audition* sent another spike of fear through Mackenzie's heart like a shard of ice. Claire was talking about the Juilliard audition. 'Um, yeah. It's the Friday after next. Five PM.'

'Yeah?' Claire straightened up, tossing her short, curly bob. It was a style that would look horrible on Mac but looked pixie-like and adorable on Claire. The hint of a smirk danced across Claire's face. 'Me too. Except I'm at four. Right before you, I guess.'

Beads of sweat broke out along the back of Mackenzie's neck. Mac and Claire had met as five-year-olds at a music camp for precocious preschoolers and had been inseparable ever since. Claire was übercompetitive with Mackenzie, always trying to beat her out for first chair or dictating what they did every Friday night, but she was also the only person Mackenzie had anything in common with – even with all the pressure to be perfect at Beacon Heights High, not many people could understand the sacrifices they had to make for music. They shared everything: which boy they had secret crushes on, which music teachers they hated – how, sometimes, they didn't feel like playing at all.

Now they were both vying to get a spot at Juilliard, though the conservatory had never taken two cellists from the same school before. More than likely, there wouldn't be room for both. And given everything that had happened with them in the past year, Mackenzie wasn't sure she wanted there to be.

'Here we are.' Claire pulled over outside Cupcake Kingdom, a popular spot in Beacon Heights, right on the town square. The afternoon rain had slackened, but the pavement was still wet and slick, and the trees and street-lights dripped water to the sidewalk below in arrhythmic patterns. 'Have fun at band practice.'

'Thanks for the ride,' Mackenzie said, opening the door to the backseat and carefully sliding out her cello case. Her parents had promised to buy her a top-quality professional instrument from Germany if she got into Juilliard – she'd need one if she was going to play with professionals – but she loved her current cello. She knew every little scratch and scuff in the glossy maple wood, every weird quirk it had. She'd even given it a name: Moomintroll.

'Anytime!' Claire yelled out the window. 'Tell Blake I love him!'

'Right, I'll be sure to do that,' Mackenzie mumbled as Claire zoomed off.

Then she looked in the window of Cupcake Kingdom. And there he was, wiping off the counter, looking sexy even in a pink-and-white-striped apron. Blake Strustek, the reason for

Claire and Mac's friend-mageddon.

Mac had become friends with Blake in junior high and joined his band, Black Lodge. They practiced weekly, but it was only in sophomore year that Mac realized she liked him as *more* than a friend . . . though she had no idea what to do with that. She stayed late at band practice, went out of her way to be in his ensembles for chamber music festivals, and at strings camp she'd linger near him every opportunity she got. The only person she confessed her crush to was Claire.

That was why it'd been such a shock when Claire came to her last year during the orchestra's trip to Disneyland. 'Blake just kissed me,' she'd announced breathlessly. 'I didn't kiss him back, because I know *you* like him, too.'

'Like him, *too?*' Mackenzie had echoed hollowly, thinking of Blake with his wide, curving lips, his thick, shaggy hair. His pale blue eyes, long-lashed and intense. Mackenzie had liked him forever, yes, but Claire had never mentioned liking him, too. Not ever.

'I'll just tell him no, right? That you like him, so even though I really, really like him, too, it'd be weird if we went out?' Claire went on.

'No!' Mackenzie had gasped, mortified. The only thing worse than Claire liking Blake was Blake knowing Mac liked him. 'It's fine . . .' she said haltingly. 'You should go for it.'

It's better this way, and you know it, Mackenzie told herself. Boys were a distraction from what really mattered. But that didn't mean she'd totally forgiven Claire. Claire was supposed to be her *best* friend, her confidant. Claire should have known better.

Blake noticed Mac and opened the door. 'Hey. You coming?'

She pointed at the cupcake on his torso. 'Nice apron,' she teased.

Blake scoffed. 'Hey. It takes a secure man to wear a pink cupcake on his chest.' He reached behind him and started to untie the strings. 'Come on in. I'm just closing up, and then we can head back.'

She followed him into the shop, which resembled a Candy Land game board. The walls were painted with pink glitter. Bright-colored prints hung everywhere, with sayings like LET THEM EAT CUPCAKES! and LIFE IS SWEET! in simple fonts. Two vintage bistro tables sat under frosted-glass sconces, and a warm, buttery aroma set her mouth watering. In the glass case counter, a handful of beautiful frosted cupcakes sat in long rows. The 'flavors' all had names like 'The Fat Elvis' or 'The Cherry Bomb.' The cupcakes were pretty picked-over – it looked like they'd almost sold out over the course of the day – but the leftover ones still looked scrumptious.

'Where's your sister?' Mac asked as Blake turned the OPEN sign around to CLOSED. His sister, Marion, had opened this shop last year.

Blake rolled his eyes. 'Taking the day off. She's probably getting a mani-pedi.'

'Let me guess. Matching bubble-gum pink?'

'You know it.' Marion was borderline obsessed with the color – she even had pink streaks in her hair.

Blake balled up his apron, tossed it into the back, and smiled wryly. 'Remember when we dared her to wear all black?'

Mac burst out laughing. 'I thought she was going to have a seizure.'

'Good times, Macks,' Blake said, using his old nickname for her, his gaze remaining on Mac for a beat. She pushed her black-framed glasses up her nose and stared at the floor, feeling suddenly guilty. Those memories with Blake were from *before* he was dating Claire. When Blake was still all hers.

He opened the door to the back room. Mackenzie followed him through a cramped industrial kitchen filled with mixers and bowls, and then through another set of double doors, into a midsize storage room. Enormous sacks of flour and sugar, bags of napkins and cupcake holders, and stacks of receipt paper were piled on the shelves. In the center of the room was enough space for a drum set, a couple of chairs, and an amp. Blake's violin was resting on top of a low file cabinet in its open case.

'Where's the rest of the band?' she asked, glancing around as if the other band members might be hiding behind the shelves.

Blake made a face, counting on his fingers. 'Javier had an SAT cram session, Dave is rewriting his Yale essay for the fifth time, and Warren has, quote, "a thing with a lady," though I bet they're just going to study for an AP Chem exam together.' He rolled his eyes. 'So it's just you and me tonight.'

Mackenzie swallowed. Her and Blake . . . alone? That hadn't happened since he started dating Claire.

Forcing herself to be normal, Mac sat down, and they started going through the set list for an upcoming gig song by song. There were a few covers – Coldplay, Mumford & Sons, even a Beyoncé arrangement – but a lot of the songs were written by Blake himself. Blake had quit orchestra at the beginning of junior year, but he was more musically talented than almost anyone she knew.

Mac played and played, trying to get that heady buzz that hit her whenever she was in the zone. That was what she lived for: making music, *feeling* music. She'd been playing the cello since she was four years old, when her parents had sat her down to listen to *The Young Person's Guide to the Orchestra* and told her to choose the instrument she wanted to learn. They had a vested interest, of course: Her mother played the flute in the Seattle Symphony, and her father was a professional piano accompanist who'd worked with Yo-Yo Ma, James Galway, and Itzhak Perlman.

Mackenzie had chosen the cello – she loved the warm, rich sounds and the enormous range the instrument produced. When she was focused, she felt like she was a part of the music, her instrument an extension of her. When she played, she could almost forget about the big Spanish test she still hadn't started studying for, or the Audition with a capital *A*, *or* Nolan.

Almost.

After the first time she saw Claire and Blake holding hands at the spring concert, Mackenzie started deliberately avoiding both of them – not that they noticed. She'd holed up in her family's airy practice room, going over every single song in her repertoire. Her parents had been thrilled. No one seemed to notice how lonely she was.

And then, about a week into her heartbreak, Nolan Hotchkiss approached her in the hall. *Mackenzie, right?* he'd said.

That's right, she'd answered shyly.

His smile grew wider. *You look cute today,* he said. And then he spun on his heel and walked away.

The Nolan Hotchkiss. Captain of the lacrosse team, first in line for valedictorian. Cute, confident Nolan, with his strong jawline and intoxicating grin. He thought *Mac* looked cute. Suddenly Blake didn't seem so amazing anymore. The one comment led to a lunchtime talk . . . and then to texting . . . and then an actual *phone call*. Mac might have lost Blake, but maybe that was okay? Maybe she should have been aiming higher all along?

So when Nolan asked her out on a date to Le Poisson, the most extravagant restaurant in all of Beacon Heights, and told her to 'wear a dress,' she did.

Nolan was so charming that first time . . . and the second, too. And so, when he asked for those pictures, she barely hesitated. She . . . *posed* . . . and then she hit send on her phone before she could think twice. It wasn't until he showed up at her door the next day that she realized she'd been tricked.

'Thanks,' he said, waving something in front of her face. It was the pictures, printed out on shiny paper. Most of her body was hidden behind her cello, but it was obvious that she was naked. Mac looked past him to his car; his friends hung out the windows, laughing at her. Her heart had sunk.

'I just wanted to let you know you won me an important bet.' Nolan chuckled, then tossed something else at Mac – a wad of bills. Before she could put the pieces together, before she could throw the money back at him, he hooted again and sauntered back to his car, pics tucked in his back pocket. When Mac came to her senses, she burned that money in the backyard. And then she'd cried for what felt like days.

No *wonder* she'd wanted revenge.

When she finished the piece and opened her eyes again, Blake was staring at her. 'That was . . . wow.'

Mac ran her hands down the length of her face, trying to refocus. She'd been so lost in the music that she'd forgotten Blake was there. She glanced away, his gaze too intense, too potent.

'Why do you always do that?' he asked.

She glanced at him again. 'What?'

'Look away. Hide.' He was watching her closely now, his eyes a piercing blue. 'It's so weird. When you play, you look so . . . so confident. Like nothing could faze you. But then you stop, and you get quiet and hidden. It's like you save the best of yourself for your music.'

Color rose in her cheeks, her heart stuttering in her chest. 'I'm not hiding anything.'

'No?' He reached toward her and carefully took off her glasses, folding the stems in and setting them on top of the amp. She blinked, the world blurred without her lenses – but Blake was so close to her she could see him perfectly. His eyes moved slowly across her features, like he was committing her to memory.

'Do you even know how beautiful you are when you play?' Then, to her shock, his lips were on hers, soft but insistent.

For a moment, she sat perfectly still, too confused to react. Blake tasted faintly of chocolate and peanut butter, his unshaven jaw lightly scratchy against her chin. Mac knew she was supposed to do something, to stop this, but soon everything fell away: her jitters, her concerns, what happened to Nolan. It just felt . . . right.

That was when a Feist song erupted from his phone. Mac knew the ringtone: it was Claire's favorite song. She pulled away fast, her cheeks red.

Blake broke away, too, a guilty expression crossing his face. 'Shoot.'

He walked uneasily through the door to the kitchen, but not before she overheard him say, 'Hey, baby, what's up?'

Mackenzie sat frozen, her lips still tasting like peanut butter. She squirmed, as though Claire could see her through the phone. As if Claire *knew*.

She shot up, grabbed her things, and stole out of the cupcake shop before Blake could stop her. She banged through the front door, the bells jingling. As soon as she got outside, the rain misting her face, she realized the enormity of what she'd done.

She'd kissed her best friend's boyfriend. And she'd liked it.

CHAPTER FOUR

Ava Jalali slid into her desk in the film studies classroom just as the bell rang for fourth period on Friday. She was usually fashionably late to class, but she'd had so much on her mind this week that it was worse than usual.

'Cutting it close, Miss Jalali,' said Mr. Granger, but she could tell he was mostly teasing. Mr. Granger was one of the youngest teachers in school, just a year or so out of college. He couldn't even pretend to have an authoritarian air when his students were only five years younger than him.

Ava turned her thousand-watt smile on her teacher. 'Sorry, Mr. Granger. Vending machine emergency. Sour Patch Kids are back in stock, everyone!'

A ripple of laughter cut through the classroom. Her boyfriend, Alex, craned around from the seat in front of her and winked. A different teacher might have gotten mad, but that was what Ava liked about Mr. Granger – and why she knew she could get away with this stuff. He just gave her a dry smile.

'Well, now that our candy-shortage crisis has ended, we can focus on what we're here to do.' Mr. Granger picked up a piece of chalk and started to write in sloppy handwriting across the chalkboard: MORALITY AND ETHICS IN CRIME FILM. 'We're starting a new unit today.'

Ava flipped her notebook to a blank page and poised her pen to take notes, ready to think about something else other than Nolan. His picture was plastered every two feet in the hallways, and she'd barely made it through the assembly yesterday. Advanced film studies was her favorite class – she'd originally signed up because it sounded like an easy A, a chance to watch movies all semester, but she'd ended up really getting into the classic films they watched. So far, they'd talked about representations of women in early monster movies, the way World War II–era Bugs Bunny cartoons had been used as American propaganda, and identity and trauma in psychological thrillers. There was so much to learn. Under the glitzy, glamorous surface of the simplest popcorn flick, there were often hidden depths of meaning.

Just like with her, she thought.

Ava hadn't always taken school seriously. Her freshman year, she'd thought studying was for losers. Nerds. Geeks. Uglies. Ava was gorgeous, and she knew it. Half Iranian and half Irish, she had striking almond-shaped eyes, smooth caramel-colored skin, and a long-limbed figure with impressive curves. She'd even worked a few modeling gigs, posing for an upscale make-up company based in Seattle and shimmying into skintight designer jeans for a department store's ad campaign. Who cared about getting into Yale or Stanford – maybe she didn't even need to go to college.

Then her mom had died, hit by a drunk driver one night on her way home from campus. Her mom had always insisted that

Ava was smarter than her report cards. Every time Ava brought home another mediocre test score, Ava's mom defended her to her dad: 'She's figuring out who she is, Firouz. She obviously has a great role model for how to be brilliant' – she pointed to herself ironically – 'but no one around here can show her how to be brilliant *and* beautiful at the same time. That's a burden only she can bear.' Ava's dad would laugh, and the storm would pass.

In the void after her mom's death, Ava had found herself wanting to study for the first time. And it turned out her mom was right – she *was* smart. Her dad noticed the change in her behavior and her GPA, and constantly told her how proud he was. Teachers began to take her seriously.

That is, until Nolan Hotchkiss sent all her hard-won efforts crumbling to sand.

'The crime genre is one that's changed shape dozens of times over the years, always morphing to provide a commentary on the moral stance Americans take at any given point in time.' Mr. Granger's voice pulled Ava back to the present. 'A lot of crime movies investigate the idea of a gray area of morality, where heroes would be challenged to behave as criminals – and vice versa. Some people love this about crime film, and some people hate it.'

Ava glanced down at her notes. She'd written the words *heroes*, *criminals*, and *hate*. She realized with a sinking feeling that the *hate* she'd written looked far too similar to the *hate* she wrote on Nolan's face last weekend, the one that was featured in newspapers and newscasts and nationwide blogs. She quickly flipped to a new page before anyone could notice.

'Now, before we keep going, I'll hand back your papers on *And Then There Were None.*'

Everyone in class sat up, on alert, as most kids did when a teacher was handing back a paper or a test. Ava knew that in the next few moments, there would be huge smiles . . . and some tears, too. Yes, even a class like film studies mattered. *Every* grade mattered at Beacon.

'Some of you did very well,' Mr. Granger murmured, peeling a paper off the stack. Ava was sure Mr. Granger looked right at her as he said that, and she sat up a little straighter in her chair. 'Some of you, however, need to be challenged. The moral questions this movie asks are complicated and maybe even a little subversive. I'd like to see you really push your arguments on this next unit.' Mr. Granger picked up a stack of papers from his desk and started to move around the room.

When he got to her row, Mr. Granger set her paper facedown on the desk. Ava turned it over, eager to see his notes – and gasped at the bright red C scrawled across the top.

A C? She couldn't believe it. She put lots of effort into this class, watching long-winded interviews with directors and reading film theory articles online. Her papers on the first movies they'd watched, *Psycho* and *Vertigo*, had earned her A-pluses. Then again, she'd written the *And Then There Were None* paper after that eerie group discussion in class – and after she'd lured Nolan upstairs at his party. She remembered the heaviness of his body as he leaned on her, the smell of beer on his breath as he tried to kiss her sloppily. The moment his muscles had gone lax . . .

She shook her head. The last thing she had wanted to do

was think about Nolan, the movie, or what she'd done.

'How'd you do?'

She glanced up to see Alex, his arm resting on the back of the seat. His expression changed quickly when he saw that she was upset.

'Um, not so great,' she mumbled.

'It's okay. Maybe he'll let you rewrite it. We can watch the movie again together –'

'No,' Ava said quickly, then winced at the flash of hurt in his warm brown eyes. She just didn't want to see that movie again, no matter what. 'Sorry, I just –'

'Miss Jalali, if you don't mind, we have more material to cover.' Mr. Granger was watching them both with a frown. Alex quickly turned back to face front.

Ava barely heard the rest of the lecture. She turned through the pages of her essay, staring at the red ink in the margins. *What point are you trying to make?* Mr. Granger had written next to one paragraph. *This argument doesn't hold up* was scribbled next to another. She felt crushed. It had been so, *so* long since she'd gotten a C. The grade almost made her feel dirty, and she stuffed the paper into her Hervé Chapelier tote bag, not wanting to look at it anymore.

Finally, the bell rang for lunch. 'We'll be assigning new groups for this next unit,' Mr. Granger called out over the buzz of people standing up and starting to pack their bags. 'Get ready for a new project next week.'

Thank god, Ava thought, looking up to see her relief mirrored on the faces of her other *And Then There Were None* group members. Julie took a heavy breath. Mackenzie drummed her fingers against the desk. Ava looked away. She didn't have anything against any of those girls. She just wanted to put that whole project – and what it had led to – behind her. She knew it was unfair, but if it hadn't been for those girls and that one conversation, everything would be different. She wouldn't have gotten a C. She wouldn't be racked by guilt.

And Nolan, maybe, wouldn't be dead.

CHAPTER FIVE

Friday night, Julie Redding walked up to Matthew Hill's house. Although the house was large and stately, and well stocked with beer and the typical party snacks, it didn't even begin to compare with Nolan Hotchkiss's bash last week.

Julie shivered, dark memories wafting back to her. But she forced them away just as quickly. She definitely didn't want to think about Nolan right now.

She shouldered through the gate to the back patio, feeling that same buzz in her chest she got before every party. *Will this one go okay? What if someone sees through me? What if someone guesses?* So she did what she always did, a calming trick she'd read about years ago in a book called *The Zen Master's Guide to Calm:* she counted, she breathed, she tried to quiet her mind. *One. Two. Three. Four. Five.* Then she shook out her hands, took a deep breath, and pasted her brightest smile on her face. The party smile. The *I'm-Julie-and-everyone-loves-me* smile.

The heavy thud of a dubstep track pulsed, punctuated by laughter and squeals. The stone fountain was already full of discarded red Solo cups, along with someone's iPhone. A couple of kids sat on lawn chairs talking intensely, the smoke of their clove cigarettes coiling around them. As people saw Julie, they waved, their faces brightening.

'You look amazing!' cooed Renata Thomas, a waifish girl who captained the gymnastics team.

'Jules!' said Helene Robinson from chemistry class, giving her a huge hug. Three other girls hugged her next. She inhaled their fruity-smelling hair and accepted their loving squeezes. By the time she'd made it inside the house, it seemed like the whole party had greeted her.

Julie's pulse began to slow. Of course it was going to be fine. She didn't need to worry. No one was going to figure out all the things she was hiding. Everyone *adored* her, and it was going to stay that way.

Early on she'd learned how to make people admire her. It'd come in handy over the years – because if they were busy noticing how fun she was, how stylish she was, how sweet she was, they didn't have time to notice that there were some things about her that were a little . . . off. How she never had anyone to her house. How people didn't even *know* where she lived. But that didn't matter, because Julie was a benevolent queen bee, unlike a lot of the rich, snobby students at Beacon Heights High. She made it easy for people to like her – and so they did.

'Oh my god, Julie!' cried a voice, breaking Julie from her thoughts. 'We're twinsies! How crazy is that?'

Julie stared into the eyes of Ashley Ferguson, a junior at Beacon and the one person whom she found it very, *very* hard to be nice to.

At least, Julie *thought* it was Ashley – eerily, it was kind of like she was looking in a mirror. The two girls were about the same height and weight, and Ashley had recently dyed her hair to almost the exact auburn of Julie's. She also used the same glittery nut-brown shadow on her eyelids and the same neutral gloss on her lips. And tonight – how, Julie wasn't sure – she was wearing the same BCBG dress Julie had on. Their shoes were different – Ashley's looked like Jimmy Choos, while Julie wore a pair of Nine West sling-backs she'd gotten on sale.

It wasn't unusual for girls to copy Julie's style. If Julie wore blue glitter nail polish on a Friday, by Monday half the school would be wearing it, too. Usually it made her feel special, powerful, but with Ashley, Julie just felt Single-White-Femaled. The girl tried *so* hard. It was embarrassing. If she told her therapist, Elliot Fielder, about it, he'd probably say Ashley was what Julie feared she would become if her secret ever got out: mocked, lame, *desperate*.

She wondered if Parker had ever looked at Julie like that. When Julie moved to Beacon Heights in sixth grade, she realized immediately that Parker – blond, clear-skinned, and fearless – was the friend she needed to have. It took a few weeks, but Julie nosed her way into Parker's posse, and pretty soon she was Parker's best friend. They were both equally beautiful and outgoing, natural partners in crime at the top of the popularity pyramid. And though they talked after school daily, and though Julie had spent many nights at Parker's house, Parker had never come to hers. Julie had said it was because her mom was super strict. Thankfully, Parker hadn't questioned it.

But then that night happened with Parker. The night when keeping her secret nearly cost Parker her life. After that, they started being honest with each other.

Ashley was still staring at Julie eagerly. 'Uh, so crazy,' Julie finally said flatly, pretending to look at something on her phone. It was just about the unfriendliest she could be.

'*Red alert*,' whispered Nyssa Frankel, who grabbed her arm and yanked her to the left. 'Let's get you out of here before that psycho cuts off your hair and pastes it on her head, okay?'

Julie giggled and let Nyssa pull her away. She glanced at Ashley over her shoulder; she was standing there, frowning, clearly aware she'd been dissed.

'I wish she'd find someone else to copy,' Julie murmured into Nyssa's ear as they sauntered back outside.

Nyssa lit a cigarette, and the scent of tobacco wafted through the air. 'Oh, style stealing is the highest form of flattery,' she said as she exhaled, shaking out her brown curls. She offered Julie a drag, but Julie shook her head. 'Anyway, everyone knows she's a loser.' Nyssa squeezed Julie's arm. 'Want me to put an ugly picture of her on Instagram? Or start a rumor about her?'

'That's okay,' Julie said, but she appreciated Nyssa's standing up for her. Ever since Parker had stopped being Parker, Nyssa had become Julie's second in command.

Nyssa looked around, hands on her hips. 'This place is bananas, huh?'

'Seriously,' Julie answered. Through the floor-to-ceiling windows, she could see a cluster of kids dancing wildly in the den, jumping up and down in rhythm to the music. A boy in a Seahawks jersey had another guy in a headlock, both of them laughing. A potted lily lay broken on the covered patio, and people had obviously walked through the spilled soil, tracking it into the house. James Wong, Zev Schaeffer, and Karen Little were playing quarters on a foldout table in the backyard.

'Everyone made it out tonight,' Nyssa murmured, elbowing her way through a cluster of kids.

Julie looked around, spotting Ava, looking model-perfect, holding tight to Alex's hand. Caitlin was here, wearing a no-nonsense striped dress and her shiny black hair pulled into a ponytail, laughing with some girls on her soccer team. Even Mackenzie was here with her friend Claire and Claire's boyfriend, Blake. But not everyone was here. Nolan wasn't. And neither was Parker.

Julie hadn't actually thought Parker would come. It was awesome that she'd shown up at Nolan's bash – but then, that wasn't because she'd wanted to socialize. She felt a pang. Parker had been through so much – of course she'd changed, and of course she was having a hard time adjusting. And after the Nolan thing, Parker seemed more tormented than ever.

Jessa Cooper and Will Mika, two of the newspaper editors, stood next to Julie and Nyssa, speaking in hushed tones. 'You can still find them online if you look hard enough,' Will whispered.

'So you've actually *looked* at the photos?' Jessa's eyes were wide. 'Of Nolan *dead?*'

Julie's stomach swooped. She knew what photos they were talking about.

Will shrugged. 'A lot of people did.'

Julie cleared her throat. 'How do you know he was actually *dead* when those photos were taken?'

Both kids turned to her. Their expressions grew reverent and respectful – she was Julie Redding, after all, and they were juniors. 'Uh, I guess I *don't* know for sure,' Will admitted. 'But, I mean, why else would the school demand they be taken down?'

'Maybe because Nolan had mean shit written on him?' Jessa piped up. 'I wonder who wrote those things on his face.'

Nyssa snorted. 'My money's on Mark Brody,' she said, referring to Nolan's friend on the lacrosse team. 'Don't guys always pull stupid pranks like that on each other?'

Julie's heart was thudding fast. *She* knew who had written on Nolan, and it wasn't Mark. She turned away and instantly collided into someone. Cold beer spilled down her back and onto her shoes. Julie cried out, jumping away.

Julie turned around and found herself face-to-face with Carson Wells, the new boy from Australia. He was something of a mystery to everyone at Beacon. The only verifiable fact was that he was drop-dead gorgeous, with coffee-colored skin, a close-shaved head, olive-green eyes, and a killer accent.

'I am *so* sorry,' he said.

'It's okay,' Julie breathed, and Carson scuttled for some napkins and began to blot Julie's shoes. 'Oh my goodness,' Julie said, suddenly embarrassed. 'Don't worry about it. You hardly got me.'

'Are you sure?' Carson stood up again. His eyes were still apologetic. 'You're Julie, right?'

'That's right,' Julie said softly.

'I'm Carson,' he said. Then he looked at the now empty beer cup. 'I guess I'm due for a refill, huh? Can I get you one, too?'

Julie felt heat rise to her cheeks. 'I suppose it'd be the least you could do.'

They walked to the back of the keg line, which led through

57

the living room to the bathroom. Music blared, and an enormous flat-screen TV was on but muted.

'So is this your first party in Beacon?' Julie asked.

Carson shook his head. 'Actually, the one last week was. Nolan's.'

'Oh.' Julie looked down. She hadn't noticed Carson there – of course, she'd had other things on her mind. 'That wasn't a great start to the year, unfortunately.'

'Seriously.' Carson shoved his hands in his pockets. 'I should have stuck to my planned evening of chamomile tea and Jane Austen novels.'

'Right.' Julie laughed. 'So how do you like it here so far?' She almost slapped her forehead once she'd said it. *That's a question your grandmother might ask!*

'Not too bad,' Carson said. 'Aside from the fact that the first question most people ask me is either what I got on my SATs, how many APs I've already taken, or, when I tell them I'm a runner, what my mile PR is.'

Julie snickered. 'That's Beacon High for you.'

Carson grimaced. 'And the weather's awful. I don't know how I'm going to get through six months of rain.'

'Try nine,' she said with a laugh. 'Yeah, it gets to me, too. I used to live in California.'

'You lived in California?' He perked up. 'Man, I'd love to live there. Dad almost took a job at USC, but UDub offered him a better deal. I was kind of bummed at first. But it's all good. If I were in California, I wouldn't be here talking to you.' He smiled. 'Why'd you move?'

'Uh, family,' she said vaguely. 'My mom wanted to be closer

to my grandmother.' It was partially true, after all. 'She passed away,' she added, in case Carson asked if they still saw each other.

'Sorry to hear about that.' Carson's voice was gentle.

Julie's throat began to feel itchy, which it always did when she lied. She wondered what he'd say if she told him the truth: that they'd *had* to move. That her dad had abandoned them years ago. That even her grandmother couldn't deal with her mother.

This was why she'd never had a boyfriend. She could get away with not telling her friend about her home life, but a boyfriend would be a different story. There would be questions she couldn't answer, the 'meet the parents' her mother could never manage. Only Parker knew the truth about Julie's mom, and Julie had only told her after the accident. By then it was clear that Parker's home life was worse – and more dangerous – than Julie's. Now Parker had her own key to Julie's place, and she protected Julie's secret fiercely. 'To the grave,' Parker had vowed, and Julie couldn't imagine trusting anyone else like she trusted Parker. Someday, in college maybe, when she'd gotten the hell out of here and was on her own, *then* she could consider falling in love and bearing her soul. But not now. Not when she risked so much. Not when someone could see . . . *everything.*

And now there was an even bigger secret to hide.

Just like that, a crack formed in her mind, and Julie was suddenly back in the film studies classroom on the day everything started. In all other respects, it had been a completely ordinary day. Nolan Hotchkiss had made fun of three kids in rapid succession in the first minute of class – first Laurie Odenton, who had a lazy eye; then Ursula Winters, who had ham-hock legs and was, Nolan said, basically undateable; and then Oliver Hodges, who was gay and proud and pretty much immune to teasing at that point. Mr. Granger had put on a movie called *And Then There Were None*, the third movie in their mystery series.

The movie was in black and white, with a booming, old-fashioned sound track. It was about eight strangers who were all called to an island by a mysterious host – but when they arrived, their host was nowhere to be seen. Instead, a recorded message accused each of them of murder.

One by one, the guests on the island started to die: the general who ordered his wife's lover into a suicide mission. The servant who'd killed his crippled employer. The crusty old maid who had her nephew locked away in the reformatory until he committed suicide. Someone was punishing them for their crimes. By the end of the movie, Julie was perched on the edge of her seat, wide-eyed. It was weirdly satisfying to watch each person get what he or she deserved. Could you even call it murder?

When the lights finally came up, Julie had blinked in the sudden brightness. Granger assigned the discussion groups immediately, and she'd found herself facing Parker, Mackenzie, Ava, and Caitlin. Besides Parker, she barely knew the others except in passing.

Caitlin had stretched her muscular arms over her head. 'That was kind of intense.'

Ava opened her notebook to a blank page, pushing her dark

hair off her face. 'But it makes sense. It's all about the rule of law, right? How dangerous it is for judgment to come from a vigilante.'

Mackenzie chimed in. 'I didn't think some of those people deserved to be punished. What's-her-name, Miss Brent? She didn't kill anyone. She just had her nephew put in jail. It wasn't her fault he killed himself.'

'Sure it was.' Caitlin's voice was sharp. Her lips were a straight, rigid line, her jaw tight. Julie thought about her brother's suicide – everyone knew Nolan had teased him relentlessly, and then her brother had killed himself.

The other girls seemed to remember Taylor at the same time. Mackenzie wrapped her chunky knit sweater tighter around her body. 'I didn't mean . . .'

'In fact, she's one of the worst of them,' Caitlin went on. 'Because she didn't even care. She didn't even feel bad.' An awkward silence fell. Mackenzie stared miserably down at her hands. Julie glanced from one girl to the next. Ava clicked her pen, again and again.

Then Parker took a deep breath. 'I know it's kind of sick,' she said, her voice low, 'but sometimes I think the judge was right. Some people deserve to be punished.'

Tears almost formed in Julie's eyes – it was the first time Parker had spoken in class in ages. But then she glanced around at the shocked faces. Okay, maybe what Parker said was a little harsh, but Julie didn't want her to recede into her shell again.

'Right?' she piped up. 'I mean, *I* know some people who deserve punishment. Personally, first on my list would be Parker's dad. The judge let him off too easy.'

The girls' muscles stiffened, the way everyone's always did when Parker's accident came up. The whole school knew what Parker's dad had done to her that night – the evidence was all over her face, for starters, plus he'd ended up in jail, which never happened in a place like Beacon.

They continued talking, mentioning people in their lives who'd wronged them – each of the girls had someone who had hurt them, too – when suddenly Caitlin leaned forward.

'You know who I'd get rid of?' Her eyes glinted as she looked across the room, toward another group's table. Nolan Hotchkiss leaned back in his chair, his arms crossed over his chest. He laughed loudly at something, a mocking sneer on his handsome face. 'Him,' she said in a dark voice.

The table went silent again. Admitting that Nolan was a jerk seemed dangerous somehow. If he ever found out, they'd be his next targets.

'Nolan *is* an asshole,' Ava breathed. 'He started rumors about me. *Awful* ones.'

Mackenzie's cheeks were blazing red. She stared down at her hands, picking at the edge of her cuticle. 'He's got . . . something he's been holding over me, too.'

Julie nodded. She hated Nolan for his role in Parker's incident. If it hadn't been for him, maybe none of it would have happened. Parker would still be her old self.

Ava scratched her pen along the table. 'How would you do it? If you were going to kill him, I mean?'

A light came on behind Caitlin's eyes. 'You know how I'd do it? Oxy. Everyone knows it's his drug of choice.'

'And then he'd be . . . *gone*,' Parker said wistfully.

62

'Or cyanide,' Caitlin had continued. 'Just like in the old movies. It's completely odorless and colorless. Difficult to detect. He'd be dead in minutes.'

Mackenzie had snickered. 'That certainly would do it.'

'Finally.'

Julie looked up. She and Carson had reached the front of the line, and Carson was pumping beer into a red Solo cup. He handed it to Julie. 'Well, cheers, Julie Redding,' he said, touching his cup to hers. 'I hope to get to know you better.'

'I hope so, too . . .' Julie was about to say more when something on the television in the den caught her eye. The chief of police stood at a podium in front of dozens of reporters, his face lit by camera flashes. Across the bottom of the screen, the text read: POLICE HOLD PRESS CONFERENCE ABOUT HOTCHKISS DEATH.

'Oh my god,' she said. Without thinking, she left the keg, grabbed the remote off the side table, and turned the volume up.

More kids drifted over, too. 'Cut the music,' Asher Collins yelled. Matt Hill did as he'd asked, and Rihanna was silenced mid-lyric. The entire room fell quiet, and clearly sensing that something big was happening, the kids from outside drifted in to watch as well.

On-screen, the chief cleared his throat and spoke into the microphone. 'The autopsy report on Nolan Hotchkiss is in at this time,' he said. A flashbulb popped. A microphone moved closer to his face. 'While we are not able to reveal the details at this point, evidence of foul play was found, and we no longer believe his death to have been caused by an accidental overdose.'

'What the . . .?' someone breathed.

'Intense,' said Nyssa, her face pale. She had sidled up to Julie without her noticing. And Julie watched as Claire Coldwell clutched Blake's hand, tears streaming down her face. Across the room, Mackenzie's eyes fluttered rapidly behind her glasses. Caitlin and Ava exchanged horrified glances. Alex glared at the TV screen, looking dazed.

Julie sat down hard on the edge of the couch, her heart seizing in her chest. *No*, she thought. *This can't be happening.* She thought about the conversation in the film classroom. All those people around them. All those listening ears.

The officer cleared his throat, staring stonily out at the crowd of reporters for a beat. When he spoke again, it was in a matter-of-fact voice, calm and deliberate. 'We're investigating all leads.' He paused for a moment, glancing at his notes. 'At this time, we're treating this as a homicide investigation. Someone – or *someones* – killed Nolan Hotchkiss. And we won't rest until we find them.'

CHAPTER SIX

It was Sunday morning, and the Beacon Heights Episcopal Church was filled to capacity for Nolan Hotchkiss's funeral. Parker stood at the back, tugging at the black wool slacks she'd borrowed from Julie. The air was warm and pungent, the waxy smell of candles mixing with expensive perfumes. High overhead, the gilded ceilings and ornate columns gleamed in the murky light. In front of the altar sat a glossy wooden coffin, heaped with lilies, roses, and hydrangea blossoms. The funeral was closed-casket. Parker couldn't help but wonder if that was because the marker hadn't washed off Nolan's skin.

Now you're as scarred as I am, she couldn't help thinking, and then hated herself for her bitterness.

The pews were packed with kids, some sitting with their parents, others clustered with their friends. Everyone in school had turned up, especially now that the news had come out that Nolan had been murdered. All sorts of theories swirled. That Nolan had gotten in too deep with a bunch of drug dealers, and they'd offed him while people were partying downstairs. That Nolan had stolen a Mafia don's girlfriend, and mobsters had crept through the window. That one of Mr. Hotchkiss's disgruntled employees had finally gotten his revenge.

Parker herself didn't know what to think. She knew who'd drawn on Nolan, but as for who killed him . . . It hadn't been her and the film studies girls. It couldn't have been.

Right?

In the front row, Mrs. Hotchkiss gave a loud and anguished wail. Then Parker felt someone's hand on her arm and turned. It was Julie. 'Come on,' she whispered. 'This is almost over. And we need to talk.'

She tripped over her feet as Julie pulled her out to the lawn and around the corner to the parking lot, which was deserted. The flagstones were silver from the rain. A wet chill hung on the air.

Ava, Mackenzie, and Caitlin were already waiting by an alcove lush with myrtle bushes and sedge grass. A weather-beaten statue of Saint Francis stood in the center, a bird feeder full of seeds in the palm of his hands.

Julie unfolded her green-and-pink plaid umbrella, and she and Parker huddled beneath it. 'Hey,' they mumbled to the girls as they approached. Parker yanked her hoodie over her head. These girls were nice – they looked at her directly without staring, as though there was nothing wrong with her – but still she felt uncomfortable around them.

'What the hell are we going to do?' Ava burst out, her voice tinged with tears.

'We should stay calm,' Julie said evenly, though she was gripping Parker's hand so hard Parker thought her nails might slice straight through her skin. 'I mean, look. We didn't *do* anything. We gave him one Oxy pill – that's all. It's not enough to kill anyone. Especially not him.'

'But that conversation we had.' Caitlin's gaze flicked back and forth. 'The things I'd *said*. The things we *did*.'

'I know,' Parker interrupted, thinking back to that night.

For hours leading up to it, she'd considered not going at all, but the temptation of getting Nolan back – really getting him back – was too great. She'd slipped into the party unseen, her hoodie up over her head. She'd found Julie instantly. 'Ready for this?' she'd asked her, her smile wide.

Julie's smile had been much more nervous. 'I think so.'

They'd gone upstairs one by one. On the landing, Parker had looked down into the crowd, but *no one* was watching them – they were either texting, or chugging beers, or hooking up with someone. She remembered seeing Asher in the corner, flirting with a girl from Brillwood Prep, and, Ursula, talking to a JV player. Julie's friend Nyssa was making out with a basketball player while her wannabe clone, Ashley, was talking to the hot new guy from Australia. Parker had continued up the dark stairwell, downing a beer and dropping the cup on one of the risers.

The others joined her in the third-floor bathroom. A vase of fresh yellow asters sat on the vanity counter.

Mackenzie had looked at Caitlin. 'You have it, right?'

Caitlin pulled out an orange prescription bottle with her name across the top. 'Yep.'

'How much should we give him?' Ava asked.

'Just one,' Parker said knowingly, thinking back to what Nolan had done to her. 'It's strong, especially with booze.'

Caitlin shook one pill onto the counter and used the cap of the bottle to grind it into a powder. Julie handed her a cup of beer, and she brushed the powder in and stirred with her finger.

67

And then they turned off the lights. The cup passed from girl to girl: they each spat in it for good measure. Their voices mingled together. *He deserves everything that's coming to him. Everyone's going to thank us for this.*

They watched in silence from the balustrade as Ava took the cup and drifted downstairs. It took them a few minutes to pick Nolan out of the crowd – he was filling his beer at the keg.

Nolan seemed surprised to see Ava, but took the drink unquestioningly from her hand. *'Hey there,'* said Mackenzie in a whispery voice faux-narrating as Ava leaned forward to murmur in Nolan's ear. *'Having fun tonight?'*

Then Mac switched to Nolan's part, pitching her voice deep. *'Now that you're here I am. What's this delicious drink you've brought me? So good! Glug glug glug.'*

The other girls, Parker included, giggled. She held her breath as Nolan took his first sip.

'Tonight's been awesome,' Mackenzie continued the joke. *'I've already pantsed a freshman, poured beer all over a girl so I could see through her shirt, and pushed four of my so-called friends into the pool. Luckily I'm super rich and all these pathetic douchebags spend all their time pandering to my every need, so there are no repercussions to my totally asinine behavior.'*

Below them, Ava touched his bicep, a coy smile playing across her lips. She knew how to keep a boy's attention, that was for sure. It was a skill Parker used to have, too.

Suddenly, they were coming upstairs. The girls dodged back into the bathroom, closing the door except for a fraction of an inch. A moment later, Ava half escorted, half dragged Nolan past. He looked wasted already.

'I've missed you so much, baby,' she purred. They could hear him mumble something in response.

They all ran out into the hall. From there, through an open bedroom door, they could see Nolan lying on his bed, Ava standing over him.

At first he was pawing at her, but then his eyelids started to droop sleepily and his words began to slur. Parker recalled glancing over her shoulder nervously, hoping no one would come up the stairs and see this. All of them gathered to watch, and for a second, it seemed wrong, like they'd turned into bullies.

Then he noticed the others in the doorway. He picked them out one by one, saying something about each of them. Parker's heart had hardened again. She was almost glad when his eyelids fluttered and he drifted off.

He's fine, she'd heard one of their voices say. *He passes out every weekend. Let's get to work.*

That had been when Mackenzie pulled the bright-colored Sharpies out of her bag. They each had taken a pen and crept closer. Caitlin had swept in first, drawing *Not to be trusted* across his forehead. Mackenzie had started to write *Liar*, and Julie had written *Monster*.

'The police are going to question everyone at that party,' Ava broke in now. 'What if someone saw us go up there with him? And, I mean, it's not like we were careful. Our fingerprints were probably all over that bathroom and the beer he'd drank. They could go back and collect everything for crime investigation.'

Mac put her hands on her hips. 'You're saying this as if we actually *did* something. We only gave him one pill, Ava,

69

something he did himself all the time. Just because we talked about killing him doesn't make us guilty. The police found evidence of foul play – there's no way *one pill* could be foul play.'

'But we did do something! We still gave him *a* pill. And we wrote all over him,' Caitlin exclaimed hysterically, raising her hands.

Parker twisted her mouth. But she couldn't quite look at the issue head-on. She could barely relive that night without getting a headache.

'Maybe we should tell someone about this,' Mac suggested. 'Like, you know, come clean about how we pranked him.'

Ava's eyes boggled. 'We *still* gave him Oxy, and that's *still* pretty bad. What if they don't believe us? What if they think we did it anyway?'

'I agree,' Julie admitted. 'We could get in a lot of trouble. I mean' – she swallowed – 'we all have a lot to lose.'

They were all silent again, thinking of what was on the line – their reputations, graduation, college, their parents' approval.

'I don't understand what *actually* happened,' Caitlin finally whispered, glancing nervously back and forth. 'I mean, everyone's saying it was Oxy. If so, someone else must have given him more drugs after we left, don't you think?'

'A lot of people hated him,' Mac whispered, glancing uncertainly at the packed parking lot.

Then Parker had a horrible thought. 'Do you think someone's trying to pin it on us?'

'I wondered the same thing,' Ava said.

Mackenzie fiddled with her glasses. 'No one was near us when we were talking in class.'

'The room isn't *that* big,' Caitlin said shakily. 'Who's in film studies with us?'

'Nolan,' Julie said. 'Or he *was.*'

'Alex,' Ava said. 'He'd never do something like that, even if he was eavesdropping.'

'Oliver Hodges,' Caitlin named. 'Ben Riddle. Quentin Aaron. They're off Nolan's radar. Ursula Winters on my soccer team. Fiona Ridge, who's vegan.'

Parker rolled her eyes. 'Just because she's vegan doesn't mean she wouldn't murder someone.'

Caitlin nodded, too. 'Fiona wouldn't hurt a fly.'

'My friend Claire's in the class, but I'm sure *she* didn't hear us,' Mackenzie offered. 'She was across the room.'

For a long moment, nobody spoke. Finches and waxwings chased one another across the courtyard, fighting over seeds. Beyond the yard's stone walls, they heard the slick hum of traffic on wet roads.

'This is so messed up.' Ava paced back and forth, her high, spiky heels wobbling precariously on the wet stones. 'What are we going to do?'

'We keep our heads down,' Julie said in a steady voice. 'We know we didn't kill anyone. This is all some kind of . . . coincidence, maybe. Or else someone is trying to get us in trouble. Either way, we should just pretend none of it happened.'

'So we . . . lie?' Mackenzie asked, biting the corner of her lip.

'We lie,' Julie said firmly.

Parker took a quick, shuddering breath. All at once, she felt eyes on the back of her neck, boring into her. She glanced back toward the entrance to the courtyard, but no one was there.

No one was watching except Saint Francis, his empty stone gaze cold and distant. A shiver traveled through her body, and a telltale white-hot spike of pain jabbed through one eye. She cradled her head in her hands.

Keep it together, she thought. *You can't fall apart now.*

'Are you going to the reception?' Ava was asking, glancing around at the others. The Hotchkisses had made a big deal about inviting everyone to their tony country club across town.

Mackenzie nodded miserably. 'We're performing there with the ensemble. I have to go. What about you?'

Ava shrugged. 'I guess it's probably a good idea to be seen there. We'll just make an appearance. Eat some crudités.' She gave a short, bitter bark of laughter. 'It's going to be the party of the year.'

Another shooting pain cut through Parker's skull, raking over her vision with lightning-white streaks. She felt Julie's hand on her back and looked up to see that her friend had noticed what was wrong. Her eyes were wide. There was a worried look on her face.

'Meet you guys over there,' Julie said, then turned away, helping Parker to a bench. In seconds, she and Julie were alone.

'Are you okay?' Julie asked, rubbing Parker's back.

Parker swallowed, her mouth sticky with bile. Nausea started to spread through her body. She thought she might be sick. 'I don't think I can manage the reception,' she whispered, pulling her knees up on the bench and resting her forehead against them. 'Headache. Bad one. I need to go lie down.'

'Okay,' Julie said softly. 'That's all right. I don't think anyone at the party saw you anywhere near Nolan, anyway. You don't have to worry.'

'I'm not worried.' Parker's voice came out angrier than she'd intended.

But her stomach writhed. Julie was right – no one had seen her at the party. She was the invisible girl, after all. There was no reason to be paranoid.

Julie stood up. 'Let's get you home, okay? *My* home, I mean. You look awful.'

'No.' Parker shook her head, then immediately regretted it as another wave of pain washed over her. 'You go. Ava's right. You should get to the reception. I can make it back to your place on my own.'

Julie gave her a long, measuring look. Then she hugged her. 'Call me if you need anything, okay?'

'Okay. I promise.'

Julie handed her the umbrella, then tugged up the hood of her jacket and walked quickly through the rain toward the street where she'd parked her car. Parker sat unmoving for a long moment, staring after her. She noticed a gargoyle in a high cornice on the side of the church, sticking its tongue out at her. A shiver ran through her as she met its malicious little eyes.

There's nothing to worry about, she told herself. *There's no reason anyone would even suspect you were involved*.

But she couldn't shake the feeling that her already damaged life was about to get a whole lot worse.

CHAPTER SEVEN

'Strings, I can barely hear you!' Mrs. Rabinowitz shouted, gesturing at the violins. 'That *crescendo* needs to be powerful!'

Mac sat in a small chair in the Beacon Heights High music wing, her cello wedged between her knees. It was Monday and Mrs. Rabinowitz was making them rehearse Mahler's funeral march. She'd added it to the fall concert program, in memory of Nolan.

The room smelled like the floral Febreze spray Mrs. Rabinowitz always sprayed before practice, and there were pictures of famous conductors and composers on the wall – a persnickety Mozart, a scattered-looking Beethoven, a haughty Scarlatti, who Mackenzie thought was always following her around the room with his discerning gaze. Today she felt as if they were all glaring at her, condemning her for what she'd done to Nolan. She still couldn't wrap her mind around it. Was someone really trying to frame them?

You were the one who sent out those photos, a punishing voice in her head said. *You really think that trick that techie guy from band camp taught you to set up a fake e-mail address is going to fly with the cops? They're going to find you.*

Next to her, Claire – currently the second-chair cellist to Mac's first-chair – leaned back and forth with the music as they played. When they got to the end of the page in the sheet music, Claire hurriedly flipped the page and fumbled her bow. It was always the second chair who turned the pages. Mac knew the duty well: she and Claire were always swapping positions, the two of them almost equally talented.

When Mac glanced up again, the room was silent, and Mrs. R was staring at her. 'Mackenzie, you're a half-beat off.'

Mac blinked. 'I am?'

Mrs. R nodded. 'You didn't notice?'

Mac started to panic. Was she *that* out of it?

Claire glanced at Mac sympathetically. 'We're all a little distracted today.'

That was an understatement. All day, Mac had been on the verge of hyperventilating. What made it worse was Principal Obata's announcement when everyone returned to class after lunch. *Social workers are on call for anyone who needs extra support right now. And please, if you have any information about the party, please talk to a teacher or a counselor – no questions asked.*

No questions asked. The words kept swirling through Mac's mind as she ran her bow across her strings. Maybe they *should* step forward. What if they'd seen something important, something they didn't even realize? Maybe they could help catch the real killer.

'*Psst.*'

Mac looked over. Claire sat next to her, her cello bow resting lightly on her instrument. She pulled out a brown paper bag and handed it over.

75

'I got these for you,' Claire whispered.

Mac peeked inside. Mini gummy violins lay in a pile almost to the top. Gummies were her favorite food, and the violins were hard to find – you could only get them at a specialty candy shop in Seattle.

She looked at Claire. 'What's this for?'

Her friend shrugged. 'A pick-me-up. You've seemed down lately.'

There was no malice in her expression. No snarky, underhanded manipulation, only a kind, earnest look. A sour taste welled in Mac's mouth. *You kissed her boyfriend*, a voice chided. *You said something terrible about her in film studies. And it's too late to take any of it back.*

For the first time in her life, Mac wondered if she was a truly awful person.

Suddenly, the door to the music room swung open, and all heads swiveled up. Two men in suits stepped inside. They looked around for a moment, their eyes raking over the symphony. Mrs. Rabinowitz gave a little jump and turned to face them, too.

'Sorry to interrupt,' the first man said. He was huge – at least six foot six – and dark-skinned, in a charcoal-gray suit. His voice was a booming baritone that filled the space effortlessly.

Mrs. Rabinowitz stepped off the riser. Next to him she looked tiny, like a little round teddy bear in her fuzzy brown cardigan. 'What can we do for you?'

'I'm Detective Peters. This is my partner, Detective McMinnamin. We're trying to gather some information about what happened at the party the other night. Can we take a few minutes of your class's time?'

Mrs. Rabinowitz gestured for him to take over, but McMinnamin stepped forward instead. He was a skinny, pale man with rabbity front teeth, and he held a stack of four-by-six index cards in his hand. He looked around the room, his eyes narrowed.

'I'm going to pass out these cards, and I want all of you to write the alphabet on one side and your names on the other.' His voice was brisk and no-nonsense. 'Uppercase letters, please. Print, not cursive.'

Kenleigh Robbins, who played viola, raised her hand. 'Do I *have* to?'

'Of course not,' McMinnamin said almost automatically. 'But we will take note of anyone who doesn't participate.'

He started handing out the cards. Mackenzie stiffened as he passed by her music stand, his eyes lingering on her for a moment before he moved on.

She knew what was going on. They needed a handwriting sample. Her mind scattered, and she tried to remember exactly what she'd written on Nolan's body that Friday night. She'd started a frowny face with heavy eyebrows, then written *LIAR* in all caps.

Slowly, she lowered her cello to its stand and grabbed her sheet-music folder to write on. With trembling hands, she printed out the letters one by one, trying to make them slightly more slanted than the block lettering she'd used on Nolan's skin.

When everyone was finished, McMinnamin picked up the index cards. Peters took a dry-erase marker and scrawled a phone number and his name on the whiteboard. 'I know how these parties go,' he said affably, a trace of a smile playing around his lips. 'No one wants to admit they were there, because it'll get everyone in trouble.' Then his affect changed, his mouth turning downward, his eyes serious. 'But something bad happened to one of your own.' He paused to let that sink in. 'We want to know what happened. And we need your help for that. I am asking anyone who was at the party that night – whether you saw Nolan or not – to give me a call at this number. You might know details that will help us get a sense of the timeline. Everything you tell me will be completely confidential.'

Mackenzie swallowed hard. Then she felt someone's hand in hers. Claire's fingers held tight. Her lips were trembling.

Mac gawked at her, surprised. 'Are you okay?'

Claire shook her head. 'We were at that party. It means we'll have to talk to them. *I'll* have to talk to them.'

So? Mac wanted to say. What did *Claire* have to feel guilty about? They'd gone to Nolan's party together, but Claire had disappeared the minute she caught sight of Blake.

Officer Peters gave their teacher a pleasant nod. 'Thanks so much for your time.' He exchanged a meaningful glance with Officer McMinnamin, and they both slipped out into the hallway.

Mac peeked at Claire again. Her knees were jumpy, and she was biting her thumbnail to the quick. 'Hey,' Mac said softly, touching Claire's hand. 'If you're worried about talking to the cops, don't be. I'm sure it will be fine. They're going to be nice. You didn't do anything.' *But I did*, a voice in her head said.

Claire's throat bobbed as she swallowed. 'Thanks,' she said shakily. 'I don't know why I'm so nervous.' She squeezed Mac's hand again and took a few deep breaths.

Mackenzie's phone beeped. She peeked into her bag at the screen. *New text from Blake*, it read.

Her heart started to pound. She whipped it out and read it, hiding it from Claire's view.

Hey, Blake wrote. *Need to work on new sets. Extra practice this week? My house, tomorrow night at 7?*

Mac held the phone between her hands, deliberating. She didn't understand what had happened between them that night at Cupcake Kingdom. The only time she'd seen him since the kiss was at Matt Hill's party, where Claire had led Blake toward the big cushion-filled den, leaving Mackenzie alone by the snack table, holding both their beers. Reminding her that yes, Blake had kissed her, but he was with Claire, and Claire was her best friend.

Her gaze fell to the bag of gummy violins on the ground. She looked at Claire next, her face so vulnerable and open. From this day forward, Mac would be a different person. A *better* person. Which meant she'd never kiss Blake again.

I guess so, but it'll have to be quick. Audition's looming, she typed, and sent off the text. There. Hopefully that sounded clinical. Uninterested. Like she was just another member of his band.

Then she deleted his text, wishing she could erase the memory of their kiss just as easily.

CHAPTER EIGHT

After school that day, Caitlin pulled into her driveway to grab her soccer cleats, which she'd forgotten for practice. She found them right away and rushed out of her room, back to her car – with any luck, she'd only miss warm-ups. But then she noticed the TV on in the den. A news reporter stood in front of Nolan Hotchkiss's house, which was now surrounded by yellow police tape, sawhorses, and gawkers.

'At the moment, the police are just asking questions, gathering facts, and canvassing the Hotchkiss home,' the reporter said. 'There were a lot of students at the Hotchkiss home the night of the party, and it's unclear exactly what happened – and when.'

Ursula Winters appeared on the screen. 'I loved Nolan so much,' she said, her voice full of feeling. 'Everyone did. It's such a horrible blow.'

Caitlin's mouth hung open. Ursula hated Nolan. Not because of what he did to Taylor, but because he'd rejected her when she asked him out. She even remembered Ursula bad-mouthing him on the soccer field shortly after he died: *You can talk about a dead guy if he was an asshole.* And then she'd looked at Caitlin pointedly, as if those were *her* words. Which they kind of were.

Then came a shot of Mrs. Hotchkiss, a thin, severe-looking, overly Botoxed woman who had a plaid headband holding back her ash-blond hair. Her eyes were red, and her mouth wobbled. 'I just don't understand who would do this to my boy. He was everyone's friend.'

'Are you freaking *kidding* me?' Caitlin snarled.

'*Ahem.*'

She looked up. One of her moms, Sibyl, was sitting in the slipper chair in the corner, a stack of papers and a calculator balanced on her lap. Her mom was an accountant, so she often kept odd hours, coming home in the middle of the day for lunch, rushing off to finish a tax return on a weekend, practically absent from March to April.

'Caitlin,' Sibyl said gently, but also firmly.

'What?' Caitlin glared at her. 'I'm sorry if I sound callous, but Nolan was *not* everyone's friend. You know it, too.'

Sibyl put the papers on the table next to her and stared at her lap. 'I know what I know,' she said gently. 'But I let go of the fury I had for that boy a long time ago. If I didn't, it would consume me. Like perhaps it's consuming you.'

Caitlin crossed her arms over her chest. 'Yeah, well. You're a stronger person than I am.'

Her mother rose from the chair and came over to stand next to Caitlin. Up close, she had minute lines around her eyes and threads of gray through her hair. Her body was soft, comfortable, the way a mom's should be. Her lips parted, and she said, 'You were at that party, weren't you? Michelle and I were talking about it. She said you and Josh went together.'

81

'A lot of people were at that party,' Caitlin said quickly, her heart starting to pound.

'I know, I know. I just hate that something so . . . *awful* happened somewhere so close to you. Again.' Her mother looked at her hard. 'You know, sometimes, when I'm angry, I do things that I shouldn't. I've told you I was teased a lot in high school for being gay. One time, I got revenge on one of the girls who teased me the most. Her name was Lindsey.'

'What did you do?'

Her mother fiddled with the Bic pen in her hand. 'During gym class, I snuck into the locker room and cut out the crotch of her jeans and stole her underwear. No one locked up their stuff – I didn't even have to break in.'

'Mom!' Caitlin's eyes widened. 'That's horrible!'

'I know.' Sibyl's brow furrowed. 'It *is* horrible. And you know what? I felt awful as soon as I did it. It just wasn't worth it at all.'

Caitlin could feel her mother watching her. There was a long silence, like maybe her mom was waiting for her to confess something.

A memory flashed in her mind of that night. Nolan had collapsed woozily onto his bed. For a moment afterward, Caitlin felt a pang of guilt. Lying there, Nolan looked almost vulnerable, sort of like how her brother looked when he used to fall asleep on the couch.

But then he'd gazed at Caitlin and smiled. 'You know what your brother sounded like when I swirlied him?' Then he'd made this horrible, girlish wail, a sound so humiliating that she'd almost slapped him. Instead, she'd written *Not to be trusted* across his face.

82

She turned away. 'I didn't do anything to Nolan, if that's what you're getting at,' she lied.

Her mother held her gaze for a beat longer, then nodded. 'Of course you didn't.'

Then she stood up, gathered her things, and walked out of the room. 'I'm running to the office,' she called over her shoulder. 'I've got a late meeting. Be back later.'

The door slammed. Caitlin sat with her hands in her lap, feeling jumpy and strange. She hated lying to her mom, but what was she supposed to do?

She still was struggling with the fact that someone really *had* killed Nolan. So many kids had been at the party. But was there someone who hated *her*, specifically? Someone who would have wanted Nolan gone – and wanted her to be blamed? Someone who was in her film studies class *and* at that party?

Ursula, she realized with a start. The girl sat in the back of film studies and usually nodded off as soon as Granger turned out the lights. But they were just soccer rivals. Ursula wasn't nutty enough to kill someone and frame Caitlin just to get her spot on the high school team. *Was* she?

Caitlin stood and shook out her hands, itching to get on the field. Maybe it would help her blow off some steam. She grabbed her cleats, strode to her car, and swung into the driver's seat.

When she turned the key in the ignition, though, nothing happened. Caitlin frowned. No lights came on. The radio didn't come on. The car charger didn't glow blue. She tried the ignition again and again, but it seemed as though the battery was dead. 'Crap,' she whispered, glancing around the driveway. Sibyl had already left. Could anything *else* go wrong today?

Pulling out her phone, she tried to think. First she called Vanessa, but she didn't pick up, probably already on the field for warm-ups. Shannon, Sujatha, and Gina didn't answer, either. Voice mail, voice mail, voice mail.

'Damn it,' Caitlin whispered, pacing around the car. After a moment, she pressed the number two on her speed dial – Josh. He didn't have practice today; the boys' coach was out sick.

Josh's cell went to voice mail, though that was typical – half the time, he left the thing at home. She dialed his landline next. It rang a few times, and then a gravelly voice picked up and mumbled hello.

'Hey,' Caitlin said gratefully, the words coming out in a rush. 'My car won't start, and I really have to get to practice.'

'Oh, I'll drive you,' the voice on the other end said.

Caitlin blinked. 'Jeremy?' He and Josh sounded eerily similar. 'Wait, is Josh there?'

'No.' Jeremy sounded a little disappointed. 'But really, Caitlin. I can drive you. It's no big deal.'

'Uh, are you sure you don't mind?' Caitlin asked.

Jeremy laughed on the other end. 'If I minded, I wouldn't have offered. I'll be there in five.'

'Okay.' Caitlin hung up and tried to start the car a few more times, but it didn't magically work just because she wanted it to. As she got out and slammed the door hard, she heard a faint buzzing sound in the distance. A pale green Vespa scooter appeared at the end of the road. Caitlin squinted as it drove right for her house, the helmeted driver hunched forward.

Caitlin drew in a small breath at the sight of him. He wore a pair of cargo shorts and a puffy North Face vest over a long-sleeved shirt, his longish hair falling into his eyes. She couldn't help but notice how muscular his bare legs were. *He looks hot*, she thought. Then she shut her eyes, surprised at the notion.

'So. How'd you break your car?' Jeremy asked.

Caitlin stared at the ground. All at once, she felt her eyes fill with tears.

'Hey.' Jeremy's voice dropped. 'Oh my god. Caitlin. What is it?'

Caitlin didn't even know what it was. Her mom's weird confession about that girl who picked on her? Taylor? Nolan? *Definitely* Nolan. All of it, all of it.

Jeremy had stepped closer. He put his hand on her arm. 'I get it,' he said softly. 'You need to get to soccer. You need to run around and get loose and lose yourself. Right?'

She blinked at him. It was as though she'd said the words herself.

'I feel like that sometimes,' Jeremy admitted. 'Like . . . if I don't do something, and I don't do it right that second, I'm going to explode.'

She blinked hard, willing her tears back. 'So what do you do?'

Jeremy shrugged. 'Usually, I get on this and just go.' He patted the Vespa. 'You cool with this? Or do you still think these things are for losers?'

'I don't –' Then Caitlin clapped her mouth shut. She remembered the day Jeremy had gotten the Vespa. He'd been fourteen years old, not technically old enough to even ride one, and he'd bought it secondhand from someone on Craigslist. The thing was thirty years old and didn't run, but he'd taken it to his parents' garage, downloaded an old manual, and asked questions on a bunch of discussion forums. He had it running in a few months.

Those things are for pussies, Josh had said. *It's a freaking scooter.* And Caitlin had giggled, too. Jeremy's face had fallen. That was back in the day when Josh's opinion had mattered to him.

Now, as she looked at the bike, she fully realized the effort he'd put into restoring it to its former glory . . . and how *cool* it looked. Could *she* do something so amazing? Could Josh? Maybe that was why he'd teased: because, in a funny way, he'd been jealous.

Caitlin had laughed along with Josh's jokes at Jeremy's expense because it seemed unfaithful to side with her boyfriend's little brother. But now she realized how immature that had been. Jeremy was a person – a seemingly interesting person. She'd known him for years now, and she was just realizing that. It struck her as the same, blindsided way she'd dealt with Taylor – not really *seeing* him, understanding him, until it was too late.

'Can I wear your helmet?' she asked.

'I insist.' Jeremy's eyes shone as he handed it to her. It was warm from his wearing it moments before. It smelled of some sort of hair product.

Jeremy stuffed her gear into a canvas saddlebag, then straddled the bike. Caitlin climbed on behind him, his torso warm against hers as she slid her arms around his waist. His shirt smelled like wood smoke and fir trees, as though he'd taken a long nature walk. She'd never noticed that about him.

'Hold on,' Jeremy instructed.

They swooped out of Caitlin's subdivision and onto a

wooded, undeveloped road. The watery sunlight filtered down through the treetops, making everything greenish-gold below. Caitlin felt like they were flying.

'This is amazing,' she admitted when they slowed for a traffic light.

'Right?' Jeremy glanced at her and grinned. 'Riding is my favorite thing in the world. You know what I'd love to do someday? Take a trip across the country. Like Jack Kerouac in *On the Road*. Meet all kinds of crazy people. Have adventures.'

'I read that, too,' Caitlin said with appreciation. 'But, um, wasn't Kerouac in a car?'

'Eh, close enough.' Jeremy shrugged. 'Don't you think that would be fun?'

'Actually, I do,' Caitlin said faintly. She'd had the same dreams of wanderlust after finishing the book. *Maybe I could travel before college*, she'd thought.

But when she'd voiced the idea to Josh, he'd looked at her crazily. 'What about All-Stars?' he'd asked her. 'And they're going to need you in July at UDub for training.'

Lake Washington opened up before them, steel blue and sparkling. Jeremy drove them down a quiet path into the Kikisoblu Bay Park, which met the water in a jagged, rocky beach. Caitlin loved going this way to practice. It took a little longer, but it was so beautiful. She wished, suddenly, that she could do this all day: drift down the road on the back of this scooter, her hair flowing behind her, the wind whipping through her, the sounds rushing past her so loudly that she didn't have time to think about any of her troubles. And, oh yeah, her arms wrapped tightly around a boy, his body pressed

87

close to hers, too, keeping her safe from falling off.

Jeremy spoke as they slowed down. 'Do you happen to remember me freshman year?'

She snorted. 'Um, of course I do.'

'I was a skinny little nerd back then. Taking three junior-level AP classes, doing debate and model UN. You know, all the stuff skinny little nerds do. But we were in study hall together. You and me.'

Caitlin squinted. 'Yeah,' she said slowly. 'I remember that.'

'And this one time, you lent me your pen because I didn't have one. And when I looked at it, I was astonished – it was a Dungeons & Dragons pen. The coolest thing I'd ever seen.'

Caitlin laughed. 'It was probably Taylor's.'

'Yeah, but you'd been using it before you gave it to me,' Jeremy pointed out. 'It didn't even occur to you that it was, I don't know, weird.'

Caitlin shrugged. 'Okay.'

'I just . . . remember that about you,' Jeremy said. 'I liked that. You were different. I mean, good at soccer for sure, but you had depth, too.'

Caitlin thought about this for a while. She tried to fight against the compliment, but it was a nice thing to say about someone. Had Josh ever talked about her being deep or different? Surely, right? Only, she couldn't think of an instance.

'Thanks,' she said, smiling.

Jeremy pulled into the school and hit the brakes for a moment. He glanced back and grinned at her. 'You know, it's good to see you smiling. You've had this tough-girl attitude since Taylor died,' he said gently. Then he moved even closer.

Almost like he was going to kiss her.

Caitlin told herself to move, but her limbs didn't cooperate. She just stared into Jeremy's large, inquisitive eyes, wondering what might happen next.

'There you are!'

Caitlin's head whipped around.

Vanessa, her red hair glinting in the sunlight, rushed toward them across the parking lot, her cleats clacking on the pavement. 'Coach Leah was just about to send out a search party!' Then she looked at who Caitlin was riding with and did a double take. 'Oh, hey, Jeremy.'

'Sorry. Just some car trouble.' Caitlin hopped off the Vespa, her cheeks flaming. She felt guilty, as if she'd somehow done something wrong.

Vanessa turned. 'Well, let's hustle. Coach is in a mood.'

Caitlin ran after her friend. It wasn't until she reached the practice field that she realized she hadn't said thank you to Jeremy – or acknowledged, maybe, what they'd been about to do. But of course she didn't acknowledge *that*. He was Josh's *brother*. Nothing more.

Still, she looked back to the curb. Jeremy was still idling there, helmet in hand. He gave Caitlin a long, lingering look. She froze as his warm brown eyes found hers. Somehow, it was like he was looking right into her soul.

And like he could tell that she'd almost let him kiss her.

CHAPTER NINE

On Monday night, Ava and Alex were curled up on the giant L-shaped couch in Ava's den. A *Harry Potter* movie marathon was on, but the two of them were paying more attention to each other. Ava would've rather brought him into her bedroom, of course; but her dad and stepmom were home, and there were strict rules in Ava's house about boyfriend-girlfriend contact in unsupervised spaces.

'Have I told you lately how gorgeous you are?' Alex murmured, pulling her close. He smelled like clean cashmere sweater and Old Spice.

Ava nudged him playfully. 'Flattery will get you nowhere, my friend.'

'No ulterior motives.' Alex shook his curly brown head emphatically. 'It's just the truth. You, Ava Jalali, are a complete knockout. Just don't let it go to your head.'

'Don't worry,' Ava teased, touching the tip of his nose. 'With you around to keep my ego in check, there's no chance of that.'

Alex leaned forward and kissed her. Ava shut her eyes and reached her arms around his shoulders to pull him closer. She and Alex had been dating for a year, but their kisses never, *ever* got old.

Neither did the compliments. It was weird: all her life, Ava had known she was beautiful. Plenty of people told her so: photographers, modeling managers, even a guy who once wanted to make an avatar of her for a video game he was creating. But only when Alex said it did it actually feel real – because, unlike everyone else, he actually cared about *her*, Ava, not just what she looked like. Alex made her feel special all the time, and he had the unique ability to keep her sane and grounded in the overly competitive world of Beacon Heights.

Alex's phone buzzed in his pocket, and he pulled away to look at the screen. 'Crap,' he said. 'I didn't realize how late it was. My parents will kill me if I miss curfew.'

'Stay,' she said. 'You know your parents love you.' *Much more than mine do right now.* The truth was, she hated being alone right now. Whenever she was, panic about Nolan – and about her slipping grades – began to overtake her. Thanks to her evil stepmother, her relationship with her father was tenuous at best. If he ever caught wind of the Nolan rumors, that would be it.

'Are you still upset about that paper?' he asked, as if reading her mind, his brown eyes warm with concern. 'That was really harsh of Mr. Granger.'

Ava suddenly flashed back to that day in class, when she and the other girls in the group had discussed vengeance and ended up talking about Nolan. *What if we dose him with Oxy?* she heard their voices say. *Not too much – just enough to knock him out. Just enough to take some incriminating pictures.*

She gritted her teeth. *Stop thinking about it.*

'Yeah, that sucked,' she said aloud. 'I wonder if I should talk to him. See if I can rewrite it?'

Alex's gaze darted to the left. 'Are you sure that's a good idea?'

Ava looked at him sharply. 'Why would you say that?' Instantly she thought of the rumors about her. But Alex didn't buy into them. 'It was *your* idea,' she added.

Alex shrugged. 'Never mind. You're right. You should try to change the grade.'

'Okay.' Ava gave Alex's hand a squeeze. She felt a little uncertain after Alex's comment, but maybe Granger rubbed guys the wrong way for the same reason all the girls liked him. 'I'll ask him on Monday.'

They walked down the grand staircase to the first floor. Instantly, the heady scent of the room spray Ava's stepmother used assaulted her nostrils. Even though her father had been married to Leslie for several years, Ava still found the smell offensive. God forbid the house smell like the Iranian spices her father used in his cooking. That would be too foreign and weird.

Of course, the rest of the place had changed as well. Gone were the Persian rugs her father and mother had bought in Tehran during their last visit, replaced with two beige couches and a leather recliner that Leslie had picked out. Gone were the gold-footed coffee table and the silk swags on the windows that Ava used to play among when she was little; in their place was a glass table and modern wooden blinds. Ava wasn't sure what Leslie was trying to erase – her husband's heritage, or his ex-wife's legacy.

They reached the front door, and Ava went up on her tiptoes to give Alex one more goodbye kiss. Ava was tall, but he still had a good six inches on her. 'Call me when you get home,' she said.

He nodded. 'Love you,' he said, kissing her lightly on the forehead before stepping outside.

'Ava?' she heard from upstairs, as she shut the door behind him. 'Is that you?'

Her father appeared at the top of the staircase wearing a white terrycloth robe he would have never bought for himself – clearly a Leslie purchase. His graying hair was mussed, the way it always looked when he was working late, and his wire-frame glasses hung low on his nose.

'How's my girl?' he asked, just the hint of an accent left in his voice.

'Everything is *great!*' Ava winced, realizing she'd injected far too much enthusiasm in the lie. But to her surprise, her father didn't catch it.

'I'm glad. Good night, *jigar,*' he said, using their old Iranian term of endearment. Ava felt a sudden rush of affection for her father. With all her stress about the Nolan stuff, she hadn't spent enough time with him lately. She resolved to change that.

'Good night,' she replied, watching as he headed back into his room. She started up the stairs, then changed her mind and went to the kitchen for a glass of water, fumbling for the light switch on the wall.

'Hi, Ava,' came a slurred voice from the darkness.

'Leslie!' Ava jumped at least a foot into the air. *Why are you sitting in the pitch-darkness like a total creep?* she wanted to ask. Her fingers found the switch, and the kitchen was suddenly flooded with light, revealing another room she barely recognized, with its glossy granite countertops and new cabinetry. Leslie sat perched on one of the stools, her long, tanned legs crossed, her blond hair loose around her face, and an empty bottle of Chardonnay next to her on the table.

Just looking at Leslie filled Ava with frustration. Her mother had been short and frumpy, with frizzy reddish hair that she kept in a bun. Nothing like this hard, brittle woman. And her father had loved her mother for her mind: she'd been the head of the math department at UDub, brilliant and flustered and funny. Ava still wasn't sure if Leslie even *had* a mind. And what brains she did have, she seemed intent on drinking away.

'I think the question is, what were *you* doing, sneaking your boyfriend out late at night?' Leslie challenged.

'It's nine PM, and we were watching a movie in the den. Last I checked, that was still allowed.' Ava crossed her arms over her chest defensively.

'I think you're spending too much time with him. I'd like it if he didn't come around here anymore,' Leslie said slowly.

'Oh yeah?' Ava shot back. 'Well, good thing it's not really up to you.'

Leslie barely flinched. 'I'm worried about you, Ava.' Her voice dripped with false concern. 'I heard some troubling things about you recently, about the sudden . . . *upturn* in your GPA. I'd hate to have to share them with your father.'

Ava gasped. How in the world would *Leslie* hear those rumors? Another mother? Did lots of parents know? 'Th-those are just nasty rumors that an ex-boyfriend started,' she stammered.

'See?' Leslie smiled, showing her too-white teeth. 'It's always about boys with you, Ava. What am I supposed to do except ask you to stop seeing this Alex person?'

Ava's hands clutched into fists at her sides, and she struggled to control her breathing. Even in death, Nolan Hotchkiss was still managing to ruin her life.

The spring of sophomore year, Ava and Nolan had dated for several months – Ava didn't normally run with his crowd, but Nolan had sought her out and had been so persistent that Ava couldn't say no. And while certain things about Nolan annoyed her, she had to admit it had been, well, *fun* being Nolan Hotchkiss's girlfriend. Freshman girls parted for her in the hallway, the way they normally did for Julie Redding and Parker Duvall and their minions. Everyone kept offering her things, study guides and hall passes and invitations to country clubs and lake houses. When she heard that Nolan was bragging about how he was going to sleep with her after junior prom, she wasn't even as bothered by it as she should've been – and she hated that now, hated that she hadn't had the self-respect to see what a scumbag he was. She'd been too wrapped up in his dazzling smile and his lying words, and she went ahead and did everything he wanted.

It was afterward, while Nolan was in the shower, that she picked up his iPhone to put on some music – and saw the texts. There were naked shots from dozens of girls in their class, including one from Delia Marks just an hour earlier. *I want to see you*, she had texted. *Tomorrow night*, Nolan had replied – while he'd been with Ava. *Can't wait to see you. Every inch of you.*

Much more calmly than she felt, Ava had stood up, pulled

on her rumpled Zac Posen dress, and slammed the door on her way out.

But Ava had learned the hard way that no one broke up with Nolan Hotchkiss without suffering the consequences. In retaliation, he told everyone that she'd been sleeping her way through the male faculty at Beacon Heights High – and maybe one or two of the females, too. Everyone knew that Ava had been getting better grades for the past year, and they were more than happy to believe Nolan's explanation. 'Pretty girls don't need brains,' Nolan would say loudly in the hallway whenever Ava was around. 'They have other ways to get what they want.'

It was awful at first – people wrote SLUT on her locker every day for a week. Guys followed her around asking for details of her exploits. Girls stopped talking when she came into a room. She'd texted Nolan in a blind rage: *If you keep telling lies about me, I'll kill you*. But this was Beacon Heights, and the damage had already been done.

Most of it had blown over by the beginning of junior year – everyone had moved on to other scandals, and Ava's friends knew Nolan was a lying scumbag anyway. And then she'd started dating Alex, who loved her for who she was, not how she looked. But Ava knew that the rumors were never truly gone. Every time she caught a group of girls whispering and shooting glances her way, or saw a boy giving her a once-over for a second too long, she wondered if it was because of what Nolan had made up about her.

She thought back to that night, at Nolan's party, when Caitlin had talked her into leading him upstairs. *It has to be you, Ava. Say you want to get back together with him. He'll love that. He thinks he's God's gift to women.*

And Caitlin had been right.

A cold, hard pit formed in her stomach, just like it always did when she thought about the prank. Nolan had been so willing to go upstairs with her, like he really believed she wanted him back. Ava didn't dare tell Alex about what she'd done; she was sure he'd get a little jealous about her seducing her ex. But more than that, he'd be afraid now of how it connected her to Nolan's death. Ava certainly was scared. The others kept insisting that his death was a coincidence, but she felt haunted. *She* had been the one to lead Nolan upstairs. *She* had been the one to feed him that spiked drink. But she knew exactly how much Oxy Caitlin had put in there, though: one measly pill. Just enough to make Nolan loopy. Not to kill him.

So how *had* it?

'Fine.' Ava turned to Leslie and sighed. 'You win. I won't bring Alex over here anymore. Just don't tell my dad about those stupid rumors.'

Leslie smiled, looking pleased and amused. 'I'm so glad we agree, Ava. I just want what's best for you. You know that.' She turned and headed up the stairs without another word.

Ava was so angry she was shaking. *This shouldn't really be a surprise*, she thought. Nolan's rumors had been tormenting her for over a year now. Why would the tormenting stop, just because he was dead?

CHAPTER TEN

After school on Tuesday, Julie sat in her sleek, spotless bedroom, wedged between two cushy throw pillows with a faux-fur blanket wrapped around her legs. Light poured through the window, making the room look clean and cheerful and, most of all, normal. Like the nice, normal bedroom of a normal girl, who had a normal mother and a normal house. A normal girl who had not possibly accidentally killed a classmate in a prank gone terribly wrong.

Don't think about it, she commanded herself. It was a coincidence. A horrible, awful coincidence that they had written on him just before he died. But nobody would believe that if she didn't believe it herself.

Police officers had popped into classrooms yesterday, asking questions. A few kids said they'd already been interviewed about the night of the party, though Julie hadn't been called in. What if someone had seen her go upstairs? What if someone had heard their conversation in film studies? Someone *must* have, right?

Only . . . who?

Now, all Julie wanted to do was lie in her bed with her head under the covers, but she had to be normal, perfect Julie. And normal, perfect Julie was happy and popular. So she had Nyssa on her phone and her friend Colette on hold. Natalie was IMing her on her MacBook Air, she had fifteen Facebook messages to read, and she had three hundred 'likes' on an Instagram selfie she'd posted only last night.

'And someone told me they were making out in the photography darkroom,' Nyssa was saying in Julie's ear, punctuating the gossip with a snicker. She was talking about Rebecca Hallswell and Corey Grier, the newest couple at Beacon, scandalous because they'd both cheated on their exes. 'I mean, get a *little* creative, Corey! The poor girl's hair is going to smell like fixer for the rest of the day!'

'Seriously,' Julie said, rolling her eyes. 'Although there *is* something romantic about the darkroom, you know? That dim lighting. And all those black-and-white photos hanging on clothespins . . .'

'Julie!' a voice called.

'Weirdo,' Nyssa joked. 'Although I'd go to any darkroom with Mr. Granger. Photography is hands down the best club ever.'

'*Julie!*' said the voice again. Then she heard a hacking cough.

'Who's *that?*' Nyssa asked, sounding a little grossed out.

'Um, our cleaning lady,' Julie said, her heart beating hard.

'You should send her home. She sounds sick,' Nyssa said. Then she groaned. 'My mom's calling me. What are you doing this afternoon?'

'Julie!'

'Um . . .' Julie needed off the phone fast. 'Actually, I gotta go, too. Call you later.'

99

She hung up. Then she stood from her desk, her heart beating harder and harder. Her mother called her one more time, her voice rising with urgency. 'Coming,' Julie said, her voice choked with a sob.

And then she opened the door.

Every square foot of carpet was crammed with boxes or furniture or Rubbermaid crates full of random collections. She squeezed through the hallway, shoving her way through a maze of boxes. Plastic garbage bags were piled so high they blocked out the sconces. Her heart thudded against her sternum, a familiar nausea blooming in her stomach.

Every step she took she felt cats brushing her shins, swarming around her ankles. In the kitchen, broken appliances cluttered the floor, old stand mixers and ice-cream makers nestled between paper sacks full of the fragments of shattered dishes. An unusable vintage stove Julie's mother had scavenged from somewhere sat under the window, piled high with stained and swollen cookbooks. Stacks of old newspapers and magazines tied with twine stood five feet tall against the walls. A dingy white cat was curled sleeping on top of one pile, while another sharpened its claws on the stack, leaving tendrils of newsprint drifting across the floor. Cat hair hovered in the air around them, swirling up in eddies every time Julie moved.

Calm down, Julie told herself. She began to count. *One, two, three . . .*

A cat's tail brushed against Julie's bare leg. She thought she might lose her mind. *Four, five, six . . .*

'Julie? Are you coming?'

Dwarfed by the teetering piles, her mother sat at the table, letting a small gray tabby lap the milk out of her cereal bowl. Four more cats swam around the woman's pudgy ankles, mewling for food. Mrs. Redding wore a pink quilted housedress, gray at the hem and stained with food. Her face was soft and doughy, her skin dull-looking. Julie fought the urge to run the kitchen scrub brush over her mother's flesh, to scrape away the outside layer of dirt and neglect. And then turn her sights on the rest of the house. Throw out everything. Burn the place to the ground.

'I'm here,' Julie said, sweeping into the room. Julie snatched the bowl and brought it to the sink, knowing that if she didn't clean it, it would sit there for weeks, or maybe even months.

'I wasn't finished!' her mother cried. Then her eyes boggled. 'And don't throw that away!'

She gestured to Julie's hand, which held a crumpled-up piece of newspaper on the sink as well as a newspaper circular boasting sales that had ended weeks ago. *Why* her mother needed those two items, she had no idea. But, wilting, she placed them back on the counter. On top of some stacked dirty dishes and a pile of other newspaper circulars that were probably equally as obsolete.

Nine. Ten. Eleven. Don't get mad. You'll make her cry, and that's the worst. Twelve. Thirteen. Julie squeezed the sponge tightly, watching the suds ooze out of its pores.

'I was just trying to help, Mom,' she said, her voice steady. She rinsed the last of the breakfast pans and unplugged the drain. Of course there was nowhere to stack the clean dishes – except for on top of the other dishes. She wiped them down with a dish towel, and then carefully stacked them on the teetering pile. 'So, um, you were calling me?'

'Yes. Can you deposit my check today?' her mother said. 'And get some kitty litter from the store?'

Fourteen. Fifteen. Sixteen. Of course her mother needed kitty litter. And god forbid she left the house *herself.* Then again, Julie was grateful for that: her mother might admit Julie was her daughter to someone who'd pass it along to kids at school. And then the jig would be up. 'Uh, sure.'

'And can you get me an *Entertainment Weekly* while you're out?'

A sudden hysterical need to laugh bubbled up in Julie's throat as her eyes slid over the towers of paper around the kitchen. 'I don't know, Mom,' she snapped, unable to resist. 'Maybe you want to catch up on your back issues first?'

She had a fleeting glimpse of her mother's hurt face before she managed to wiggle her way past a cardboard box of Christmas ornaments and into the hallway. Guilt flooded her. She knew her mom was sick, that this was an *illness,* as Dr. Fielder had said, but Julie couldn't help but feel angry at her.

She squeezed into the bathroom, which smelled like the bleach she'd scoured the small room with and was stuffed full of bulk boxes of macaroni and cheese, opened bags of kitty litter, used toothbrushes, empty shampoo bottles, and god knew what else.

She took a deep breath and looked at herself in the mirror. Her glossy auburn hair was sleek and straight. Her pale green blouse was crisp and wrinkle-free.

'You are not your mom. You will not become her,' Julie repeated to herself. She calmed down a little, but she knew she had to get out of the house to keep from losing it. Pulling out her phone, she dialed Parker. 'I need some retail therapy – stat. You in?' Julie said when Parker answered.

'Sure. Pick me up?' Parker said huskily. 'But I have to be done by six. I'm seeing Dr. Fielder then.'

Julie shut her eyes and said a silent *thank goodness*. 'Done. I'm leaving now.'

Twenty minutes later, Julie and Parker were cruising the aisles of Tara's Consignment, a secondhand boutique in Beacon whose owner had a thing for *Gone with the Wind* – there were posters of the movie all over the walls, famous quotes in the dressing rooms, and a Scarlett O'Hara doll behind the counter. It was Julie's favorite store, partly because it was on a nondescript side street away from the main shops – meaning she could slip in without her friends seeing her and asking the obvious questions of why someone like *her* would shop consignment – and also because it was where the rich residents brought last year's castoffs to make room for this season's line. Tara's was how Julie, who basically lived off her lifeguarding wages, could afford Joe's Jeans, Diane von Furstenberg dresses, Joie blouses, and Elizabeth and James accessories.

'How about this?' Julie asked, holding a canary-yellow dress up to Parker's skinny frame.

Parker made a face. 'Have I *ever* worn yellow?'

'Not in a while,' Julie said quietly. 'I'm glad you're seeing Dr. Fielder today. Are you nervous?'

Parker shrugged and walked toward the shoe racks at the back of the store. Julie followed her, knowing she shouldn't push.

She thought of her own session with Elliot Fielder. Unlike

a lot of things that were a stigma in Beacon Heights, having a shrink wasn't one of them. Nyssa, who'd had eating issues, talked about hers all the time. There was even a rumor that Nolan had had a shrink, though Julie doubted it was true. The guy wasn't human enough to need counseling.

Call me Elliot, Dr. Fielder had said, his eyes crinkling as he smiled. Julie had been surprised at how young he was when she opened the door to his small but cozy office.

Elliot had made Julie feel so comfortable as she'd explained her family history to him. All her worries about her mom. *I'm scared that I'm going to be like her,* she'd said. *She used to be so gorgeous, successful, perfect. But then . . . something changed.*

Long ago, her mother had looked just like her. Acted just like her, too, caring about her looks and her home. Caring about what people thought. Julie wasn't sure when she'd started to slip, only that it had been bit by bit. If someone had told her ten years ago that they'd be evicted by the California health board because their house was unsafe to live in – *because of her mother's cats* – Julie would have told them they were a big, fat liar. She hadn't seen her mother's condition coming. And now, she had no way of dealing with it except to breathe . . . and count . . . and hide.

'Have you talked to anyone else about this?' Elliot had asked her.

Julie lowered her eyes. Her secret was *horrible*. People had dropped her in California, made fun of her relentlessly, teasing her on the playground, writing gossip about her on the chalkboard when the class broke for lunch. They all assumed she was as dirty as the house she lived in. That last year felt like a prison – she'd had no friends. Her mom was a stranger now. She literally had no one.

'Only my friend Parker. And now I just need to know if what happened to my mom will happen to me,' she said softly, gathering her courage.

Elliot had been understanding and reassuring. 'You know, from a clinical perspective, you don't fit the mold of someone poised for a mental break,' he'd said. 'You seem like a high-functioning, extremely smart teenager who is balancing a lot of really heavy problems.' In other words: *You are not your mother.*

Julie paused in front of a photograph of Vivien Leigh standing in the doorway of Tara, a wistful expression on her face. If only she could adopt the *Gone with the Wind* mentality that tomorrow was another day. Another day without worries of Nolan or her dirty little secret.

Julie cleared her throat and picked up a studded bracelet from a tray of jewelry on a table. 'What do you think about this?'

Parker frowned. 'That looks like more me than you, don't you think?'

'Well then, I'll buy it for you,' Julie said, marching up to the counter. She slid it across the table to the same college-age girl with green streaks in her hair who always worked there. 'I'd like to get this for my friend,' she said, gesturing to Parker behind her.

Something fluttered across the cashier's face when she looked behind Julie at her friend. People could be so *shallow*. Julie clenched her fist.

Afterward, they stepped out onto the pavement, walked down the block, and turned onto the main shopping drag.

There was a high-end jewelry store, a furnishings place with birdcage chandeliers and thousand-dollar cashmere blankets, a Madewell, a Coach store, a Williams-Sonoma, and several restaurants.

'Julie?'

'Oh, shit,' Parker mumbled.

Julie whirled around. Nyssa stood at the corner, several shopping bags looped around her wrist. Natalie Houma was with her, cell phone in hand.

'It *is* you!' Nyssa cried. She skipped up to her happily and took Julie's hand. 'You got off the phone earlier too quickly for me to ask, but we're just about to meet some people at Judy's Diner. You *have* to come. Carson is there. He's been asking about you.' She winked.

Julie blushed. She glanced at Parker, wondering if she'd come, too. But her friend was already gone. *Typical.*

'Sure,' she said, lowering her shoulders. It might have seemed like she was ditching Parker, but she knew Parker didn't want to be there. Julie resolved to catch up with her after the appointment. Maybe it would help. Maybe in time Parker would open herself back up to the world and let everyone else see the girl only Julie now knew.

CHAPTER ELEVEN

At six that night, Parker pushed open the door of a nondescript office building in downtown Beacon Heights. The waiting room was empty, save for a few other chairs, a vase of flowers, and some dog-eared magazines. She looked at the second door that led into another hallway. ELLIOT FIELDER, MSW, it said in big letters at the top.

The headshrinker. She *so* wasn't looking forward to this, but she'd promised Julie. And now that Nolan's death was being investigated, it was more important than ever that she learn to keep it together.

The door opened, and a man appeared. He had tousled dark hair, and his eyes were slightly shadowed in a serious, brooding way. He had a lean, muscular runner's frame. He blinked at her. 'Um . . .' he said.

Parker stood up, embarrassed by all the thoughts that had just rushed through her mind. 'I'm Parker,' she said. 'Parker Duvall. Julie's friend?'

His gaze remained on her. It wasn't a gawk, though, just a half squint, as if he was trying to figure out something about her. Then he cleared his throat and took her clipboard. 'Oh, right.

Julie mentioned you'd be coming. Come on in and sit down.'

She walked past him into the office. The overhead fluorescent light was off, but a few floor lamps gave off a gentle glow from the corners of the room. Outside the window, the sky was as flat and gray as her mood.

She flopped down on the loveseat, throwing her legs up over one arm.

Dr. Fielder shut the door and sat down on a desk chair, pulling it out to the middle of the room. For a few moments, he stared at her with an expression she couldn't read. The wall clock ticked off the minutes of silence.

'Why do you keep staring at me?' she finally snapped. 'I realize I have scars. You don't have to make me feel like more of a freak.'

Fielder frowned. 'Scars?'

Parker scoffed. 'Good party trick, doctor. But they're right here.' She gestured to her face, half hidden under her hoodie. 'I know my face looks like it went through a meat processor, okay?'

'I don't see any scars,' Fielder said defiantly. He licked his lips. 'I'm sorry, Parker. It's just that Julie has told me a little about you, and I have to admit I'm a little surprised you came today.'

What had Julie said? Probably the same crap she said to Parker every day – *It's like you've just given up. If you'd just make an effort. Blah, blah, blah.* 'Julie's my best friend, and she thinks she knows it all. But sometimes, she's wrong.'

He smiled a little. 'Julie is worried about you, Parker.'

She snorted. 'Julie worries about everything. I can take care of myself. I mean, I've been through hell, and I'm still standing. That's got to count for something, Dr. Fielder.'

He nodded slowly, stroking his chin. 'Please, call me Elliot. And I'm not actually a doctor. I'm a counselor, which means I'm more interested in listening to you than fixing you. Okay?'

Parker frowned warily. *Call me Elliot. I'm interested in listening. I don't see any scars.* This guy was full of lines.

'And you're right,' he continued. 'You're obviously a tough girl, Parker. A fighter. But that doesn't mean that you have to deal with all this alone.'

She looked away, down her long, slender legs in their scuffed motorcycle boots.

'Do you want to talk about what happened?' Elliot's voice was soft, gentle.

She gave a dismissive shrug. 'It's not a big deal.'

'You sure about that?'

She looked at him again. A hollow ache pulsed in her sternum. It'd been a long time since anyone but Julie had treated her like a human being.

She cleared her throat. 'So my dad used to hit me. No biggie.'

Elliot's eyes widened. 'It seems like a big deal to me.'

A bark of laughter fought out of her throat. 'I deserved it. That's what my mom always told me – I antagonized him. I was always messing up. He'd overhear me talking about some party on the phone, or he'd catch me coming out of school with my skirt hitched up higher than was allowed. There was always one reason or another.' She kept her eyes down, away from the therapist, twisting a lock of hair around one finger.

Elliot crossed his arms over his chest. 'It's never right for someone to hurt you. No matter *what* you do. You know that, right?'

Parker scoffed. 'Well, apparently the cops thought the same

thing. Because he's in prison now. Problem solved, right?'

Elliot scratched his nose. 'Julie mentioned an attack.'

Of course Julie would sell her out like that. 'Yep. The turning point. The night the cops came and took him away.'

'Can you describe that night?'

She shrugged. 'He snapped. Went berserk. And *this* happened.' She gestured to her face and then tried to laugh, like it didn't matter, but of course it did. Of course it mattered that her once perfect face now looked like *this*.

She remembered the party, remembered Julie finding her in Nolan's bedroom, bombed out of her mind. That was the night he'd slipped her an Oxy – she'd never done that drug before. 'Come on, I'm taking you home,' Julie had said.

Parker had begged her not to. 'What if my dad is up? Can't I just stay at your place?'

Julie had bit her lip; it was before she'd told Parker her secret. 'He won't be up. You've snuck in before. Just be really quiet and sleep it off.'

She remembered getting out of Julie's car and walking shakily toward her house. But she actually didn't remember much of what happened once she got inside. Still, she'd seen her dad angry enough times to fill in the blanks.

'It was awful, wasn't it?' Elliot said gently.

Parker stared at her hands in her lap.

'And what happened after that? You were in the hospital, right?'

Jesus, had Julie told him *everything*?

'And then your dad was in prison, I believe? How did you feel about that?'

Parker snorted. 'What do *you* think?' Then her gaze shifted

110

to the window. 'My mom hates me for it. She thinks that night was my fault. Maybe it was. But it was *his* fault, too.'

'Your dad's?'

'No.' Her voice caught. 'M-my friend's.'

'What do you mean?'

Parker shut her eyes. Nolan's face swam in her mind. She considered not saying anything, but she'd come so far already. 'I had another best friend besides Julie. That night, the night of the attack, he gave me Oxy, even though he knew my dad would kill me if he ever caught me high.'

Elliot frowned. 'Why would your friend do that?'

Parker's shoulders shot up and then down. 'That's Nolan for you. Sometimes he played God just for the hell of it.'

Elliot squinted. 'Nolan . . . Hotchkiss?'

Parker stared at him, her heart rate picking up. 'Did you know him?'

Elliot shook his head. 'Just what I've read in the papers. How have you been holding up?'

Parker leaned back in the chair and hugged one of the jacquard pillows to her chest. 'I didn't exactly love the guy.'

Elliot frowned slightly. 'So you weren't friends at the end?'

'No way. He wouldn't even look at me after everything happened.'

'Did you go to the funeral?'

Parker shrugged. 'Yeah. I mean, it's not like I wanted him to get hurt. But am I ready to, like, hold a candle-light vigil? Not so much.' A shudder ran up her spine. 'All the crying and histrionics. It's been . . . bringing back bad memories.'

Elliot nodded slowly. 'That's not unusual.'

111

'It's not?'

Elliot looked down at his notepad. 'Julie mentioned once that you have spells. Headaches. Panic attacks. How often are you having those?'

She shrugged. 'A few times a week. The headaches come and go. The panic attacks . . . those happen when something startles me. Loud noises, sudden movements. Cars backfiring. That kind of thing. And sometimes it's hard for me to remember things. There are huge gaps . . .'

'That sounds a lot like post-traumatic stress disorder,' he said, leaning back in his chair. 'Which shouldn't be surprising, given all you've been through.'

She glanced up at him. 'Isn't that what vets have when they come back from war?'

'That's where we see it a lot, it's true. But PTSD can happen to anybody who's been through a severe trauma. Your body gets stuck reacting to what it perceives as threats, even if those threats aren't valid. But the good news is it's totally treatable.'

Parker sat up, putting her feet flat on the ground and turning to face him. Her head was swimming. She'd come here to placate Julie, sure that nothing – no one – could put her back together. But the way Elliot was talking, maybe he could help her. Maybe she wasn't a lost cause.

It'd been a long time since she'd felt that way.

'Here's the thing, Parker.' Elliot's voice was gentle. She wiped her eyes and looked at him. 'This doesn't mean you're damaged. It just means your mind has adapted to feelings of being unsafe. It's a coping mechanism.'

'That sounds a lot like damage to me,' she said, taking a

112

deep, shuddering breath. 'Great. I'm doubly damaged. Face *and* mind.'

He clucked his tongue. 'Parker, all of us are damaged in our own ways. It's just that most people call it "experience." And you've had a lot of experience. With your father. With your mother. And with Nolan.'

She nodded.

Suddenly she felt his hand on hers. It was warm and slightly calloused near the tips, as if he played an instrument in his spare time. He gave her hand a quick squeeze, and then let go.

'Parker, you have all the reasons in the world not to trust anyone,' he murmured. 'No one can blame you for being cautious. But you have nothing to be afraid of. I promise you, if you give me just a little trust . . . if you can take a leap of faith . . . I will do my best to help you.'

'How?' Parker blurted, sure her cheeks were red.

'We can work through things together. The first step of any therapy is a little self-awareness. I want you to think about the ways your habits, your belief systems, your personality quirks have been developed to help you and protect you. Then ask yourself if they are truly working or if they're hurting you. For instance, when you feel a headache coming on, focus on something in front of you. Something real, like your hand, to keep you in the moment. It sounds small, but it helps, I promise.'

She searched his face. He looked so sincere. She wanted more than anything to believe him. To believe that things didn't always have to be so desperate, so painful. To believe she didn't always have to be alone. To believe that maybe, just maybe, one day, everything would be okay.

CHAPTER TWELVE

That same night, after a few hours of practicing the material in the Juilliard audition packet, Mac parked at the curb at Blake's house. He lived in a neighborhood of old Victorians near the Beacon Heights library; she used to come here all the time and play on his trampoline in the backyard. They'd held competitions to see who could jump the highest and who could do the best flip. Had Claire ever joined them? Mac wondered. She couldn't remember.

She slammed the door to her car and took a deep, resolved breath. *Okay. It's just band practice. And that kiss? Never happened. And it's never going to happen again.* Besides, the whole band would be here this time. Blake wouldn't kiss her in front of all those people.

She grabbed her cello case from the trunk and walked briskly up the front path to the door. Blake's doorbell was the same as always, deep chimes playing the first few notes of Beethoven's Fifth Symphony. The door flung open, and Blake stood in his socks, a pair of dark jeans, and a forest-green T-shirt. His smile was cagey and shy.

'Hello,' Mac said coolly.

'Hey.' Blake was just as breezy and cavalier. He opened the door wider. 'Come on in.'

See? Mac thought as she followed him, her cello case bumping against her knees. Blake *did* want to forget. This was going to go easier than she thought. And as she passed a line of pictures in the hallway, she spied one of Blake and Claire on the trip the orchestra had taken to Disneyland last year – Blake had quit orchestra by then, but he'd begged his parents to buy him a ticket anyway. He wore Mickey Mouse ears and was making a devil's sign to the camera. Claire was kissing his cheek, her face pink.

They were supposed to be together, Mac told herself with determination. And she was just the friend.

Blake led her through the old country kitchen and opened the door to the refinished basement. As Mac tromped down the stairs after him, it occurred to her how quiet the house was. She walked into the large basement room, which smelled a little musty and had a dehumidifier chugging in the corner. Several music stands and amps were set up by the TV, but the room was empty.

'The others aren't here yet?' she asked.

Blake hopped off the last step and turned around and faced her. 'They canceled again. Stuff to do, I guess.'

Mac blinked. Blake didn't seem as bummed about it as he had the last time. Had he *told* them not to come?

She squeezed the handle of her cello case hard. 'Oh. Well, in that case, I should probably go practice for my audition.'

He nodded, but Mac thought she detected disappointment flash across his face. 'Yeah, I bet you're stressed. What are you playing?'

Mackenzie bit her lip. 'I'm debating between the first

movement and the fourth of Elgar's Concerto in E Minor. And I think I'll do Tchaikovsky's *Pezzo capriccioso* for the big finish. I don't know, though. I've been second-guessing myself a lot. I did Popper's *Spinning Song* for the state solo competition last year, and it's still in good shape. Maybe I'll do that instead.' She pinched the bridge of her nose. 'My mom has this friend Darlene who works at Juilliard and has an in with the admissions. If I wanted to, I suppose I could just ask her what she thought. But that seems like cheating.' The only thing worse than not getting into Juilliard, she thought, was getting in dishonestly.

'Well, Claire's going with Popper,' he advised. 'You should stick with Tchaikovsky. You'll stand out more.'

He grimaced slightly, as if he realized that he'd said Claire's name.

'Yeah, um, okay,' Mac said awkwardly, ready to walk back up the stairs.

Blake grabbed her arm. 'Mac, wait. Stay. *Please.* Even just for one song.'

She was surprised at the emphasis in his voice. Her heart thudded against her chest. But she cleared her throat. 'I don't think this is a good idea,' she said. 'Not after . . . you know. Last week.' She definitely wasn't going to say *kiss* out loud.

Blake's gaze dropped to the floor. 'I was afraid you were going to say that. I totally shouldn't have kissed you, right? You're not . . . *into* me.'

'No – I mean, *yes.* I am.' Mac slapped her forehead. 'Wait. I mean, *no.* You shouldn't have kissed me, though. Claire's my best friend, Blake. I can't do that to her.'

He put his hands on his hips. 'Wait, back up to that first part. You *are* into me?'

Mac lifted one shoulder. She thought that was painfully obvious.

'And if Claire wasn't in the picture, you wouldn't be saying this right now?'

Mac stared at her embroidered flats. She couldn't get mixed up in this. She needed to focus on Juilliard. It was bad enough she would probably be interviewed by the police soon. It was bad enough someone probably *had* seen her go upstairs shortly before Nolan did. And then there were those pictures she'd posted . . . She was going to be questioned, she knew it. Too much stuff was going on already – she couldn't get mixed up with Blake, too.

But when she felt Blake take her hand, she didn't pull away. His touch seemed to weaken her, her limbs suddenly feeling like noodles. He pulled her to the couch, which was soft and plush and had a crocheted afghan on it that Mac had always loved. He cupped her face in his hands and gave her a tender smile. 'You are *so* beautiful,' he gushed. 'I can't stop thinking about you and me at the cupcake shop.'

His breath tickled her earlobe. He smelled like Ivory soap, and a little bit like sugar – the cupcake smell lingered even when he wasn't at work. She felt light-headed.

'Me, too,' she heard herself admit. But then she turned her head. 'What are we *doing*, though? You have a girlfriend, Blake. This isn't right.'

Blake shook his head. 'I'm trying to end things. I want to be with you.'

Mac blinked hard. 'You *do*? *Why*?'

'Because you're so . . . *you*.' He nodded.

Mac smiled wryly. 'Unfortunately.'

'That's a good thing.' Blake sat up and took her hands. 'I've *always* wanted you.'

'Then why did you kiss Claire at Disneyland?' she blurted.

For a moment, Blake looked genuinely confused. 'What are you talking about? Claire kissed *me.*'

'What?' Mackenzie said, peering at him through her glasses. 'Claire said you kissed her on a ride, but that she stopped it because she had to clear it with me first.'

Blake shook his head slowly. 'Um, no. We were on Pirates of the Caribbean. And I asked her if, you know, she thought you would ever go out with me.' Blake's cheeks were red. 'She said you were interested in someone else, but that she liked me – and she kissed me then and there.' He looked at Mackenzie earnestly, lifting her chin. 'I *never* would have gone for her if I thought I had a chance with you.'

Mac's mouth fell open. That hadn't been what Claire told her. In fact, it had been quite the *opposite*. And all this time, she had hidden herself away, letting them have their space. Her blood began to boil.

He slid his arms around her waist and pulled her suddenly down on his lap. 'Let's not talk about Claire right now, okay?'

Then they were kissing again. And Mac did as she was told: her mind went blank. For once, she wasn't worrying about how she looked or sounded – or about what she was doing to Claire. She wasn't thinking about anything but Blake's lips, Blake's hands, and Blake's body. In that moment, nothing and no one existed except her and the boy she'd loved for so many years from afar.

CHAPTER THIRTEEN

On Wednesday, Ava showed up to film studies class early, hoping to talk to Mr. Granger, but he didn't come into the classroom until the final bell rang.

'Okay, everyone,' he said, and turned to write on the chalkboard. 'Today we're going to start a new film. This one is called *The Bad Seed*. Anyone heard of it?'

A lot of eager hands shot up, Ava's included. He turned around and his eyes landed on her. 'It's the one about the little girl who commits murder,' she said, encouraged.

Granger nodded. 'A perfect-seeming child. Daughter of a perfect family. How on earth could she be capable of something so awful?'

Ava's stomach clenched. It was a strange choice of film after one of his students was murdered. She glanced at the others. Mac shifted. Julie tapped her toe incessantly.

Granger walked over to the television and turned it on. 'Those of you who have seen it, what would you say are some of the main themes?'

Ava's hand shot up again. She was determined to redeem herself after that big red C. 'Nature versus nurture,' she volunteered. 'A perfect family should, in theory, raise a perfect girl. What went wrong?'

'Indeed.' Granger's smiled gleamed. 'So what *could* go wrong, Ava? Any thoughts?'

'Well.' Ava could feel everyone looking at her. 'Maybe some people are just born evil. They can't help it.'

Granger snapped his fingers. 'That's one of the central arguments in this film: *Are people born evil, or good?* Very smart, Ava.'

She sat back and grinned. Alex caught her eye and raised his brow. *Show-off,* he mouthed teasingly.

'We can even think of examples in our own life,' Granger went on. 'There might be people we know about whom we ask that very question.'

Granger dimmed the lights, and everyone quieted down as the film came on the screen. It was just as scary as Ava had remembered, and the little girl in the movie reminded her a lot of Nolan. When the final bell rang, she started to pack up her books, pulling nervously at the hem of the gray Theory dress she'd worn because she knew it made her look serious.

'Hey,' Alex said, turning around with a grin. 'Want to go off campus for lunch today?'

She smiled at him. 'Thanks. But I need to talk to Mr. Granger.'

'Oh, right. Good luck.' He gave her hand a reassuring squeeze.

Ava waited until everyone else had left the classroom before she stood up and slowly walked to the front of the room. Mr. Granger was erasing the chalkboard, his back to her. Outside the classroom she heard the hallway filling with the chaos of freed students, lockers slamming and kids shouting. When

Mr. Granger finally turned, he looked surprised to see her there.

'Ava. What can I do for you?'

The essay trembled in her hands, the big red C at the top catching her eye. She bit her lip and tried to sound as confident as possible. 'I wanted to talk to you about this grade, Mr. Granger.'

He sat down on the edge of his desk. 'I see. Do my comments make sense to you?'

She shrugged, still staring down at the paper. 'I guess so. You thought it was stupid.'

'Not stupid.' He stood up off the desk quickly, and all at once they were standing so close together she had to look up to meet his gaze. A warm, citrusy smell came off him, like tangerines sitting in sunlight. She swallowed.

'The essay was very well written, Ava. Your prose is among the most sophisticated in the class. But the arguments were unfocused, nothing like your previous papers.'

Ava nodded. 'Yeah. I was kind of distracted when I wrote it.'

'It was a tough topic, and this was a tough week,' Granger said, his green eyes steady on her. 'It's hard to lose a classmate – or, in my case, a student.'

Ava nodded, casting her eyes down.

Granger leaned back against the desk. 'Perhaps you were at a disadvantage because of your group.'

'Um . . . right.' Ava tried to gauge his expression. What did he mean by that?

He looked at her expectantly, and she tried not to sound shaky as she forged ahead. 'What I came to ask is, I'd like to rewrite the essay for a new grade.'

Mr. Granger paused for a second, then nodded. 'That sounds fair,' he said. 'Why don't we meet and talk about it. What's your schedule like this week?'

'I'm free whenever works for you,' Ava said agreeably.

Granger pulled out his iPhone to check his schedule, then frowned. 'Actually this week is pretty difficult for me, especially right after school. Would Friday work – maybe around seven?' He smiled at her encouragingly.

Ava's shoulders relaxed, the tension flooding out of her. 'Oh, yes. Of course. Thank you so much, Mr. Granger. Should I meet you here?'

He glanced at the wall, giving it a wry smile. 'Unfortunately for me, the drama club is in dress rehearsals for *Guys and Dolls*, and the auditorium is flush with that wall. It'll be pretty loud in here.' He thought for a moment. 'What about my house? I'm just a few blocks from here. Besides, I have a book on villains by Chuck Klosterman I'd really like to lend you.'

Ava blinked. She'd never been to a teacher's house before. But he was going out of his way to help her with her paper, so the least she could do was come to him.

'Okay,' she said. 'I'll be there.'

'Great.' He put his phone back in his pocket and quickly wrote down his address for her. 'I think you're really talented, Ava. You have a lot of potential.'

'Thanks, Mr. Granger.' She squared her shoulders and turned to walk out of the classroom just as the door opened from the hallway.

'Excuse me?' a man said, stepping into the room.

'Yes?' Granger stood up fast, straightening his papers.

The man strode across the room. 'I'm Detective Peters. I'm wondering if I could speak to Miss Jalali.'

His gaze turned to Ava. Ava shrank back, wondering how he knew her name – but then, maybe it was a cop's job to know. Her head felt faint. What *else* did he know?

'I just have a few questions for you, Miss Jalali,' Peters said, perhaps noticing the nervous look on Ava's face.

'That's fine with me,' Granger said, his smile mild. 'We're finished here. You can use the classroom.'

'Actually, I need to take her down to the station,' Peters said.

Ava's heart sank. 'Th-the station?' She could feel Granger staring at her.

'We can't technically conduct interviews on school grounds, but I got permission from the office to come into the school.'

'W-will you tell my parents?' Ava blurted.

Peters's mild expression didn't change. 'That you're being questioned, yes. But everyone is being questioned, Miss Jalali. Is there *more* I should tell them?'

Ava shook her head faintly. 'Of course not.' Then she turned to follow the cop out of the room. Alex was waiting just outside the door. When he saw her with the cop, his mouth dropped open.

'They're just asking me some questions,' she said quickly, trying to erase the concern from his eyes.

'Um, okay.' Alex gently touched her arm. 'Do you want me to come with you?'

She blinked, considering. Then she snapped her expression into something much more confident and brave. She had to get a grip. She couldn't afford to look guilty. She'd done nothing *wrong*.

'It's okay,' she said brightly, giving Alex a peck on the cheek. 'I'm sure it's all just a formality. I'll be back soon.'

And then she turned her smile on the detective and followed him outside to where his squad car was parked at the curb. She paused at the backseat, and the detective laughed lightly. 'You can sit up front with me. Unless you're a criminal?'

Ava's cheeks reddened, and she managed to laugh as she scrambled to the passenger door. 'Of course not,' she mumbled as she climbed in.

Not yet, anyway.

Ava had never been to a police station before, but it wasn't that different from what she'd imagined: drab blue walls, people behind desks, WANTED posters, linoleum. The detective took Ava into a small room at the back and asked if she wanted coffee. She declined, afraid that it would make her hands shake even more badly than they already were. There was a long mirror on one side of the room; her wide-eyed, dark-haired, beautiful face stared back at her. She wondered if the mirror was actually translucent on the other side of the wall. Were officers standing there, ready to watch her?

Her phone beeped. *You okay?* Alex texted.

Ava turned her phone over, too freaked to type back. She looked at her expression in the mirror again. She needed to focus.

Peters returned with his coffee and shut the door. 'So. Ava Jalali. J-A-L-A-L-I, is that right?'

Ava nodded. 'Uh-huh.'

Peters leaned forward. 'Okay. It's come to our attention

that you were the last person anyone remembers with Nolan Hotchkiss the night of his death.'

Ava frowned, her pulse racing double time. 'I doubt that.'

Peters didn't blink. 'An eyewitness said they saw you on the dance floor with him. You were "all over him," as he describes it.'

Thank *god* Alex hadn't come here with her. All at once, the memory of Nolan's close, hot body pressed up against hers on the dance floor flashed into her mind. *Does your boyfriend know you're flirting with me?* he'd said, his breath smelling like booze. It had taken everything in Ava's power to keep it together. *What he doesn't know won't hurt him.* She remembered how hard her heart was pounding. How she kept peeking over her shoulder, terrified that Alex would step into the room and see what she was doing – she'd sent him on a wild-goose chase for her phone, which she said she'd left in his car, which was parked far at the end of the street. When Ava led Nolan upstairs, Alex was still probably searching for the phone that wasn't there.

'Who told you that?' she blurted.

'Is it true?' Peters countered.

Ava twisted a strand of hair around her finger. 'I had too much to drink that night. But I have a boyfriend, and he knows Nolan and I were together a few years ago. He's still jealous. I'd rather he didn't know.'

'None of this will get back to him,' Peters assured her. 'So you *were* flirting with Nolan?'

Ava weighed her options. If kids on the dance floor saw her, it might not be smart to lie. 'I'm a flirt,' she said matter-of-factly. 'Especially after a few beers.'

'Did you go upstairs with him?'

She drew back and made a face. 'I wasn't *that* drunk.'

'Someone said they saw you.'

From her bravest, strongest depths, Ava found the courage to look the detective in the eye. 'Did one of Nolan's buddies tell you that?' She leaned forward, batting her eyelashes. 'Not every girl goes upstairs with guys at parties. Some of us have some dignity.'

'Okay, okay.' The detective flipped some pages of his notebook, staring at scrawl. 'But *someone* went upstairs with Nolan that night – several eyewitnesses said they were sure they saw him going up with a girl. Any ideas who that might be?'

Ava shook her head, her long hair swishing back and forth. Her heart beat hard. 'Nope.'

'And you weren't . . . mad at Nolan for some reason? Because I heard you two had a bad break-up. Nolan even started some rumors about you, if I'm not mistaken? Rumors that you were . . . more than a "flirt," as you say. And maybe Nolan brushed you off at the party, wasn't into what you wanted. Maybe you got angry.'

'I assure you, Nolan wasn't the one who did the brushing off.' Ava paused, wondering if she'd been too sarcastic. 'I'm sorry, Detective. But that's all I know.'

'Can you tell me where you went after you danced with Nolan?'

'Back to my boyfriend. Where I belonged.'

'And he can vouch for you?'

'Of course,' Ava said, looking Peters straight in the eye. Alex had returned shortly after she'd snuck back downstairs; she'd found him in the kitchen after the prank. It was, mostly, the truth.

126

The detective stared at her for what felt like ages. Ava stared back, willing herself not to blink. *They don't know anything,* she kept repeating to herself. *All they know is that he went upstairs with a girl. And they don't even know that, not really.*

Finally, Peters drew back. 'Okay, then,' he said. He tossed his empty coffee cup in a small trash can in the corner. 'I'll drive you back to school. Thanks for your time.'

Ava's legs felt like Jell-O as she followed him down the long hall and climbed back into his squad car once more. After Peters slammed the door behind him and started the engine, he draped his arm over the back of the seats and smiled at her. 'But you'll tell me if you remember anything else, right? Anything at all?'

'Of course,' Ava said, smiling her brightest, most helpful smile back at him.

But what she really meant was, *Like hell I will*.

CHAPTER FOURTEEN

'So it's the seventy-sixth minute of the game, and we're tied with Kirkland. And we're all on edge, because this is the game that decides who goes on to state. I'm hanging back in midfield, and here comes their forward.'

Caitlin poked at her salmon with the edge of her fork, only half listening as Josh recounted one of his soccer victories to the table. Next to her, her mother Sibyl laughed.

'I remember that kid,' she said. 'He was massive. I couldn't believe he could move that fast.'

'Yeah, he's at Indiana this year. Full ride,' Josh said. He took another huge bite of his Dungeness crabcakes. 'Anyway, so the clock is ticking, and this guy is huge and fast and heading straight for the goal. No one else is even close to him.' He paused dramatically. 'I'm the only one who's got a chance to stop him.'

Across the table from Caitlin, Josh's dad, Ted, sipped a glass of red wine, his face flushed and pleasant. Next to him, Josh's mom, Michelle, watched her son with a rapt expression. Caitlin's moms were on her side of the table – Sibyl next to her, and Mary Ann on the other side of Sibyl. They were gathered at the Martell-Lewises' house for their weekly Wednesday dinner. Jeremy wasn't there, and Caitlin couldn't help but wonder where he was.

Just two days ago they'd almost kissed. Or ... *had* they? Maybe she'd misinterpreted. Maybe he was going to lean forward just to give her a friendly, platonic hug. That *had* to be it.

'What happened then?' breathed Michelle, looking at Josh.

Caitlin fought the urge to roll her eyes. She was proud of Josh, too, but that game had been almost a year ago, and they'd all been there. They'd all *seen* what happened next.

Josh put down his fork and leaned in to the table. 'There was no way I could overtake him – I could see that. He was too fast, and I was, like, thirty yards away. But suddenly, out of nowhere, it just hit me like a bolt from the blue. I could see the path stretched out at my feet, like someone had laid it out just for me. It was almost glowing, it was so vivid. And I knew – if I could just follow the path, I would head him off, just in time.'

Caitlin tried to hang on to Josh's words, but she found her mind drifting. She thought instead about what Ava had told her when she called her an hour ago. All those things Ava had said about getting called into the police station. About people seeing Ava go upstairs with Nolan. And if the police were onto Ava, how long before she mentioned who she was with and what they'd done? Then what would her parents do? Caitlin was all they had left now. This would destroy them.

Suddenly she heard Josh clearing his throat. She gave a little start as she realized that everyone at the table had gone still. Looking up, she saw that Josh had pulled a small black velvet

129

box from his pocket. Smiling confidently, he slid it across the table toward her.

Caitlin's mouth went dry. Her eyes darted around the table. Ted had a knowing smile beneath his full salt-and-pepper beard, but next to him, Michelle's hands had flown to her lips. Mary Ann grabbed Sibyl's hand as they both watched, wide-eyed. Across from her, Josh gave her a *come-on-open-it-already* nod.

Only, Caitlin didn't *want* to open it. She was afraid to see what it was. Everyone was looking at her, though, and every second that ticked by made the moment seem even weirder. She took a deep breath and flipped the lid.

Inside was a pendant, hanging on a slender golden chain. It was in the shape of a small glass ball – inside was a small chunk of something green. The air flooded back into her lungs, and the tension at the table was broken.

'It's a chunk of turf,' Josh said, giving her his lopsided grin. 'From Husky Stadium.'

'That's lovely,' Mary Ann exclaimed, leaning across Sibyl to peer down into the box. Caitlin thought she sounded a tiny bit disappointed. Did her moms actually want her to get *engaged* . . . when she was still in high school? Then again, that way, she and Josh would be the perfect soccer-playing couple . . . forever.

Caitlin didn't even want to think about it, though. And it freaked her out, a little, when she realized how *much* she didn't want to think about it. *Should* she be thinking about it?

'Thanks,' she said, finally finding her voice. She shut the box. 'That's really . . . cool.'

Josh grinned. 'You're going to dominate at semifinals,' he said. 'I can't wait.'

Caitlin stared down at her plate, a blur of green and red. She knew this was a nice gesture. She knew it was supposed to make her happy. But for some reason, it just made her feel . . . trapped. Something about the way her moms were staring at her – like she was their last hope, like they *needed* her to be happy – and the way Josh was looking at her, so sweet but so unaware of anything she was going through, prickled at her in ways she couldn't even explain. She needed out of here before she started crying at the table.

'Um, can you excuse me for a minute?' she mumbled, jumping up. 'I'm not feeling well.'

She turned and headed out of the kitchen and ran upstairs. But instead of going to her room, she went to Taylor's. She and her moms hadn't changed his room at all; there were still books on the floor where he'd left them, and the calendar was still turned to the month he died. They kept saying they would clean it out and turn it into a guest room, but somehow they never seemed to get around to it.

Images of Taylor came floating back to her as she fell onto his twin bed. Her little brother's habit of carrying all his textbooks at once in his backpack instead of using his locker like a normal person, so that he looked like a turtle under the giant hump of his bag. The way he looked bent over a Dungeons & Dragons figurine, painting the armor with a tiny, delicate brush, his tongue between his lips in concentration. The way he screamed, high-pitched and girlish, if someone startled him. Caitlin had loved to sneak up on him and poke him in the ribs just to see him jump.

Then she thought about Nolan shutting him into a locker

for three hours, just as he'd documented in *Reasons Death Is Better Than School*. When Nolan had tripped him in the hall, sending him flat across the filthy linoleum. When Nolan had stepped on Taylor's iPhone to break it, or ripped the pages out of his Robert Jordan novel right in front of him. Caitlin hadn't seen most of these things happen – she'd only read about them in Taylor's journal after the fact. Taylor had swallowed all of it so bravely. He'd kept it to himself, the last entries both hopeless and resolute. To him, death *was* a better option than high school. He would escape Nolan.

No wonder she'd been so up for that prank at the party. No wonder she'd taken Julie by the arm when they all convened by Nolan's stairs, her body thrumming with adrenaline. Even now, even knowing she could be blamed for his death, she had no regrets for giving Nolan a taste of his own medicine.

'Caitlin.'

Startled out of her thoughts, she sat. Mary Ann stood in the doorway.

She thought her body language would drive her mom away, but Mary Ann walked in and paused next to the bed. She could feel her gaze on her. Her eyes were the same dark brown as Caitlin's. Whenever strangers saw her with Mary Ann and asked if Caitlin was adopted, Mary Ann would always say, 'No, she's mine. Can't you tell by the eyes?'

Mary Ann sat next to Caitlin on the bed and folded her hands. 'Is everything okay, honey?' she asked in a small voice. 'Are you missing Taylor?'

'No,' she said sullenly. 'I mean, yes, I always miss him. But no more tonight than usual.'

'Is it something with Josh?' Mary Ann sighed. 'You two shouldn't fight. You're so good together.'

Caitlin stared at her mother, frustration building inside her. Why were her moms so obsessed with her and Josh's love life? 'I'm not fighting with Josh. Why would you think that?'

Mary Ann smiled sadly. 'It's just not like you to walk away from the table. And you've been acting strange lately, sweetheart. I'm just worried about you.' She hesitated. 'Have you taken any of that OxyContin Dr. Magnuson prescribed?'

Caitlin did a double take. 'What? Why?'

'I'm just . . . curious.' Her mother didn't meet her gaze.

Caitlin wound a piece of dark hair around her finger, her pulse suddenly racing. 'A few,' she said carefully.

'When?'

'I don't know.' Caitlin threw up her hands.

Her mother exhaled loudly. 'Well, I was hoping you hadn't. If you still had all your prescription, you'd be in the clear.'

Her heart skipped a beat. 'What are you talking about?'

Something about her expression was strange, almost suspicious. 'Well, the police called earlier. They're calling everyone from your school with an Oxy prescription. They subpoenaed records from all the local pharmacies. Obviously, your name came up.'

Caitlin's heart was thudding fast. 'Nolan was a notorious pill popper. He had his own stash.'

'Maybe so.' Mary Ann nodded like she wanted to believe that. But the expression on her face seemed timorous, like she was about to burst into tears. 'It's just . . . can you do something for me?'

133

'Sure. What?'

'Bring me the rest of your OxyContin prescription?'

Caitlin stared at her. 'Why?'

'Just humor me, honey.' Mary Ann looked uncomfortable. 'You don't need it anymore, right? I'm going to dispose of it for you.'

Caitlin blinked. 'Do you think I had something to do with what happened to Nolan?'

'No!' Mary Ann said quickly, her eyes widening. 'Honey, I'm not accusing you of anything. I just . . . well, you haven't been yourself lately. And Coach Leah called to say she had to kick you out of practice the other day. Sometimes that medication causes changes in people. I just would rather we have the pills, okay? Just in case . . .'

Just in case what? Caitlin wanted to ask, fearful of how her mother had drifted off.

Instead, she rose robotically, walked to the bathroom she used to share with Taylor, and grabbed the pills, carefully examining the bottle. All kinds of paranoid thoughts entered her mind: what if there was a tracking device on the thing? What if the bottle could *tell* you, somehow, where it had been – and that it had logged time in the Hotchkisses' house? She shut her eyes and saw herself shaking out a single pill into her palm. Grinding it up and brushing it into that cup. Was all Oxy the same, or was each pill unique, like a snowflake? What if there was a way to track down that the pill in Nolan's stomach had come from her?

But if she balked now, her moms would surely suspect that something was up. Swallowing hard, Caitlin brought the bottle to Mary Ann.

'Here you go,' she said despondently. 'I hope that eases your mind.'

'Oh, honey, you know I just want what's best for you,' Mary Ann said, and tried to grab Caitlin for a hug. Caitlin shook free, darting under her arm and slipping into her bedroom, locking the door swiftly behind her. She collapsed on her bed and pushed a pillow against her face, her whole body shaking. The police had already talked to Ava. It was only a matter of time before they called her in, too. And if her own mother thought she had it in her to kill Nolan, why would anyone else think she was innocent?

CHAPTER FIFTEEN

Wednesday afternoon, Parker sat on her front porch in South Kenwood, a town just outside the Beacon Heights line, smoking a cigarette and looking out at the rain. It felt weird to be sitting here; she hated coming home so much that she was rarely here anymore. This neighborhood was a far cry from their old one in Beacon. After her dad went to jail, her mom had sold their sprawling five-bedroom house and moved into this bungalow. The paint was peeling off in long strips. A neglected begonia slumped in a pot on the railing. All the houses on the street were small and crumbling, with overgrown little lawns surrounded by sagging chain-link fences. Empty beer cans rolled in the gutters, and more than one yard had a car up on blocks.

She took a quick, nervous drag, exhaling a sharp burst of smoke. A shadow flashed in the doorway of the house across the street, and she tensed. *Stop the whole paranoid act*, she scolded herself. *No one's after you.*

But that was easier said than done. For the past few days she'd been a complete mess. Everywhere she went, she could feel eyes on her. *Why*, she wasn't sure . . . but she just felt watched. Cops were crawling all over the school, and students were being called in right and left to confess anything they knew about the party. It was turning into a witch hunt – kids were dropping the names of rivals and enemies to try to get them hauled in for questioning, claiming they'd seen so-and-so talking to Nolan that Friday night.

Ava had called everyone this afternoon to tell them that someone had seen her taking Nolan upstairs. 'I denied it,' she'd said flatly. 'But we have to be careful. People might have seen more than we think.'

So far, no one had asked Parker any questions – and she could only hope it would stay that way. But what about all the pictures kids had taken that night? What if someone had caught her black-hoodied figure slumping in the background? Someone might whisper to the cops about how sullen and withdrawn she'd become after her attack. The rumors might swirl about how Nolan had drugged her the night she was beaten. *Parker Duvall has a motive*, people might say.

And then there was an even more horrible thought: although Parker wanted to trust these new friends of hers, *could* she? Who was to say one of them wouldn't crack and give her up? She didn't think Caitlin would be a problem – Caitlin still hated Nolan's guts too much to go out of her way to help the cops. And of course Parker could count on Julie. But Mackenzie? She'd looked ready to spill her guts at the funeral. And Ava . . . well, the cops already *were* onto her – Parker doubted that princess would hold up well in jail. It wasn't as if Parker contributed much to the circle of friends. Maybe they'd see her as expendable. An easy scapegoat. An already damaged girl with nothing left to lose.

Her thoughts were interrupted when a Lexus – five years old, but still way nicer than any of the other cars in this neighborhood – pulled into the driveway. Her mother stepped out, slamming the door behind her, and stared at Parker.

'What are you doing here?' she snapped, hands on her hips.

Parker made a face. 'Nice to see you, too.'

Mrs. Duvall opened the back door of her car and started pulling out bags of groceries. Parker watched her mother coolly, not offering to help.

If the house was a step down in the world, her mother's outfit was a total fall from grace. Since the trial, Mrs. Duvall had worn the same long-sleeved shirt and yoga pants almost every day, though they'd gotten baggier and baggier on her bony frame as she wasted away. Her once perfectly colored hair had grown out to a dull, graying mousy brown, and it hung in limp locks around her face. And more than that, she just looked . . . *tired*. Like she'd battled the world and the world had won. She never smiled anymore. Never laughed. Everything was a struggle.

Mrs. Duvall looped the bags over her arm and struggled up the steps with them.

'Are you just going to sit out here on the porch all day?' she snapped.

It was surprising how much this still stung. She shot to her feet. 'You're the one who messed up, you know,' she sputtered, not sure what had come over her. Maybe it was her talk with Elliot, but she felt bolder than usual. 'It's a mother's job to protect her family. But you just *let it happen.*'

The color drained from Mrs. Duvall's cheeks. For a moment,

she looked as if Parker had slapped her. Then she pressed her lips together and unlocked the door. 'Jesus Christ,' she snarled. 'Haven't you done enough already?'

She pushed her way in the door and dragged the grocery bags behind her. Before Parker could follow her, she slammed the door shut. Parker heard the firm *click* of the lock from the other side.

Parker stood there for a moment, staring at the faded welcome mat. *Fine. Whatever.* She turned around and kicked the potted begonia with the tip of her steel-toed boots. It made a satisfying shattering sound against the slate pathway below.

Well then, back to Julie's. She headed up the street toward the bus stop, past the dilapidated houses and the convenience store. But then her hands started to shake. What had she done that had been so bad that she'd deserved such horrible treatment? Why did *both* her parents hate her so badly?

She remembered one night when she'd been sitting at the kitchen table, not long before the night that changed everything. She'd been on the phone with Julie, laughing about something Nolan had done at school that day. Then she'd heard the door slam hard – her father was home. His footsteps were heavy, his breathing hard. Parker knew the signs, but instead of getting up and scurrying to her room like she usually did, she'd stayed at the table, the phone pressed to her ear. *It's my house, too*, she'd thought defiantly. *I shouldn't have to hide.*

She didn't even have time to hang up the phone before he hit her. After her father was through with her, her mother had crouched next to her on the floor, placing a bag of frozen peas on her bruised ribs – her dad had learned to hurt her where others couldn't see. 'You need to learn to stay out of your father's way,' her mom had admonished. 'You're making it worse.'

Snap.

Parker wasn't sure where the sound had come from. She swiveled around and stared down the street, the hairs on the back of her neck standing up. Was someone following her? Taking pictures? *Watching?* Three teenagers came out of the convenience store holding slushies and talking loudly in Spanish. A block away, an old woman hobbled out to her mailbox. Three birds lifted off the telephone wire all at once.

No one is watching, she told herself angrily. *Do you really think anyone cares about you?*

The bus grumbled from the next block. Parker picked up speed to get to the stop on time. Suddenly, all she wanted was to be on the bus in an anonymous crowd of commuters, hoodie pulled around her face, headphones on her ears with the music turned up loud. The bus whizzed past the stop just as she turned the corner. 'Hey!' Parker cried, waving her hands at the driver as she sprinted to catch up. The driver kept going.

'No!' Parker screamed, slapping her arms to her sides. Now she'd have to wait twenty minutes for the next bus.

Snap.

Parker's skin prickled again. She looked around, watching as a Nissan Maxima peeled away from the curb. As it passed, she caught a glimpse of the driver through the tinted windows, but she couldn't make out the face. It looked like a man. Almost like her father.

She could feel that sinking, pounding sensation of another

headache coming on, but she tried to fight it. What had Elliot told her to do as a coping mechanism during their session? She couldn't remember a thing. Her vision felt swirled and distorted. Dizzily, she fumbled for her phone, finding herself dialing a number.

'Hello?' came Elliot's voice.

'Uh, Dr. Fielder – Elliot?' Her voice was high and thin, nothing like her own.

'Julie?' Elliot said uncertainly.

'N-no, it's Parker. Parker Duvall.'

'Ah. Parker. Of course.' There was a swishing sound behind him, as though he were in traffic, perhaps, talking on a cell phone. Parker wondered if this was a terrible time to call. He had a healthy life. A *normal* life. He didn't want to be bothered by her.

'You're busy,' she said. 'I'll go.'

'Wait, Parker,' Elliot said. 'I'll always take a call from you. Are you okay? What's up?'

'It's . . .' Parker swallowed hard. 'Everything. My mom . . . this neighborhood I'm in . . . I feel like someone's following me . . . I'm sort of having a hard time coping. I can feel myself slipping away, and you said to call, so . . .'

'And I'm glad you did.' Elliot's voice sounded closer now, not so muffled. 'You've got to hold on, Parker. Try to stay in the here and now. Focus on something real – your hand, your foot – and tell yourself that it's going to be fine.'

She was sitting on the bench at the bus stop now, her head between her knees. 'But I don't *feel* fine,' she admitted. 'I feel like no one sees me.'

'You know that's not true.' His voice was steady and trustworthy. 'I see you, Parker.'

Parker gazed shakily out at the road, staring at the median divider until she came back into herself. Cars passed steadily now, none of them looking suspicious. Her heart rate began to slow. Her breathing wasn't so shallow anymore, either. It was amazing: just hearing Elliot's voice had brought her back to earth.

A few moments passed. 'How are you feeling now?' Elliot asked.

'Better,' Parker admitted. 'Not as . . . tight. I can see everything again. I feel focused.'

'Good,' Elliot said. 'Listen, Parker, let's move up your next appointment. Do you think you can make some time?'

Parker's throat felt dry. 'I – I think so,' she said.

'Great,' Elliot said. 'And listen. If you feel any more attacks coming on, if you need me for *any reason*, I'm always here. Please call. I always want to talk.'

'O-okay,' Parker said. She hung up and hugged her chest tightly. The paranoid feelings had disappeared completely, and in their place were visions of Elliot's therapy room. That comfy couch. That soothing lighting. And Elliot's safe, open face, smiling at her, helping her, saving her.

But then a police car drove by. The officer peered out the window at her, giving her a long once-over. Parker pulled her hoodie lower over her face, holding her breath until the car passed. She exhaled heavily, looking down at her phone. Elliot might want to save her, but if the police found out what she and her friends had done to Nolan, he might not have time.

CHAPTER SIXTEEN

It was raining on Friday as Ava drove toward Mr. Granger's house. At the end of the block, she turned onto Shadywood Road, a familiar street of small, quaint houses. As she passed Alex's, she gave it a little wave, even though she knew Alex was out at the mall, shopping for a new pair of Vans. Then she pulled into the driveway just two houses down. It was funny: Alex had mentioned once that he'd seen Mr. Granger running on his block, but Ava hadn't realized how close their houses were until she pulled into the driveway.

Granger's house had blue shutters and a red front door. Rolling back her shoulders, Ava walked to the front stoop and rang the doorbell, adjusting the strap of her bag, which was filled with spiral notebooks and her laptop and even note cards, since she hadn't been sure what she would need.

She heard footsteps, and the door flung open. 'Miss Jalali,' Granger said with a smile. 'Please come in.' Ava followed him inside, looking curiously around. His living room was warm, with two low-slung leather couches around a square teak coffee table. There were film noir posters on the walls, a bunch of ancient-looking cameras, and an old film projector on a side table.

'Does that actually show movies?' Ava asked, gesturing to it.

'Yep. I've thought about bringing it into class, actually. Maybe next unit.'

'I'd love to see something on it,' she said, then wondered if that sounded like she was inviting herself over again. 'I mean, I bet it's the best way to see old movies, the way they were designed.'

'Exactly.' For a split second, his gaze seemed to travel down her body, taking in her smooth skin. Her ample cleavage. Ava felt her cheeks growing warm – but a moment later she was sure she'd imagined it. Nolan's stupid rumor was making her paranoid.

'Thank you for letting me rewrite the essay,' she said. The sooner they got started, the sooner she could call Alex.

'I think you're a wonderful writer. I'd love to see you do more with it.'

She frowned, looking down at her clasped hands. 'Thank you. But I don't think good writers get Cs.'

'Ava.' Granger seemed suddenly earnest. 'I didn't give you a C because your work was *bad*. I gave it to you because I know you can do better. You're special – I expect more from you than I do from the other kids in class.' He cocked his head. 'Do you write anything aside from school stuff?'

'I've written a few, um, essay-type things,' Ava admitted. 'About things that happen to me. You know, stuff about my mom. Stuff about my family.' She shrugged awkwardly. 'Not that anyone's seen it.'

Granger nodded. 'If something is weighing on you, writing is a great way to relieve the tension. So you like narrative nonfiction?'

'I guess so,' she said. 'But I guess I see it more like a diary. It's really just for me – no one else has ever read it.'

'Not even your boyfriend?'

'Not yet,' Ava said. Was that weird, that Granger was bringing up Alex? She tried not to let it bother her. Maybe he was just trying to be cool, show that he knew some of the school gossip.

'Well, *I'd* really like to read them.' Granger crossed his arms over his chest. 'You've got a fascinating mind, Ava. You're beautiful *and* brilliant.'

'Thank you?' Ava said uncertainly. A teacher shouldn't say she was beautiful. A teacher shouldn't even *notice* what she looked like. But the way he was looking at her, Mr. Granger definitely noticed.

'So, um, my paper?' she blurted out, her voice squeaking.

'Of course.' Granger blinked as if coming out of a trance. 'Let's get to work on that.' But then he leaned forward. 'Listen. If you don't mind me asking, was everything okay with the police the other day? I was worried about you.'

A sour taste welled in Ava's mouth. 'Um, everything was fine,' she said in a small voice. 'Just routine questions.'

Granger sniffed. 'The cops shouldn't be questioning kids. It's scary and intimidating, and they're never going to get anyone to talk that way.' His smile was kind on the surface, but Ava sensed another emotion below. 'But enough of that. I just made a pot of Caffe Vita coffee. Best in all of Seattle. Can I get you a cup?'

Ava was too jittery for coffee, but she felt like it would be rude to say no. 'Um, sure.'

She followed him into a kitchen with white ceramic

countertops and a long, rough-wood table covered in camera parts and developing equipment. Pulling the coffeepot from its warmer, Granger poured two mugs and brought one to Ava. 'I'm sorry about the mess.'

'What is it for?' she asked.

'Oh, hobby stuff. Let me just go ahead and move all this, okay? I need to remember to bring it to school for photography club anyway.' He scooped boxes labeled B&H PHOTOGRAPHY SUPPLIES into his arms. 'Then we'll get to your paper.'

'Sure.' Ava sat down on the edge of a chair when Granger stepped out of the room. She looked around his clean, efficient kitchen, noting the line of canisters by the sink, the red-and-yellow-striped dish towels hanging from the oven door, and a picture of Marlene Dietrich looking particularly mysterious.

Beep.

Granger's iPhone, which he had left on the table, lit up. Ava looked at it and froze. On it was a picture message . . . of someone's boobs.

She glanced in the direction of the front door, then slowly slid the phone toward her and looked again at the photo. It was a boob shot, all right . . . and there was a familiar poster of *Casablanca* on the wall. Ava felt her stomach turn.

This picture had been taken in their film studies classroom.

She unlocked the screen, and the icons flooded into place. With shaking hands, Ava clicked the *Messages* icon. Dozens of texts, most of them *pictures* of topless girls, filled the screen. Ava flicked through sext after sext, horrified. The numbers hadn't been saved as contacts, and the girls never showed their faces, but Beacon was small. She recognized Jenny Thiel's Texas

146

belt buckle in one of them. There was Mimi Colt's beloved Chanel tote on the desk behind her in another. There were Polly Kramer's henna-tattooed hands, which she had meticulously redone every few weeks. She recognized seniors from last year, when Granger had started teaching at Beacon High.

Ava's mouth was agape. He'd gotten all these girls to send him these pictures? What else had they done for him?

There was a small clicking sound, and Ava's head popped up. Granger's front door was still shut, but he was bound to come out any minute now. She was about to set the phone back down and get out when something else caught her eye – a number that she recognized.

What had *Nolan Hotchkiss* texted Mr. Granger?

Ava clicked open the text thread and saw that it consisted of only one thing – a video. She pressed play.

The video started in Granger's classroom. Justine Williams, a brunette senior with puffy beesting lips, sat on the edge of his desk. Granger stood in front of her, between her slightly parted legs, and stroked her cheek. 'Have you ever seen *La Dolce Vita?*'

'No,' said Justine in a slightly wavering, innocent voice.

He took her hands. 'There is a scene where a couple wades into the Trevi Fountain in Rome. It's so romantic. I can see us doing the same thing.'

'R-really?' Justine said nervously, giving a high-pitched laugh.

Then he kissed her full on the lips.

It was the expression on Justine's face that made Ava almost puke. Justine looked uncomfortable and excited all at once. She also looked hopeful. Even though she knew it was wrong, she was so entranced she didn't care.

The camera started to shake. It went out of focus for a moment, and then it was turned around onto the filmmaker. It was Nolan, standing outside Granger's classroom in the hall. A slow, hostile smirk spread over his face.

'Oooh, teacher,' he cooed into the camera. 'You give such good extra credit assignments.' His tone changed abruptly. 'Speaking of assignments, I've got one or two for you. And if you don't want this going public, you'd better pay attention.'

Squeak.

Ava shot up for real this time just as Granger's door opened. She quickly placed his iPhone exactly where he'd left it, then moved back into her seat.

Granger sat in the chair next to her and scooted forward until his face was only a few inches from hers. 'Okay, let's get started,' he said. Then he looked more closely at Ava's face and frowned. 'Are you all right?'

There was no way Ava could be in this room even a moment longer. 'Um, actually, I have to go to the bathroom,' she blurted, her words coming out in a rush. She reached for her purse, nearly upending it, she grabbed it so hard.

He pointed to a door down the hall, and she walked quickly toward it, locking the door behind her. She collapsed against it, trying to process what she'd just seen. All those boob shots. All those girls he'd taken advantage of. Justine's expression. And *Nolan*. Had Nolan been *blackmailing* Granger?

The window was open, and a cool breeze broke her out of her trance. On a whim, she opened Granger's mirrored medicine cabinet. And right there, on the middle shelf, was an orange bottle clearly labeled. LUCAS GRANGER. OXYCONTIN, 20 MGS. TAKE FOR PAIN AS DIRECTED.

Oh. My. God. With shaking hands, Ava grabbed her phone from her purse and snapped a photo of the bottle. Then, heart pounding, she flushed the toilet, turned on the tap, then left the bathroom.

Mr. Granger was sitting at the table, waiting for her.

She forced an apologetic smile on her face. 'I am so sorry to do this, but I just got a text from my dad. I have to go.'

Granger stood and stepped a few paces in front of her, blocking her way. 'So soon?'

Ava's breath caught. 'We can work on the paper another time, right?'

Granger's smile was twitchy. 'But I made time for you *now*, Ava. You're being rude.'

Ava dared to look into his eyes, registering the very *un*teacherly tone. He seemed totally sure of himself. Not guilty. Not sheepish. He didn't think he was doing anything wrong.

'M-my father needs me,' she stalled, trying to remind him that she was still a *child*. With parents. And a father who would *kill* him.

'Are you sure you wouldn't at least like to earn some extra credit before you go?' he said suggestively, placing a hand on Ava's neck.

She pulled away in horror. 'I – I have a boyfriend,' she reiterated, her voice cracking.

Granger's eyes widened comically. 'Why, Miss Jalali! What do you think I'm suggesting?'

Which confused Ava even further. She didn't mean to, but

149

her gaze fell to his phone. She'd *seen* those videos. She wasn't suggesting anything that wasn't already implied.

Granger looked, too, then glanced back at her, seeming to put two and two together. His eyes darkened.

Ava tried to take a step back. 'I really need to go.'

Granger's fingers clamped hard. 'I know the rumors about you are true, Ava,' he said, all traces of warmth gone from his tone. 'And I have to say, I'm disappointed that you'd do this for other teachers but not for me.'

Time seemed to stop. *You'd do this for other teachers but not for me.* The words hung in the air, giving voice to the horrible stories Nolan had told long ago. She knew other students had heard them, but teachers? Who *hadn't* Nolan told?

Was this why she'd gotten all those As from Granger, because it was all part of his plan to get her to come over? For one horrifying moment, she wondered why the hell she bothered to work so hard. If everyone thought the worst of her anyway, what would one kiss cost her, really, if it meant she'd get an A?

Ava's blood ran cold. 'Those are just rumors,' she whispered. 'I wouldn't – I haven't –'

Granger gave her a condescending glare. 'Ava, you knew exactly what you were doing. So cut the innocent act, okay?'

And then he pulled her toward him, his grip strong. Ava managed to break free and barreled for the door, slipping out without him catching her. She sprinted to her car and slammed the door, revving the engine. Only when she'd made a few turns did she finally pull over, lean forward to rest her forehead on the steering wheel, and burst into tears.

CHAPTER SEVENTEEN

At eight o'clock on Friday night, Julie rushed into her bedroom. Parker was sitting on Julie's second twin bed, painting her nails chalkboard black. Adele crooned from the iPod dock, and the sound of rain pattered on the window outside.

'I'm so glad you're here. You'll never believe what just happened,' Julie said, flashing her phone at Parker.

On it was a text from Carson. *U like sushi? Was thinking of checking out Maru's. Tomorrow?*

Parker scanned the phone and handed it back. 'Are you going to say yes?'

'You know my rule. No boyfriends.'

Parker shrugged. 'Live a little. A date is not the same as having a boyfriend.'

'I know.' Julie rocked on her mattress. Goose pimples ran along her arms from the chill, but she barely noticed. 'But god, can you imagine what would happen if Carson found out about my mom?'

Parker shrugged. 'It's nothing a little damage control can't solve. You just have to spin the story.'

Julie shook her head. 'That's easier said than done. Think

about what happened to Ava.' Even though Ava was smart and pretty and popular, it'd been easy for Nolan to taint her reputation, even if everyone knew deep down he was full of it.

'Or even you,' Julie added, looking at her friend. Parker had been the most admired girl in school before her dad attacked her. Even as a freshman, she'd been on almost every page in the yearbook. But now, just because her dad had gone to jail, just because there were scars on her face, she was persona non grata.

If *their* reputations had been so easy to damage, Julie didn't stand a chance.

Suddenly, Katy Perry's 'Firework' came blasting out of her cell phone. She jumped, then picked it up and frowned down at the caller ID. Speak of the devil. Ava was calling. As soon as Julie picked up, she could hear Ava saying 'oh my god, oh my god' over and over. She glanced nervously at Parker.

'Hey, what's up?' Julie said tentatively.

Ava stopped *oh-my-god-ing*. 'I think Granger killed Nolan.'

Julie froze, her fingers clutching the phone. 'Our *teacher* Granger?'

'I'm almost sure of it.' Ava's voice was hushed and trembling. Julie motioned Parker over, then put the phone on speaker.

'I was in Granger's house,' Ava went on. 'He offered to help with a paper, although that was bullshit – he's a complete perv. I shouldn't have gone, but that's another story. Anyway, I found . . . pictures. On his phone . . .' She trailed off. It sounded like she was crying.

Slowly, Julie was able to get out of Ava what the pictures were of. Then Ava told her about the Nolan video where he'd threatened Granger. Julie's heart gave a lurch in her chest.

'That's probable cause,' she said slowly. 'But you really think he could have done it?'

'He wanted to kiss me when I left today,' Ava explained. 'And when I said no, his face . . .' She broke off and wailed. 'It was *awful*. And he has an Oxy prescription. I saw it in his bathroom.'

'I can't believe you went to his *house*,' Parker blurted.

'I know how it looks,' Ava wailed. 'But I was just trying to get help with my paper. Honest.'

'We believe you,' Julie insisted. She stood up off her bed and started to pace. Granger had seemed so *nice*. So . . . supportive. It was shocking that he could be such a jerk. She thought back to the day in his class once more. *Could* he have overheard?

Caitlin had leaned forward across the desk excitedly. 'Oxy. Everyone knows it's his drug of choice,' Caitlin had said. 'Or cyanide. He'd be dead in minutes.'

Julie had cleared her throat, her gaze drifting to Nolan across the room. He was in a group with Ursula; Ava's boyfriend, Alex; and a meek girl named Renee Foley, and they all looked miserable. 'We *are* just kidding, right?' she asked nervously.

'Of course,' Mackenzie said quickly, her laugh shrill.

Then Parker leaned forward, caging her fingertips together thoughtfully. 'Though we don't have to kill him to take him down.'

'What do you mean?' Ava asked slowly.

Parker thought for a moment. 'Well, the next time he hosts a party, we can prank him. Obviously we won't use cyanide, but what about Oxy? He loves the stuff anyway. Not too much – just enough to knock him out. Just enough to take some incriminating pictures.'

A gleam of excitement dawned in Caitlin's eyes. 'We could take pictures of him with his pants down. Or Sharpie his face.'

Mackenzie shifted. 'Everyone hates him. They're all just too scared to admit it. We'd be heroes if we pranked him.'

Ava straightened her back and lifted her chin. 'Should we do it?'

'I'm in,' Mackenzie whispered.

'Me, too.' Caitlin nodded.

The girls had looked at Julie. As much as she wanted to take part, it *so* wasn't her. But she took a deep breath. 'Where do we get the Oxy?'

At that moment, a shadow fell over her. Parker shot her friend a warning look, and Julie wrenched around in her seat to gaze up at Mr. Granger. For a moment, Julie was sure their teacher had heard everything. Sometimes, he had this way of sitting in on conversations as though he were a fly on the wall. Julie, like all the other girls, was flattered and a little unnerved by his attention – he was *so* good-looking and charming, and he had a vast, impressive knowledge of amazing films. But that day, he'd stared down at her with an unreadable expression on his face.

But then he'd said, 'So how's the discussion going over here, ladies?' And given them a big smile.

Now, Julie swallowed, her throat dry. 'He *did* come over right at the end of our conversation,' she said worriedly to Ava.

'Maybe he did hear everything,' Ava said.

'So how do you think this went down?' Julie thought aloud. 'Granger slipped upstairs and gave Nolan more Oxy after we left? And how? Shoved it down his throat and made him swallow?'

'Maybe Nolan woke up after we left,' Ava suggested. 'And you think Granger was watching us the whole time? Like he *heard* our conversation in class and decided to, like, piggyback off our plan?'

'Why would he pin it on us?' Parker asked. 'I mean, he doesn't seem like *that* bad a guy.'

'Uh, hello?' Ava interrupted. 'Didn't you just hear my story?'

'True,' Julie said. 'But what did *we* do? Why would Granger have it out for us? Was it simply out of convenience? Is he that much of a psycho?'

'You should go to the cops with this,' Parker said firmly.

'I can't go by myself!' Ava shrieked. 'You have to come with me. I already talked to Caitlin and Mackenzie – they said they'd come, too. I'll even pick you up.'

'No!' Julie almost screamed. Parker looked at her warningly. 'I mean, I'm not home. I'll just meet you at the station.'

Twenty minutes later, she and Parker pulled into the parking lot of the police station. The asphalt was cracked and uneven, and she stepped into a deep puddle as she got out of her car, soaking her sneakers. They ran toward the awning outside the glass double doors, where Mackenzie, Ava, and Caitlin were already huddled together.

Ava's face was swollen from crying, her make-up smeared. Caitlin had an arm around her shoulder and looked nervous but determined. Julie's hands clenched slightly, a hot rush of anger toward Mr. Granger spiking through her. 'Are you okay?' she asked Ava fiercely.

'Fine,' Ava looked miserable. 'I'm just . . . pissed off. And

155

scared.' She glanced at the others. 'I think he realized I'd seen his phone.'

Julie glanced around, half expecting Granger to be sitting in the parking lot, staring at them. But there were only rows and rows of police cars.

She turned toward the door. 'Let's go,' she said. 'You need to turn this asshole in, Ava.'

She led them into the station. It was nearly nine, and the waiting area was almost empty. A young officer with a dramatically waxed mustache sat alone at the desk, snickering at something on his computer screen. When he saw them, he raised an eyebrow.

'What can I do for you ladies?' He leaned over the desk, looking them all up and down. Julie dug her nails into her palms. The last thing Parker needed was some idiot in uniform staring at her.

Julie jutted a finger at Ava. 'She needs to talk to someone about the Nolan Hotchkiss murder,' she said, her voice ringing clearly through the room.

The cop stared from one to the other of them, gulping like a landed fish. But before he could recover, a deep baritone spoke from farther back behind the desk. 'Send them back, Deputy.'

It was Detective Peters – the one who had been going from classroom to classroom handing out his card. He'd come to Julie's calculus class, and she'd masked her handwriting as best she could, hoping it looked nothing like the happy, bubbly letters she'd penned on Nolan's chest.

Silently, the deputy opened a little gate in the desk to let them through. He led them into a large interrogation room with venetian blinds across a big plate-glass window. Julie felt Parker stiffen – the farther they got from an escape path, the tenser she got. Julie touched Parker's arm comfortingly, willing her to relax.

They sat down at uncomfortable folding chairs on one side of a rectangular table. The detective sat across from them. The room smelled faintly moldy, like something moist had gotten into the heating vent. A large poster showing Mount Saint Helens exploding hung on one wall.

'Sorry to make you sit in interrogation. My office isn't big enough for all of us.' Detective Peters smiled and leaned back slightly in his chair. 'Now, what did you want to tell me about?'

Julie shifted her weight uneasily. She'd talked to enough cops after Parker's hospitalization to know that Peters was trying to coax them into telling more than they'd planned.

Julie exchanged glances with the others. Mackenzie pressed her fingertips together in quick, nervous patterns, her dirty-blond hair in a messy side braid. Caitlin's lips were a thin line on her face. She looked even smaller than usual in an oversize USA soccer sweatshirt. Parker gripped the edge of the table as if she were on the edge of a cliff, and it was the only thing for her to hold onto.

Ava finally spoke up. 'I think I know who killed Nolan Hotchkiss.' Her voice was so soft Julie could barely hear.

Detective Peters's eyebrows shot up.

'I think it was Mr. Granger,' Julie added. 'Our advanced film studies teacher.'

The detective licked his lips, clasping his hands together on the table in front of him. 'That's a very serious accusation,

157

Miss Jalali,' he said finally. 'Why would you say such a thing?'

'He's been . . . *intimate* with a lot of the girls in our class,' Ava said. 'And Nolan knew it. He was blackmailing him.'

'I see,' said Detective Peters soberly. 'Do you have any proof of this?'

'He came on to me,' Ava said miserably. 'Today.'

'I've heard it happening with other girls, too,' Julie piped up, even though this was all news to her.

'And how do you know Nolan knew?'

This time, Parker cleared her throat. 'Because I used to be friends with him. He told me he knew. He said Granger kept pictures of girls on his iPhone.'

Julie stared at Parker, astonished by her quick thinking. They hadn't rehearsed this. The other girls looked surprised and pleased, too.

The detective scratched his head. He glanced at Parker, then quickly looked away, perhaps put off by her face. 'I see.'

'You should search his phone,' Ava piped up. 'A-and you should look through his house. For evidence of Oxy.'

'And you should at least arrest him for what he's doing to these students,' Julie added. 'It's wrong.'

Detective Peters tapped on the top of his desk. Finally, he shook his head. 'Perhaps Granger has some things to answer for, but as far as we're concerned, Nolan's death isn't one of them.' Then he leaned back in his chair again and gave them a long look that was hard to decipher. 'But we *do* have some questions for all of you.'

CHAPTER EIGHTEEN

We do *have some questions for all of you*. The words reverberated through Mackenzie's mind, but before she had the chance to wonder what he was talking about – what *type* of questions he might ask – Peters went on.

'We looked through Nolan's phone shortly after his death. We found some pretty steamy pictures of you there, Miss Wright,' he said, looking straight at Mackenzie.

Her stomach dropped. She lowered her head, too humiliated to make eye contact with the others. By their gasps, it was clear they didn't know what he was talking about. 'Nolan does that to everyone,' she mumbled.

Peters didn't look impressed. 'We also tracked down the IP address of the individual who sent out the photos of Mr. Hotchkiss . . . *defaced* . . . at that party, to an Internet café. Several people say a blond girl with your height and build was seen at the time in question.'

Mac felt her cheeks turn red. 'It wasn't me.'

Then the detective had turned to Ava. 'We also found a death threat from you.'

Ava blinked. 'What are you talking about?'

He opened the manila file on the table in front of him and took out a thick folder. When he opened it, the first page showed a printout of text messages.

'"If you tell anyone else, I'll kill you,"' he read out loud.

Ava's lips turned downward. 'He was spreading rumors about me. I just wanted him to stop.'

'Twenty different kids told me they saw you heading upstairs with him the night of the party, Miss Jalali.' He gave a mock-confused smile. 'I guess you were a little mixed-up the last time we talked, huh?'

Then the detective looked at Caitlin. 'It's no secret why *you* might want him dead, Ms. Martell-Lewis. But killing a bully isn't the way to deal with a problem.'

Caitlin turned pale. 'You don't know anything about me,' she spat.

'And I saved the best for last.' The detective then held up a photo. It was a close-up showing the words *Monster* on his face. Julie gasped. 'We're still waiting for a final report from forensics, but you see that funny-looking *M*, with a loop-de-loop up the middle? Familiar, huh?'

Then the detective stood. 'Look. I don't know what all this means, but I do know you ladies are lying. I don't know why, but I'll give you a break: tell me the truth *now*, and we can work something out. It's better to get everything out in the open before things get really crazy.'

The room was dead silent. From down the hall, they heard a phone ring. Mac's hands twitched in her lap. She considered confessing about helping to put Oxy in that drink. It was a simple prank, after all – nothing more than that. They weren't *killers*.

Julie spoke up. 'We only came here because you promised we wouldn't get in any trouble if we had information about the murder. We know it was Mr. Granger. He had the weapon – the drugs – and the motive. All you have to do is prove it.'

Detective Peters smiled again. This time it wasn't the affable, easygoing grin but a cold, hard smile. 'I assure you we'll look into Mr. Granger sexually assaulting students, ladies, and we'll talk to him about that. But I want to talk to *you* about Nolan. Nolan didn't die from OxyContin. Nolan was murdered with cyanide poisoning.'

'Cyanide poisoning?' Mac blurted, though she hadn't meant to. Ava kicked her ever-so-softly under the table.

'That's right.' Peters closed his manila folder again, his gaze moving slowly and intently over each of them. 'Now if you come up with any more theories, be sure to come see me right away. Or maybe I'll be paying you a visit before you have the chance.'

He looked at them like he knew everything. For a few seconds, nobody moved. Mac's brain cycled around the same word again and again and again. *Cyanide. Cyanide.*

Then Caitlin stood up violently from the table, shoving her chair back. She walked heavily toward the door. Mackenzie jumped up and scrambled after her, and then the others followed.

Outside, they crowded next to Mackenzie's Ford Escape. Caitlin wiped angry tears from the corners of her eyes, then angrily turned and kicked the curb.

'What the hell are we going to do?' Mackenzie's eyes were wide. 'Should we confess the prank? We didn't lace that drink with cyanide. I don't even know what cyanide looks like, let alone how to *get* it.'

'No,' Julie insisted. 'You saw him in there. He won't believe us.'

'Guys, what are the odds that someone killed Nolan *just like we planned?*' Caitlin said. Her face was red and her breath was coming rapidly like she was on the brink of hyperventilating. 'There's no way that's a coincidence. None.'

'Definitely not. Granger *must* have overheard us,' Ava broke in. 'It has to be him. Now we just need proof.' Her eyes darted back and forth. 'And I think I know where to get it.'

It was easy to get into Beacon Heights High, even late at night – so many overachievers came in for meetings and rehearsals that the security guards kept the doors open until after ten most nights. When Mac and Ava swept through the lobby, no one was even sitting at the front booth to sign them in. The halls were quiet and dark, their footsteps echoing down the empty hallways. The girls had decided it was best that only two of them went, and Mackenzie and Ava promised to call the others when they were done.

'Do you think we'll be able to find something?' Mackenzie asked as they came to a stop in front of Granger's door. They'd talked about breaking into his house but decided they'd start with the school. It seemed less extreme somehow.

'Only one way to find out.' But before she tried it, she looked curiously at Mac. 'Those pictures on Nolan's phone the cops were talking about. He was blackmailing you, right?'

Mac lowered her eyes. 'Not exactly. It was a dumb bet with his friends. And I was an idiot for falling for it.'

'We were *all* idiots when it came to him,' Ava said, gripping her hand and squeezing hard. 'You shouldn't feel embarrassed. He did that to everyone. I heard he had the same sort of pictures of your friend Claire.'

'Claire?' Mac blinked. Claire had never told her that. 'When?'

Ava shrugged. 'It was when Nolan and I were dating. But who knows? He could have been lying. He said he had pictures of tons of girls.'

Then she turned and tried the knob. Locked. But Mackenzie had a plan for that, too. Once, during a recital trip, a bassoon player from Oregon had taught her how to pick a lock with a reed. She glanced up and down the hall, then pulled the stiff wooden reed from her patchwork purse. She leaned down over the doorknob and fiddled with it. A moment later, Mackenzie heard a soft *click*. They were in.

'How do you know how to do that?' Ava breathed, astonished.

Mac smirked. 'I'm full of surprises.' She slid the reed back in her pocket, and they closed the door carefully behind them.

The ghostly outlines of not-completely-erased words lingered on the chalkboard. Ava strode to Granger's office, which was locked, too. But Mac was able to pick that lock as well, and they pried the door open and went inside.

It was darker in here, and the office was dustier than the classroom. The air smelled faintly of the cucumber Aveda hand soap Granger used, and the shelves were piled with books and old photography equipment.

Mac jerked open the top drawer. It was full of paperwork – stacks of homework, a bundle of permission slips for their upcoming field trip to the Majestic Theater in Beacon, pens, and paper clips. In one compartment, they found a pack of cigarettes and an overripe apple.

'Nothing,' Ava muttered.

Mackenzie tugged on the handle of a drawer and found that it was locked. She crouched in front of it, fiddling with the pick.

'This one's tricky,' she muttered, shaking the shim in frustration.

Outside the door, someone whistled the melody to 'Low Rider' off-key. The girls froze. A set of keys jingled musically, and something scraped in the keyhole.

Ava's eyes widened in the dark. 'We have to get out of here.'

'I've almost got it!' Mac jiggled the pick one more time, and the drawer slid open.

The doorknob on the door jerked back and forth without turning. The keys jingled again as someone looked for the right one. Ava dug her fingernails in Mac's arm. 'Come *on!*'

'Look,' Mac murmured.

The drawer had all the contraband from the past year inside. A Nintendo DS sat atop a comic book. A pearl-handled penknife, a Zippo, and a little silver flask were next to it. Ava dug through it, an anguished expression on her face.

'There's nothing here,' she mumbled. 'Nothing even remotely suspicious.'

There was another rasping sound in the keyhole. Mackenzie jerked Ava away by the back of her shirt and ducked under the office desk just as the door swung open.

Randy, the school's hippie janitor, stood in the doorway. His head was cocked, and he looked around as though he could sense someone was there.

Mac pressed her lips together, trying not to breathe. Her heart pounded fast in her chest. What was *he* doing here so late at night? If Randy caught them here, digging around in Granger's office, he would tell Granger for sure. And then Granger would tell the cops.

Slowly, Randy walked toward the office. His footsteps thudded against the floor. His whistling had stopped. Mac couldn't see him, but she sensed he was standing in the doorway. She closed her eyes and tried not to move. Ava clutched her hand tightly. Mac was almost positive she could hear Randy holding his breath, assessing the situation.

But then he breathed out. She sensed him turn, and the footsteps started up again. There was the metallic *clang* of a trash can knocking against the big trash bin he pushed around school. Moments later, there were more footsteps, and the door eased shut.

Slowly, Mac stood and stared at the empty classroom before them. As soon as she knew it was safe, she darted toward the door, eager to get the hell out of there. That had been close – too close. With the cops already onto them, one wrong move could be the end of everything they'd all worked so hard for – graduation, college, *Juilliard*. One wrong move and their perfect lives would be over.

CHAPTER NINETEEN

Saturday morning, Parker sat in Elliot's office, her hands gripping her knees. The room smelled faintly of a cinnamon candle, and a New Age song heavy on the wind chimes and didgeridoo tinkled faintly out of hidden speakers. The therapist offered Parker a gentle smile from across the room.

'So,' he said, 'how has this week been?'

'Trying,' Parker admitted.

'Can you tell me why?'

Parker shut her eyes. 'There have been a lot of police at school. It's awful.'

'Have any of them spoken to you?'

She tensed. 'Why would they talk to me?'

Elliot held up two palms. 'I assumed police officers talk to everyone in a case like this.'

Parker let her hair fall around her damaged face and twisted her mouth. *Way to go, idiot*, she thought. *Way to make yourself look superguilty. Why don't you just confess what you did?*

She cleared her throat. Elliot was sitting across from her so patiently. She almost felt like she *could* tell him everything. She needed someone to listen, and she wanted it to be him.

But then she thought of the other girls. They'd vowed to keep their secret.

'The police did talk to me, yes,' she mumbled.

Elliot tented his fingers together. 'Did they ask you about your relationship with Nolan?'

Parker raised one shoulder. 'Actually, they *didn't*.' The detective had gone through each girl's motives one by one, but he'd barely looked at Parker. 'Maybe he felt sorry for me,' she muttered. For all she knew, he remembered her from when her dad was arrested.

Elliot crossed his legs and leaned forward. 'Did you *want* him to ask you about Nolan?'

'No,' Parker said quickly. But then she glanced at the ceiling. 'Maybe.'

'Is that because you want them to know what he did? That he was kind of responsible?'

Parker peeked at him. Tears began to fill her eyes, thinking how Nolan wouldn't even look at her when she'd returned to school after her time in the hospital.

'I just wish he would have said he was sorry,' she said. 'We wouldn't have been friends after that, but I could have let it go.'

Elliot nodded thoughtfully. 'Have you ever considered forgiving Nolan?'

Parker made a face. 'I could never.'

'Hear me out, Parker. What happened has already happened; you can't take it back. Your dad is gone, Nolan is dead. Now you need to find a way to move forward.'

Parker cocked her head. 'How do I do that?'

Elliot stood and held out his hand. 'How about we take a field trip?'

'Don't you have another session?'

Elliot shook his head. 'You're all I've got today, Parker Duvall. So you're stuck with me.'

He led her down the gray-carpeted hall and out a heavy door to the parking lot. Parker's bike was chained to the rack, but Elliot bypassed it, heading to a silver car with a couple of bumper stickers for car-racing companies on the back.

'Let's go for a drive,' Elliot said, opening the passenger door for Parker.

'O-okay,' she said, but her heart was thumping. She knew Elliot in the context of one safe room. Venturing out felt different – somehow foreign. But she trusted him.

Elliot slid behind the wheel and started the engine. In moments, a fast-paced, hard-rock song by a band Parker had never heard blared through the stereo. Elliot turned down the volume, casting Parker a sheepish grin. 'Sorry.'

'It's cool,' Parker said, pushing her hair off her face for one moment. She caught a glimpse of herself in the side mirror and nearly gasped. The way the shadows angled, she almost looked . . . *normal*. She almost couldn't see her scars.

Elliot pulled onto the main road and drove a few miles over hilly terrain. They passed the main square and all the shops, several developments, the high school, and then the road Nolan had lived on, a road Parker had once known well. She looked at the turnoff, then back at Elliot.

'Uh, where are we going, anyway?' She'd thought they were going to park outside Nolan's house, and maybe Elliot would ask her to say good-bye to Nolan on his front lawn or something.

'You'll see,' Elliot announced, hitting the gas.

Parker shrugged. Maybe they would keep driving all the way to the sea. All the way out of her *life*.

But Elliot was slowing to a stop. Parker frowned at the rolling green hills in front of her, then at the wrought-iron gates to the left. In scrolled writing along the top read MCALLISTER CEMETERY.

Her heart froze.

Elliot shifted into park and cut the engine. He got out of the car, then swung around and opened Parker's door.

She stared at him. 'What are you doing?' Her voice was flinty, sharp. Parker shook her head violently. 'No. No way.'

Elliot frowned. 'What do you mean?'

'I mean I'm not going in there.' Parker got out of the car and took a few big steps away from him.

'Why?' Elliot cocked his head. 'What's happening in your mind right now?'

Parker wasn't sure what was happening – all she knew was that warning bells were going off like crazy. She saw flashes of light, then felt the painful twinge of an oncoming migraine. Nolan's face swam in her mind, his eyes narrowed. Then she saw her father's face above her. His hand coming down again and again. She heard someone screaming and only realized later that it was her. How she'd lain there, limp, lifeless, on the floor.

When she looked at Elliot, all she could do was shake her head. Pain seared from temple to temple. 'I can't go in there,' she whispered, her eyes closed tightly. 'I just can't.'

A crow flew overhead. Elliot's throat bobbed as he swallowed. 'Okay,' he said faintly. 'It's just that –'

'Parker?'

Parker whirled around. Julie stood behind her, looking angelic in a white diaphanous blouse and with her hair strewn around her shoulders. Her eyes were round with concern. 'I was just on my way to town to get something for my mom and saw you here. What's going on?'

'Thank god you're here,' Parker said, collapsing against Julie.

'Come on,' Julie said, reaching out her hand. She glanced at Elliot. 'I'm taking her home. We'll catch the next bus.'

Elliot blinked. 'Uh, sure,' he said, stepping aside. 'I was just trying to help.'

'You have to be careful with her,' Julie said protectively, carefully taking Parker's arm. The headache had come on full force, blocking Parker's vision, turning her stomach, sending waves of pain down her back. 'It's okay,' she could hear Julie's voice above her. 'You're going to be fine.'

'I couldn't do it,' Parker moaned, though every word she spoke hurt. 'I just couldn't.'

'I know,' Julie said, seemingly understanding even though Parker didn't quite get it herself. Maybe it was another hole in her memory: maybe old Parker had hated cemeteries. Maybe something bad had happened to her in one.

But she didn't care about the reason right then. All she wanted to do was sit on the bus bench with her eyes closed. All she wanted was to never think again.

CHAPTER TWENTY

That afternoon, Caitlin sat on the edge of the paper-lined bed at her orthopedic clinic, pushing her foot into her physical therapist's palm for her weekly appointment. 'Okay, now flex,' the therapist, a tall, strapping Russian whose name was Igor, said, watching her face as she moved her ankle around.

'It feels pretty good,' Caitlin said.

'Good.' Igor kept rolling her foot in different directions, his hands cool and careful.

In the corner, a local news station played, muted but with closed captions. A breaking-news alert rolled across the bottom of the screen. LOCAL BOY KILLED WITH CYANIDE.

She flinched. Igor looked at her sharply. 'Did that hurt?'

'No.' She swallowed, her mouth suddenly dry. Igor gently let go of her foot. 'Um, could you turn that up?' she asked. Igor looked confused for a second, then grabbed the remote from a nearby table and handed it to Caitlin. The sound came on instantly.

'Let's talk a little more about cyanide,' the reporter was saying, her voice strangely chipper. 'And for that, I'd like to introduce Dr. John Newlin, forensics expert. Dr. Newlin?'

The doctor cleared his throat. 'Cyanide poisoning is a classic method of both murder and suicide, mostly because the drug acts so quickly and looks like a cardiac event. The poison impedes the victim's ability to use oxygen, making the victim feel as though he is suffocating.'

'And cyanide isn't a common substance, right?' the reporter interrupted. 'In the Hotchkiss case, how could a murderer have gotten hold of it?'

'Well,' said the doctor, 'there are several professions that would allow access to cyanide in one form or another: chemists, photographers, pest control, mineral refining, dyeing, printing . . . The investigators are likely looking at people who have connections to those industries.'

Caitlin stiffened. She'd assumed cyanide would be hard to come by, but it sounded like there were a million ways to get it. What if she or the other girls had it in their garage or basement, without even knowing it? What then?

'What about the chem lab at school?' the reporter asked.

John Newlin paused. 'A chemistry professor *would* know how to obtain potassium cyanide – old chemistry sets used to include it, in fact. But it's difficult to imagine a teacher introducing such a dangerous chemical into the classroom.'

'Thank you for joining us, John. There continue to be no new leads in the Hotchkiss investigation. Now, at the top of the next hour –'

Caitlin turned off the TV and leaned back on the table. Her heart was racing.

'Were you friends with him?' Igor asked, a sympathetic look in his eyes.

Caitlin chewed on the corner of her lip. 'I didn't really know him that well.'

Igor nodded. 'Well, a crime like this affects everyone in the community, whether or not you were friends with him. It's terrible. I hope whoever did it rots in jail.'

Rots in jail. Her heart thudded in time with the words. That might be her future. Caitlin thought back to the police interrogation and the detective's face grinning when he said she clearly had motive. She shuddered at the idea that the cops were sitting around, *talking* about her.

About *them*.

She glanced at her phone. Ava had sent a message last night: *Just looked thru Bogie's shit at the lighthouse. Nada.* It was a code: *Bogie* was their name for Granger, after Humphrey Bogart, whom he was always talking about, and the *lighthouse* was Beacon Heights High. Where could they go from here? How could they pin this on Granger? Did he have access to cyanide? The reporter had said photographers used it, and Granger ran a photography club.

She quickly sent a group text. *Photographers use cyanide.*

Her phone buzzed almost instantly. She expected it to be from one of the girls, but instead it was from . . . Jeremy.

Dragon Ball marathon on. Thought you should know . . .

It brought an unexpected smile to her face. She hadn't talked to him since he'd driven her to practice last week, but they'd seen each other in the halls at school, and smiled shyly at each other.

Nerd. ☺, she wrote back.

Takes one to know one. ☺, he texted.

'Well, everything's healing up nicely,' said Igor, taking a pen out of his pocket. 'The good news is you probably only need to see me a couple more times.'

'Great.' Caitlin nodded.

'And, Caitlin?' he said jovially.

She looked up at him. 'Yeah?'

'Kick some butt in your big game, will you?' He gave her a conspiratorial wink.

'Thanks,' she said, suddenly aware that she'd barely thought about the upcoming semifinals that Wednesday. With everything else going on, it felt almost . . . trivial. She gathered her bag and walked outside. When she heard a honk at the curb, she looked up. Josh sat in his Jeep Cherokee.

'How's Igor?' he said.

Caitlin straightened up. She'd forgotten he was waiting for her. 'Russian, as usual.'

She got into the car and buckled her seat belt. Josh leaned over to kiss her hello. But when she closed her eyes and kissed him back, she imagined herself sitting on the back of Jeremy's Vespa, her arms wrapped around his. She flinched, horrified.

'So where to? Dirk's?' It was their favorite burger place, famous for its sweet potato fries.

Caitlin made a face. 'I just ate.'

Josh waved his hand. 'Well, *I'm* starving, so do you mind?' He started the car without waiting for her answer. 'Once you smell those fries, you'll totally want some.'

I said I wasn't hungry, Caitlin thought as they pulled away from the curb.

Jay Z's 'Empire State of Mind' came blasting out through

the speakers. Caitlin jumped at the sudden noise, slamming her palm against the dash as if to brace herself. Josh cranked it up even louder. 'This song always makes me think of the Cape Disappointment trip,' he yelled. 'Remember? We listened to it on the way there, like, five hundred times?'

The bass shook so hard it felt like an extra heartbeat vibrating through her body. The Cape Disappointment trip had been just after their sophomore year. Josh had just gotten his driver's license and they'd gone to the coast for a week with a bunch of other soccer players. She still remembered the sun-dappled trees whipping by outside the car window, all of them singing at the top of their lungs without a care in the world. She remembered Josh's hand on her knee, and little charges of electric attraction shooting between them. That was when Taylor was still alive, when Caitlin was still happy and innocent. That was before she'd known how much the world could hurt a person.

It felt like so long ago.

A heavy weight settled on her knee, and she looked down to see Josh's hand resting on her pant leg. She was shocked at how foreign and clumsy his hand felt on her leg. Almost *annoying*, in fact.

She stared out the window, thinking about what Jeremy had told her the other night. *Sometimes I think you need to get away to get some perspective.* She couldn't stop thinking about it. It felt like he'd told her she was living her life all wrong. What the hell was it supposed to mean, though? And what was she supposed to do about it? What was she supposed to change?

She looked over at Josh. 'Do you ever think about what

you'd do if you couldn't play soccer anymore?' The question came out in a tumble.

He frowned. 'Huh?'

The seat belt felt tight across her throat and she tugged at it. 'If you got hurt or something. Or if you burned out.'

Josh frowned. 'Why even worry about something like that? Your ankle is fine, Cate. You're definitely playing soccer.'

'Yeah, but . . .' She gave a little grunt of frustration. 'I mean, what if you hurt yourself really badly or something. Or what if you didn't *feel* like it anymore? What would you do then?'

Josh almost ran a stoplight turning to look at her. 'Are you quitting?'

'No.' She turned to look out the window. 'I'm just playing devil's advocate.'

He gave her a blank, almost nervous look, shaking his head. 'I just don't see the point in thinking about something that isn't going to happen. Soccer is life.' He grinned. It was a slogan on one of the bumper stickers plastered on the back of his car.

'But actually, Josh, it *is* going to happen.' Caitlin's heart started to beat faster. 'We're not going to be playing soccer forever. After UDub, *if* we both get in . . . well, the pros are a long shot, even if you are one of the best. We have to have *some* sort of plan.'

Josh looked hurt. 'You don't think I can go pro?'

'That's not what I said!' she insisted. 'And it's not the point. Don't you think it's a good idea to . . . I don't know. To slow down sometimes? To look around and see what you want out of life?'

He snorted. Caitlin watched him for a moment, but he didn't

176

seem to give the question any consideration. 'What's gotten into you lately, anyway?' he asked. 'You've been acting weird.'

She shrugged, then decided to say the name she'd been holding back. 'I guess I've been thinking about Taylor a lot. The Nolan thing . . . it's brought up a lot of memories. And it's like . . . life is *so* short. The only way we've spent it is running up and down the soccer field.'

Josh shook his head. 'I honestly don't see what Taylor or Nolan have to do with soccer.'

She whipped her head around to stare at him. 'They have *everything* to do with soccer. If I hadn't been so wrapped up in soccer, I might have seen what was happening to Taylor. And now I can't stop thinking about it.'

Josh still looked blank. 'Well, maybe you should. Because it's going to screw up your game. Screw up your chances at getting into UDub.'

Her mouth dropped open. 'And then . . . what? You won't like me anymore if I don't win the big game? You won't like me if I actually *think* about what happened instead of pushing it under the rug?'

Josh halted at a stoplight. 'God, Caitlin. You've been picking on me for the past two weeks. And I didn't even *do* anything.'

A thousand words froze in Caitlin's throat. *I just want you to listen to me*, she wanted to scream. *I want to be able to talk about Taylor without you getting all weird. I want you to throw your arms around me and say you'll listen, however long it takes. I want you to understand, even if you don't understand. And that's what hurts the most.*

But for some reason, she couldn't actually say it. Maybe it

177

was because they'd been together for too long; they'd developed a pattern of *not* saying so many things that it felt weird to actually be honest. Or maybe it was because it was all too true, and saying it would prove how disconnected they really were. It was a harsh thing to realize, but suddenly, Caitlin saw it in sharp focus. Besides soccer, she and Josh had *nothing in common*. Nothing at all.

She tore her seat belt off and jerked the car door open.

'What the hell?' he asked, his shocked face turning toward her.

She stepped out of the car and threw up one hand.

'Babe, get back in the car,' Josh demanded.

Caitlin shook her head, slamming the door tight. 'I need some time alone,' she snapped through the open window.

'Caitlin, what the hell did I do?'

For a moment Josh looked uncertain, and she was almost afraid he'd get out and follow her. But then the light changed. Behind him cars started to honk. He stared at her for a long moment, confused. Then he shook his head, held up his hand in a 'whatever' kind of gesture, and roared off down the street.

She stood there for a moment, breathing in the smells of exhaust and faintly rotten leaves. Her heart pounded loudly in her ears. She'd never done anything like that before – she and Josh had barely ever even squabbled. It felt scary to do something so unlike herself. But also kind of liberating.

She pulled out her phone, about to call someone to pick her up – her moms? *Jeremy?* – when she noticed someone jogging by. She did a double take. *Granger.*

He was dressed in running shorts and a long-sleeved shirt,

but his pace was slow, almost leisurely. He locked eyes with her as he passed. A small, strange smile tugged up the corners of his lips. He gave a tiny, ironic salute, and then he was gone.

Caitlin's hand shook. She knew that look. She'd given it to Nolan a thousand times after Taylor died. Its message was loud and clear: *You're going down – and there's nothing you can do about it.*

CHAPTER TWENTY-ONE

Saturday night, Julie stepped into Maru's Sushi and shook the water off the plaid umbrella she'd just borrowed. It was raining buckets, but although Julie's house was filled with, well, *everything* imaginable, she couldn't find a single umbrella in any of the piles. However, she'd run into two groups of kids from school in the parking garage, and multiple people had offered to lend her an umbrella. One girl, a junior named Sadie, said she'd *hold* the umbrella over Julie as she walked the short distance to the restaurant. 'You guys are so sweet,' Julie had said, graciously accepting Sadie's Burberry umbrella and promising to return it on Monday. Popularity did have its privileges sometimes – it was the one bright spot in her otherwise collapsing world.

Now, she looked around the crimson-and-gold restaurant. The air smelled like soy and ginger, her favorite scent combo. Paper lanterns hung over the tables, giving off a muted glow. Behind the bar a sushi chef stood frowning in concentration, his knife flying over the cutting board. She finally caught sight of Carson at a table in the corner, under an enormous *Gyotaku*-style print of a chinook salmon. He was looking down at the menu and didn't notice her. She still couldn't believe she'd let Parker talk her into this. 'You *deserve* a dream date, especially after the past few days,' she'd said, and had physically taken the phone from Julie and texted Carson back an emphatic *yes*.

'Hey,' she said as she approached, nerves clanging.

Carson's bright olive eyes flicked up to hers, and he did a double take, standing up so fast his knees hit the table. Julie hid her smile. She was wearing her favorite black dress with faux-leather detail and big sparkly earrings. It looked like something Ava might wear.

'Hi.' He moved around the table to pull out her chair. 'Um, you look fantastic.' She loved the way his accent drew out the vowels. Fan-tas-tic.

'Thanks. So do you.' He wore a gray blazer, distressed jeans, and a vintage T-shirt with a Seventies-style graphic of a sunset over palm trees. Julie was acutely aware that every girl in the restaurant kept turning to ogle him, but she pretended not to notice.

The waitress sidled up to the table, pen poised over her pad. Carson glanced back down at the menu. 'So what's good here?'

'Well, we definitely want some spicy tuna rolls and eel and salmon sashimi. And the *ebi*. Oh, and miso soup. And probably some *inari*,' Julie said.

He started to laugh. 'Just how much fish do you plan to eat?'

'You've officially been warned. This is not amateur hour.' She raised her eyebrow in a mock challenge, and he grinned up at the waitress.

'Okay. Bring us everything she said.'

'And some edamame!' Julie added as the waitress started to walk away. 'Please!'

She met Carson's eyes and smiled. He was so gorgeous, with the gold flecks in his eyes and his smooth dark skin. She almost couldn't believe he'd wanted to go out with *her*.

'So, Julie, tell me something about you that I don't know,' he said, fidgeting with the straw in his water glass.

Julie blinked. There was so much he could never know. She spooled through her life details, looking for something innocuous. 'I'm a lifeguard at the indoor pool at the Beacon Rec Center. It's just a lot of wild kids and old-lady lap swimmers.'

His eyes twinkled. 'A lifeguard? You sure you're not an Aussie?'

'An honorary one, maybe,' Julie joked. 'I guess everyone's born knowing how to swim there, huh?'

'Pretty much,' Carson said, his fist resting on his chin as he gazed at her. 'And, you know, everyone rides kangaroos to school and wrestles crocodiles.'

'And here I was thinking you all just drove around the Outback, talking in sexy accents.'

'You think my accent is sexy?' His voice was low, and a smile played around his lips.

Julie smiled back at him, filled with a sudden confidence. 'The accent, yes. I'm still deciding about everything else.'

'Well,' Carson said, leaning forward and resting his elbows on the table. 'Let me see what I can do to change your mind.'

The waitress brought out their edamame, and they swapped stories, laughing almost the entire time. Carson told her about filming comedy sketches with his friends in Sydney, and about surfing in the Tasman Sea. 'One time, a great white shark circled my surfboard for forty minutes,' he said, widening his eyes. 'I had to just stay there and wait him out. I thought I was shark bait for sure.'

'You think that's scary?' Julie teased. 'One time, my friend Parker persuaded me to hitchhike to Portland for a Taylor Swift concert. We spent hours on the highway with no luck. And then this skeevy guy picked us up. His car was full of bobbleheads – I mean *packed* – and he kept humming this weird song that sounded like it was from a horror movie. We were so creeped out we made him let us off at the next exit. And then this *other* car came along, and it ended up being Mr. Downing, our algebra teacher.' She giggled at the memory. 'Let's just say that we never made it to see Swift.'

Carson reached for an edamame pod. 'I've done some hitchhiking in Sydney and the outskirts – it can be dicey. Who's your friend you're talking about? Parker?'

'Uh-huh.' Julie's smile dimmed a little.

'Does she go to our school?'

Julie picked an imaginary ball of lint off her sleeve. But before she had to figure out how to describe Parker, the waitress walked up with their sushi and rolls, and the subject was dropped. Carson gasped in mock horror at the mountains of food on the table before them. 'How are we ever going to finish all this?'

'Have you ever *had* eel?' Julie challenged. 'Trust me. You'll be licking the plate.' She reached for a piece with her chopsticks and dunked it in soy sauce. Carson grinned and followed her example.

After some more easy conversation, Julie stood up and excused herself. She slipped into the bathroom and checked her make-up in the big round mirror over the sink. Then she

183

experimented with a big, honest, dazzled smile. Everything was going so well that she almost couldn't believe it. Maybe she really *could* do this. Maybe she could even have a relationship. It might be easy to keep her secret. Nyssa had never come to Julie's house, and Julie had been friends with her for years.

She rummaged around in the depths of her purse for the petal-pink lipstick she'd bought just for tonight, thinking about how she was going to ask Carson more questions about life in Australia. He was so playful and funny without being boastful or lame. She snapped the lid back on the lipstick and reached for a paper towel to blot. Then a face materialized in the mirror behind her.

Julie almost screamed.

'Hello to you, too,' Ashley Ferguson said, a cold smile spreading across her thin lips.

Ashley wore a short skirt that was at least a size too small for her. Her boobs peeked painfully out over the cleavage of her tight cashmere sweater. Her make-up looked almost exactly like Julie's, except she'd gotten the shades subtly wrong – her foundation was too dark, and she'd managed to spread a glittery highlighter over her entire face. It was like looking at herself through a fun-house mirror, distorted and grotesque.

'W-what are you doing here?' Julie sputtered.

Ashley silently plucked Julie's purse out of her hands, pulling the lipstick out and applying it in the mirror. It was too light for her complexion, but she smacked her lips together approvingly. Then she dropped the tube into her own purse.

'Um, excuse me, that's mine,' Julie said, staring at Ashley in disbelief.

'But you're so nice, I thought you'd want to share,' Ashley said lightly, tossing her hair over her shoulder.

'Well, I don't. Please give it back,' Julie said, holding her hand out. That lipstick had cost her two paychecks.

But Ashley just looked at her challengingly. 'No.'

Julie shifted her weight, losing patience. She had enough to deal with right now; she didn't need a stalker on top of it. 'You can't just go around stealing other people's things. *Or* looks,' she steamed. 'You're such a freaking copycat.'

Instead of looking taken aback or ashamed, Ashley just smiled at her, looking oddly excited. 'Copycat. What an interesting choice of words.'

'Whatever, Ashley. Just get a life already and stop stealing mine,' Julie said, snatching her lipstick out of Ashley's purse and striding out of the bathroom, proud that she'd finally stood up to someone. Maybe the police could push her around, but Ashley Ferguson couldn't.

And more important, she had a hot date to finish.

CHAPTER TWENTY-TWO

The following Monday, Ava slumped into film studies, her head down. That was the bitch about school: no matter what happened, no matter who you got in a fight with, who broke up with you, or whether a teacher tried to molest you at his house, you still had to go to the same freaking classes every day. Face the same demons and humiliation. You couldn't run and hide, no matter how badly you wanted to.

Case in point: there was Mr. Granger pacing up and down the aisles, his fingers laced cockily in his belt loops, a look of superiority on his face. 'So,' he spoke to the class, 'how is *The Postman Always Rings Twice* different from the other movies we've seen in this unit?'

Silence. When Granger passed Ava's desk, she intentionally looked down. To her horror, he paused next to her. He was so close she could feel the heat of his body.

'Miss Jalali?' She flinched at the sound of her name. His voice sounded ice-cold. 'What do you think?'

Ava looked up through the long curtain of her hair. 'Um. One of the things that struck me was how fatalistic it is,' she mustered. 'In *And Then There Were None*, the whole point was that the judge had to punish people because otherwise they'd never be punished. So it's about humanity scheming to have some control over its own circumstances. But in *this* movie, it's almost like fate has set a trap before any of the characters even meet. Cora and Frank are punished because they're, like, doomed to be punished.'

'Because they're, "like, doomed"?' Mr. Granger sneered. 'Very articulate. Anyone have a less obvious point to make? Colette, what do you think?'

Ava sagged in her chair, the droning of her classmates suddenly very far away. All she wanted was to find some way to prove Granger had murdered Nolan so that he would go to jail – and so that she and her friends would be safe.

But then she noticed something sitting on her desk. It was a folded-up piece of paper, seemingly dropped there a moment ago. Ava glanced around at her classmates, but no one was looking at her. The only person whose gaze was upon her, actually, was Granger's. He glared at her from the front of the room, his eyes dropping to the paper on her desk.

Ava's stomach lurched. *He'd* written it.

She slipped the piece of paper to her lap and opened it up. She recognized his scrawl from his comments on her papers.

Some people know to keep their mouths shut – I guess you're not one of them. I'd be careful if I were you.

And PS: if you show this to anyone, I'll know. You don't want to mess with me.

Ava's mouth dropped open. She looked up at Granger again,

but he was facing the board, chalk in hand. Was that a threat? How could the cops not have found those pictures? She thought back to that moment at his house, when he'd caught her glancing at his phone. He must have known she'd seen them and deleted all the evidence.

Finally, the bell rang, and Ava shot up, desperate to be out of that classroom. She had to get as far from Granger as possible.

'Hey! Hey, Ava, wait!'

Even though she knew it was Alex, Ava didn't slow down. Alex caught up with her in the hallway, gasping for breath. 'Hey, are you okay?'

'I'm fine,' she said, not slowing down.

'What was with Granger today? He was being a dick. The stuff you said was totally right on.'

She shrugged. 'I guess he was in a shitty mood.'

'Hey.' Alex caught her arm and stopped her hard in the middle of the hall. His eyes searched her face. Suddenly, Ava couldn't fight it anymore. Tears sprang to her eyes, her lower lip trembling. She started to turn away from him, but he touched her elbow.

'Hey,' he said softly, giving her a sympathetic look. 'You want to get out of here?'

She hesitated. She wasn't sure she was in the mood to hang out with *anyone*. Then again, the thought of staying on campus – where she risked bumping into Granger, or worse, Detective Peters – sent a roiling wave of nausea through her. She wiped her tears impatiently away. 'Okay,' she said. 'Let's go.'

They took Alex's car. Ava stared out the window as they passed posh boutiques and pedestrians under bright-colored umbrellas.

Alex turned the radio up a little as the Beatles' 'Here Comes the Sun' came over the air, singing along under his breath as they drove across Lake Washington and into the city. He was adorably off-key.

Finally, the two of them arrived at the Washington Park Arboretum. Alex unfurled an oversize blue-and-green plaid umbrella as he slammed the car door behind him, coming around to hold it over Ava's head as she stepped out into the rain. She inhaled deeply – the air smelled like soil and fir trees.

'I haven't been here since I was a kid,' Ava said, looking around. 'But I always loved it.'

'I thought it would cheer you up,' Alex said softly.

He bought two tickets, and they went into the park. Ava's breath caught in her throat. Seattle didn't get many fall colors – the rain kept everything green and lush through most of the year – but here a shock of gold and red leaves fluttered overhead like flames. A peaceful stream wove its way through mossy boulders, murmuring softly in the rain. They made their way down the stone pathway, the only people in the park. *The only people in the world*, Ava thought, her eyes flickering toward Alex.

'So you're letting Granger get to you,' he said. 'I can totally tell.'

Ava ducked her head. 'He was in a jerky mood. Maybe he didn't have enough girls fawning over him this morning.'

Alex shook his head, a disgusted look on his face. 'I don't get why so many girls have a crush on him. He seems like a sleaze.' He frowned. 'It seemed like you guys were getting along, though. Like, he used to praise you for *everything*. What ever happened with that paper you were going to rewrite?'

Ava looked away. She should have known Alex wouldn't forget

189

about this. She shrugged. 'He wouldn't let me rewrite after all.'

'Ava.' Alex's voice was stern. 'I *know* you. You're acting really weird right now. Something's going on, right? Please tell me. Whatever it is, I'll understand.'

Ava felt her cheeks redden. This really wasn't fair to Alex. Maybe she needed to come clean. Well, *sort of* clean, anyway. 'He kind of . . . hit on me, okay?' she blurted.

Alex's face flashed with anger. *'When?'*

She shook her head, humiliated. 'I went to see him another time. At his house.' She lowered her eyes. 'It was for the paper – or so I thought. Really, it was all a set-up.'

Alex pulled her into a hug, tracing small circles on her back. 'I'm so sorry, Ava. But you need to go to the police. You know that, right? He'll get fired.'

'I tried, actually.'

Alex pulled away and looked at her in shock. 'You did?'

Ava felt so guilty. Usually, she and Alex told each other everything. 'A few days ago. They didn't believe me.'

'Why not?'

Ava shrugged, searching for an answer that would make sense. 'Because I'm just a pretty girl making stuff up. Or maybe they'd heard the rumors, too.' She laughed awkwardly.

'That's not funny.' Alex paced around. 'God. That's so messed up. Remember how I said I had something to tell you about him? Well, I've seen girls go to his house. A *lot* of them. College age. Maybe even *our* age. And now, with him hitting on you . . . it's even worse. He needs to be punished.'

'Wait.' Ava stared at him. 'You saw girls our age go into his house? Are you *sure?*'

Alex nodded. 'Positive.'

She gripped his hand. 'Maybe *you* could go to the police.'

Alex shrugged. 'I'm not sure how that would look after you went and they didn't believe you. They'd probably think that I was just trying to stick up for you or something. It's not like I have solid proof.'

'Right,' Ava said despondently, lowering her shoulders.

'But I can watch him, if you want,' Alex said gently. 'This guy needs to be stopped. What he's doing is so wrong.'

'Thank you.' Ava peeked him. 'So you're not mad?'

'At you?' Alex shook his head. 'Ava, I *love* you.'

'I love you, too.'

He hugged Ava again, and she leaned forward into him, feeling a burst of gratitude. Maybe, if Alex kept watching Granger, he would find proof of what he was doing. And if the cops arrested him for being a sleazebag, they would look into everything else in his life, too. *Including* Nolan.

Her pulse began to race again as she realized she hadn't been one hundred percent honest with Alex. What she'd told him was *almost* the truth . . . but there was so much more she'd left out. All of it about Nolan.

Hopefully he'd never need to know.

CHAPTER TWENTY-THREE

The next day, Mackenzie and Julie huddled below Julie's car window in the Beacon Heights parking lot. It was after school, and an unusually hot sun was beating down on them through the moon roof. Mac was impressed by Julie's spotless car – there wasn't a gum wrapper or empty soda can anywhere, just a spare hoodie on the backseat. And though they were surrounded by Mercedes, BMWs, and Audis bought by parents who had more money than they knew what to do with, Julie's car was an old, manual-transmission Subaru.

'What do your parents do, anyway?' Mac asked idly. She just realized she didn't know very much about Julie's home life. The other girls moaned about their situations – Ava complained about her father and stepmother, Caitlin muttered about her good-cop, bad-cop moms, and she certainly did her fair share of grousing about her überstrict parents and her whiny sister.

Julie looked away. 'Um, my dad isn't really around. And my mom . . .' Then she stiffened. 'Get down. There he is.'

Mac ducked just as Mr. Granger walked out one of the doors under the breezeway and toward the gym, his duffel bag hanging from one hand. In moments, he disappeared through the gym's double doors.

Julie looked at her. 'I guess he's working out?'

'Looks like it,' Mac said. Beacon Heights High's workout facilities were top-notch; a lot of teachers used them, too.

'Should we go in?' Julie murmured.

Mac shrugged. They'd been following Granger for an hour and a half. The others had taken shifts yesterday and today, all in the hopes that something he did would lead them to the truth about what had happened to Nolan. But so far, their stakeouts had been a bust. Yesterday, they'd followed him to the grocery store, the public library, and to a sports bar packed with Seahawks fans . . . and he hadn't done so much as hit on the bartender. Today, they'd tailed him from the school to Starbucks and now back to the gym.

Mac leaned her head back in the seat and sighed. 'He's the most boring murderer in history.'

Julie shook her head. 'Sooner or later he'll slip up. We just have to be there when it happens.'

Mackenzie twisted her lips to one side skeptically. She wanted to believe Julie, but she wasn't so sure. Granger seemed to be going about his business without a care in the world. He didn't do *anything* suspicious. 'I just wish Ava's boyfriend had a record of the girls coming in and out of his place,' she muttered. Ava had filled them in on her boyfriend's revelation yesterday about Granger's extracurricular affairs.

'Even so, that might not tie him to Nolan,' Julie said. Then she looked at Mac. 'You can go, you know. You probably have to practice, right? No point in screwing up both of our futures.'

Mac shut her eyes. Of course she had to practice, but practicing was far from the forefront of her mind. Her phone rang softly from the depths of her backpack. She rummaged for it, and when she saw the name on the screen, her heart sped up. *Blake*.

They hadn't seen each other for a week. Actually, Mac hadn't really seen Claire for a couple of days, either – they hadn't talked over the weekend, and she wasn't in school yesterday or today. Mac had considered texting her to see if she was sick and needed her assignments – that was what they'd done in the past – but somehow she hadn't been able to bring herself to do it. All she could think about was how Claire had lied to her that day at Disneyland.

The phone kept ringing. Mac knew she shouldn't take Blake's call, but she felt her fingers reaching for the answer button on the screen anyway.

'Hey, Macks.' Blake's soft voice came through the receiver. 'What're you doing?'

'Uh, nothing,' she lied, glancing guiltily at Julie. 'What's up?'

'Come meet me at the ferry,' he said.

'What, in Seattle?' She snorted. 'I can't do that.'

Julie raised an eyebrow at her, but she turned toward the window.

'Why not?' Blake sounded disappointed.

'Because . . . because I have stuff to do.' *And because you're not mine*, she wanted to add.

'But I haven't seen you in days,' he murmured. 'Come on. There's this ice-cream place on Bainbridge Island that makes the best dulce de leche. I'll buy you a cone. I'll buy you ten cones.' He paused for a moment. 'I really miss you.'

Mac's heart jumped. How long had she wanted him to say something just like that? She glanced at Julie, covering the phone with one hand.

'Actually, *can* you finish this without me?'

Julie nodded. 'Sure.' Mac was glad Julie didn't ask her why.

Mackenzie moved her hand and talked into the phone again. 'Okay. I'm on my way.'

The pier was bustling when she arrived forty-five minutes later. Lines of commuter cars waited to get on board while tourists posed in front of Puget Sound to take pictures. Gulls squealed shrilly, wheeling overhead and diving toward the current. The sun faded and then grew brighter as wispy clouds moved across it, the light changing every few minutes like someone was playing with a dimmer that controlled the weather.

Blake met her next to the ferry's ticketing booth, his shaggy hair curling from the bottom of a black knit cap. She awkwardly raised her hand in greeting.

He looked half surprised she'd actually shown up, like he'd just won a contest or something. Then he leaned down and grabbed her hand. 'Come on.'

They walked up the long stairs and boarded. The observation deck wasn't very crowded – a large group of retirees in matching Windbreakers peered out through binoculars, and a thin girl wearing loose hemp pants sat on a bench hugging her knees, but otherwise they were alone. The ferry's horn blared across the water as it pushed off. Behind them, Seattle's skyline spread out in panorama.

'I love boats,' he said, leaning against the railing. 'Even in the middle of winter sometimes I'll come out here. I'm usually the only one on the observation deck during a freezing rain. Everyone smart is in the galley drinking hot cocoa.'

'Have you ever been to the San Juan Islands?' Mackenzie asked. When he shook his head, she went on. 'My parents have a cottage up there. We go every summer. Well, we used to. Now, between me and my sister, we have too many competitions and rehearsals to take a month off.' She smiled, remembering the little salt-stained house on the shore. 'My dad used to take us sailing every morning. I loved that.'

They stood side by side in silence for a few minutes, watching the ferry cut through the water. Ocean spray lightly flecked her face. The wind had a cold bite to it, and she was glad she'd worn her vintage peacoat.

'Look,' he said, pointing out at the water. 'Whales.' She turned to see a handful of graybacks slicing through the water. Her eyes widened as a huge gray fin breached suddenly out of the water before slapping back down and disappearing. The retirees at the railing gasped with pleasure. A second whale popped its head up out of the water and eyed the ferry beadily.

Mackenzie turned to Blake, but before she could say anything, he blurted, 'I broke up with Claire.'

Mackenzie blinked. 'You . . . what?'

'Last night. I told her we were through.'

Mackenzie clung to the railing, her limbs suddenly limp and heavy. Maybe that was why Claire hadn't been in symphony. She was probably at home, crying her eyes out. A teensy part of her felt bad for her friend, especially coupled with what she'd found out from Ava – that Nolan might have blackmailed Claire, too. But then she remembered once more how Claire had lied to Blake about her and then stolen Blake away.

'Did you have a fight?'

He shrugged. 'Not really. But like I told you, this was a long time coming.' He stared at the water. 'I didn't tell her about us, just so you know. The last thing I want is to mess up your friendship.'

Mackenzie took her glasses off and wiped water droplets off the lenses. 'Honestly, our friendship is pretty messed up as it stands.'

'What do you mean?'

'I mean, what kind of friends constantly hope for each other to fail?' She shrugged. 'We compete over everything. Even you.'

Blake's cheeks reddened. 'I'm sorry I got between you guys.'

'If it hadn't been you, it would have been something – or someone – else. Sometimes I wonder if I even really know her.'

'You know what she said when I broke up with her?' Blake said. 'That I'd come crawling back to her soon enough.'

Mac shivered. 'Really?' But then she looked down. Maybe it shouldn't surprise her. Claire bulldozed anyone who was in her path or caused her pain; she always got what she wanted. It was probably why she would get the Juilliard spot and Mac wouldn't. After all, Mac was the one here, when Claire was probably practicing. Her heart lurched. Was Blake worth her sacrificing that? Was her head in the right place?

But when she looked at him again, she thought that maybe it was. 'How are *you* feeling?' she asked, her voice soft.

He glanced up, a look of surprise flitting across his face.

Then he broke into a sheepish grin. 'Honestly . . . kind of great. I mean, I never wanted to hurt her, but it feels like I've been carrying this huge weight around.'

Mackenzie picked a piece of flaking paint off the metal railing. It felt like there was a big pink elephant sitting between them on the boat that neither of them was talking about. Mac was scared to ask the question, but she'd made this mistake before. It was what had happened the last time she had a chance with Blake. She'd pined away, staring after him in the hallways, never saying how she really felt. This was her chance. She took a deep breath.

'What does that mean for us?' Her voice almost disappeared in the wind, but she forced herself to meet his eyes.

He gazed steadily down at her. 'I think that's up to you. I think you already know I'm kind of crazy about you.'

For a split second, she thought about Claire. It was easy to picture her face, shocked and hurt and tear-streaked. But it was easy, too, to remember her smug expression when she'd shown up holding hands with Blake at the spring concert last year.

Before she could change her mind, Mackenzie leaned toward him, pressing her lips to his. The wind whipped around them, the sea spray cold on their cheeks. He slid his arms around her waist and pulled her close.

Her heart trilled in her chest. In that moment, she couldn't have said which was better: finally getting the boy – or beating Claire to do it.

CHAPTER TWENTY-FOUR

At seven AM on Wednesday, Julie woke up to birdsongs outside her window. She blinked sleepily in the sunlight filtering in through her curtains, rolling over to see if Parker was awake yet.

Only Parker was gone. Her bed had been neatly made, the pillow fluffed, and her things were nowhere to be seen. She reached across to the nightstand for her iPhone and pulled up Parker's name. *Where are you?* she texted. *Call me.*

Julie felt a pull in her chest. Where did she go? Lately, Parker was spending more and more time by herself, letting Julie in less and less. Julie wanted to think that Parker's therapy with Elliot was working, but after picking Parker up from the cemetery on Saturday, she wasn't so sure. Parker had seemed . . . *unhinged*.

Half an hour later, Julie finished wading through the wreck in the hall, trying to clean out the litter box, when the doorbell rang. Julie breathed a sigh of relief. Parker must have forgotten her key again.

She pulled her bathrobe around her shoulders and pushed her way through the hallway, trying to quell the anxiety she always felt at the sight of the towering boxes stacked against either wall. Mewling cats wove around her feet and watched from the heights of garbage everywhere. One fat, crusty-eyed tabby snored wheezily from where it'd nestled in an upturned sun hat.

'Julie! Who's at the door?' Her mother's voice was shrill and frightened from her bedroom.

'I've got it,' Julie called back, pulling the door open quickly. Then her jaw dropped.

It was *Ashley*.

'Julie!' Ashley crowed loudly. She had that same strange, pointed smile on her face from when she'd tried to crash Julie's date. 'How are you?'

Julie's heart thudded. Ashley had seen the overabundance of lawn decor in the yard. The stacks of car tires and extra porch furniture. The Christmas decorations that were still up from two years ago. A cat wandered across the grass, pausing to pee. And two stacks of boxes sat by the garage, only because the garage was too chock-full for them to fit inside. They were all mushy and almost moldy from sitting out in the rain.

'H-how did you know where I lived?' Julie blurted. Ashley cocked her head. 'Why? Is it a secret?'

Of course it's a secret! a voice in Julie's head shouted. She never put her real address for the school manual. She even received her magazine subscriptions and college brochures at a PO box. Could Ashley have followed her circuitous route home? She'd always taken extra turns just in case someone from school was behind her.

Ashley waved her hand around the house, and then pointed inside, that saccharine smile still on her face. 'I had a really long chat with your mom the other day,' she said sweetly. 'She told me about all her cats. *And* she told me about California.'

Julie's mouth dropped open. 'Y-you spoke to my mom?' she said weakly. Her head was spinning. She'd been here before? Jesus, her mom had let Ashley *inside*? She'd told her about how they'd been *evicted*?

Julie could still remember the day the health board inspectors had come to their little house, accompanied by two disgusted-looking cops with a warrant. The inspectors had worn hazmat suits. Mrs. Redding had gone into hysterics, sobbing and pulling her own hair out, begging them not to take her 'babies.' They finally handcuffed her. Julie sat next to her mother on the curb, watching as the inspectors carried cage after cage of sick, angry cats to their van. It hurt her to see her mother in so much pain. But a part of her wanted to yell, *Take me, too!*

'It was such a shock to learn. You seem so . . . together on the outside,' Ashley said. 'Just goes to show: never judge a bitch by her cover.'

Julie stared at Ashley, trembling. 'You can't tell anyone,' she whispered.

'And why not?' Ashley crossed her arms. 'Secrets are meant to be shared. Especially *dirty* ones.' Her smile turned hard. 'Enjoy your popularity while you still have it, Julie. Soon, I won't be the only one to know the real you.'

And then she waved and stepped off the porch, carefully maneuvering around the rusty umbrella table and chairs that sat on the front lawn. Julie watched her car disappear down the street, then covered her face with her hands.

Julie had worked so hard to erase her past, to hide her secret in the present, but her house of cards was crumbling down around her. Parker was freaking out. The police were trying to frame her and her friends for something they didn't do, and now it was only a matter of time before her secret came out. Julie wasn't who she said she was, and before long, everyone would know the truth.

CHAPTER TWENTY-FIVE

Wednesday evening, Caitlin stood in the girls' locker room, shaking out her arms and legs and jumping up and down to keep warm. Her uniform had been freshly washed, and it smelled like fabric softener. Her socks were pulled up, her shin guards in place. She'd checked the hair band on her ponytail at least six times to make sure it was secure. Monk, her monkey keychain, was tucked into her gear bag, and she had a stash of blue-raspberry Gatorade for time-outs.

It was go time. The biggest game of her high-school career. Outside the locker room, she could hear the stadium filling up. Before she changed, she'd met the UDub recruiter, a sporty-looking woman in her thirties named Monica. If she played well during this game, she'd be guaranteed a spot on next year's team.

And if she didn't . . .

Caitlin shut her eyes. She didn't want to think that way. She sat down and massaged her ankle, trying to ignore the twinges of pain she'd felt in the past few days. All of a sudden, she felt someone staring at her from across the room. Ursula, also in her soccer jersey and shorts, smirked at her from the water fountains.

'You feeling okay?' she teased, her gaze dropping to Caitlin's ankle.

'I'm fine,' Caitlin said tightly.

'Good. I'd hate for you to mess up!' Ursula sang. Then, halfway out the door, she stopped and whirled around. 'Oh. I forgot. Someone is looking for you.'

Caitlin frowned. 'The UDub recruiter? I already met her.'

'No . . .' Ursula smiled, smug. 'Actually, it was a cop.'

Caitlin's heart stopped. 'W-why?' she blurted.

'Oh, I guess the Nolan stuff,' Ursula said. 'They're totally getting in everyone's business.' Then she skipped out of the room. Caitlin's heart pounded. The Oxy. It had to be. *Had* they traced it to her? Or maybe they'd matched her handwriting sample. *Stop thinking about it*, she told herself. *She's just trying to get in your head.*

Setting her jaw, she shouldered her gear bag and stormed out of the locker room and into the long, echoing hallway.

Kids and their families crammed every nook. Ursula had run up to her parents and was boasting about something to her dad, a squat man in a T-shirt that said AAA POOL CARE AND LANDSCAPING.

Then Caitlin looked back and forth for a police officer, praying he wasn't staked out here, hoping to catch her. When someone pulled on her sleeve from behind, she wrenched away, her heart leaping into her chest.

'Whoa!' Jeremy backed up, a startled smile on his face. 'Sorry!'

Caitlin's shoulders dropped. 'I didn't see you.' Then she peered at him. 'What are you *doing* here?' As far as she knew,

Jeremy had never been to a soccer game – not even one of Josh's.

Jeremy cocked his head. 'This is it, right? The big game? I wanted to cheer you on.'

'Oh.' Caitlin smiled nervously, then peered around the hall and out into the small courtyard that led to the field. Was Josh here? She hadn't seen him, and they'd barely talked all week. But it seemed crazy for him not to come – he knew how much this meant to her. What if he was watching them right now?

'Uh, let's go somewhere else,' she said, suddenly feeling paranoid.

She took Jeremy's arm and led him outside and under the bleachers to a dark, secluded spot. Metallic sounds of people walking up and down the stands echoed from above. A group of kids burst into laughter. Then someone said, 'Whoa!' and a river of cola-colored liquid seeped through a hole in the stands, almost on Jeremy's head.

'Oops,' Caitlin said, shifting him out of harm's way. 'Soccer games are hazardous, you know.'

'Nervous? Excited?' Jeremy asked, his eyes shining.

'A little of both, I guess,' Caitlin admitted. She felt her cheeks redden. 'Thanks for coming to this. It means a lot to me.'

'No problem. Actually, I brought you something.' Jeremy rummaged in his pockets and extracted a long, thin object. Caitlin studied it for a moment, then realized it was a pen. Not just *any* pen, either – a Dungeons & Dragons pen.

She looked up. 'Was this the pen I lent you?'

Jeremy nodded. 'The one that was Taylor's. I thought you should have it back.'

Caitlin smiled, her eyes welling up for a second before she

blinked the tears away. 'Thanks.'

'I should add that it's brought me good luck through the years,' Jeremy said. 'I used it on my driver's test. I used it on finals last semester. I had it in my pocket when I had my nationals debate with the Model UN. I feel sort of . . . *safe* with it. Although maybe that has something to do with the fact that it used to belong to you.'

He was looking at her so sweetly, so earnestly, like she was the most important thing in his entire life. Caitlin felt her throat close, but her heart open. All of a sudden, what she needed to do seemed abundantly clear. Yes, it would be messy, but it was what she wanted. And if she'd learned anything from Taylor – or the fact that the police were breathing down her neck – it was that life was short.

She peered around to make sure no one was watching. Then she leaned forward and kissed him.

For a moment, Jeremy was stiff, his eyes wide open. But when he kissed her back, his lips were soft and warm. Caitlin inhaled the grassy scent of his clothes. She ran her hands through his hair, which was so much longer than Josh's sporty-boy buzz cut. Tingles ran up and down her body.

When they pulled away, they both grinned. 'I'm sorry,' Jeremy blurted.

Caitlin gave him a crazy look. 'For what? *I* was the one who kissed you.'

'Oh.' Jeremy lowered his eyes. There were two blooms of red on his cheeks. 'Well, yeah. I guess you did.'

The whistle blew on the field, and they looked at each other again. In a few minutes, Caitlin's game would be starting.

But something else suddenly dawned on her, too. She felt . . . lighter, somehow. Freer. Jeremy's kiss had opened up a whole new world, and she no longer felt bogged down. If she played well, great. But if she didn't . . . maybe it would still be okay. After all, she'd already won something today, no matter the game's final score.

CHAPTER TWENTY-SIX

Thursday after school, Parker hovered outside Elliot's office. The sun streamed in through the windows, making dappled patterns on the carpet. Traffic swished by out the window, creating soothing, soporific white noise. Elliot hadn't noticed her yet, but instead was staring very intensely at something on his computer screen. Parker wondered what it was. A psychologists' forum? The *Seattle Times?* Porn?

Then Elliot glanced up. He paled and jumped, then smiled awkwardly. 'Parker!' he said in a loud voice. 'I didn't see you there! Come in, come in!'

Parker slumped into the room, pulling the hoodie securely over her head. She slumped down on the couch and hugged a pillow. She could feel Elliot looking at her.

'Is everything okay?' Elliot asked with hesitation.

Parker shrugged. He could probably sense how antsy she felt. How prickly. She'd hesitated at the front door of the building for at least ten minutes before actually stepping inside, unsure she wanted to face his questioning during this session. Because she *knew* there would be questioning. Even crazy Parker was accountable for her meltdowns.

Elliot sat back and crossed his arms over his chest. 'So, Parker. I'm guessing you don't want to talk about the cemetery.'

'No,' Parker barked. She covered her ears. 'No, no, no.'

'Hey, it's okay.' Elliot rose from his seat, stepped forward, and gently lifted her hands away. He met her eyes, his bow-shaped lips curving into a smile. 'Listen. We don't have to talk about it. I promise. We can talk about something else.'

Parker blinked. 'W-why don't you want me to talk about it?' she demanded.

'Because obviously you're not ready,' Elliot said, raising his palms. 'And that's fine. You have your reasons for not liking cemeteries. We can explore that, or we'll talk about something else. I'll never push you on anything.'

Parker sat quietly for a moment, letting this sink in. It felt like reverse psychology, but annoyingly, it was *working*. 'It's like something prevented me from going in there, a mental block or something,' she stated, trying to make sense of her emotions. 'You know how psychics can tell if a place is cursed or tainted or if something bad happened there? It's a feeling like that, maybe.'

'What do you think happened there?'

Parker shrugged. 'I don't really know. People died, obviously. Maybe that's all.'

Elliot nodded, but it looked like he didn't completely believe her. Parker wasn't sure she believed herself, in fact – but she knew she didn't want to walk through those gates.

'Are you angry at me for taking you there?' Elliot asked, looking worried.

Parker shook her head. 'Not exactly,' she said quietly. 'I

mean, I guess I felt a *little* ambushed. But I didn't know I was going to react that way until I was actually there.'

'What did the reaction feel like?'

Parker shut her eyes. 'I wish I could explain it. But I can't. I'm sorry.'

'It's okay, Parker.' He smiled, looking straight at her. No one ever looked straight at her these days. 'We can take our time.' He paused and looked down at his hands. 'There's no rush.'

They smiled at each other, and Parker's heart did another leap. It wasn't like her to make emotional confessions to people. Even the old Parker kept her emotions pretty close to the vest. But she needed someone in her corner besides Julie.

Then he jumped up. 'You know, I have a book on articulating emotions that might help you. Hang on – it's in reception. Let me grab it.'

He swept out the door quickly and was gone. Parker sat back, her heart still hammering. But she felt good, too – it really felt like Elliot *got* her.

She looked around his office, thinking how little she knew about him. There wasn't a lot out on his desk – just an old-fashioned banker's lamp, an empty in-box, and a molded-plastic flower with a solar panel that wiggled its leaves in the thin sunlight. Who was Elliot Fielder? What made him tick? Did he have family in the area? Was he married? What did he like to read? What sort of music did he have on his iPod? What *was* he looking at on his computer when she came in? Wouldn't *anyone* wonder about some basic facts? Elliot knew so much about *her*, after all, it seemed only fair to reciprocate.

She glanced through the crack in the door again – he was

still looking through the books on the main bookshelf. Quietly, she stood and moved to his computer. As she wiggled the mouse, the *National Geographic* nature-photos screensaver disappeared, and a log-in screen popped up.

On a whim, she picked up the keyboard and turned it over. When she worked in the attendance office her sophomore year, she'd taped all the passwords she had a hard time remembering there. Great minds must think alike because there was a piece of paper printed with small, tight print.

FIELDER_E/pr0m3th3us_b0und

Before she could think about it twice, she typed it in.

A photograph filled the computer screen. At first, Parker blinked. She immediately recognized the location. It had been taken in the Arbor Mall just outside the food court. A girl in a black hoodie sat alone at a table, sipping Coke from a straw, her long hair peeking out over the collar of her sweatshirt.

It was . . . *her*.

She clicked on an arrow icon. Another picture sprang up – her again. She was sitting on her mom's porch, smoking a cigarette, her hoodie pulled over her face. Another arrow click. The next photo was taken from a vantage just across the street from the school as she disappeared through the big double doors. Another showed her in sneakers and shorts and that same hoodie, jogging by the lake.

It hadn't been her imagination at all. Someone *had* been following her. *Elliot*.

'What are you doing?'

Elliot stood in the doorway, a paperback book in one hand. His face was as white as a cloud, his eyes suddenly hard. She shot up, knocking something off his desk by accident, but she didn't stop to pick it up.

'What are *you* doing?' she asked, her voice shaking with barely controlled rage. 'What the hell are these pictures doing on your computer?'

'That computer is full of confidential information,' he said, slapping the book down on the couch and taking a step toward her. 'Do you realize how much trouble I could get in if you saw the wrong thing?'

She gave a high bark of laughter. 'The wrong thing? Like the fact that you're *stalking* me?'

He moved faster than she would have expected. Suddenly his hand was like a vise around her wrist. 'You have to listen to me, Parker.'

But before he could finish his sentence, a scream tore from her throat. For a moment, she didn't know where she was. She barely knew *who* she was. Panic seized her, and all she knew was that she had to get away. She kicked Elliot's knee with all her strength. A dull crack filled the air. His hand unclenched, and she bolted for the door.

Then she ran and ran, until her lungs heaved painfully in her chest and her legs felt like rubber. If she could have, she would have run forever – away from Elliot, away from Beacon, and away from her horrible life.

CHAPTER TWENTY-SEVEN

Okay. Deep breaths. It is all going to be okay.

It was Friday afternoon, and Mackenzie sat in a gray institutional hallway in the University of Washington's music building, cradling her borrowed cello against her chest. It was almost time for her audition – which meant that right now, Claire was in there, wowing the judges. Mac hadn't seen her go in, but Claire's audition time was branded into her brain. She wondered if Claire was nervous. She wondered if she'd feverishly washed her hands at least three times before she went in there, a little tic Claire had before every audition.

Because Mac was the last audition of the day, no one else was in the hall with her. She closed her eyes and tried to breathe, but panic bubbled up inside. She knew, deep in her bones, that she hadn't practiced enough. She'd been so worried about Nolan and the investigation. She'd spent so much time with Blake.

But even now, thinking about Blake tugged her lips into a smile. She pulled her phone out of her pocket to see if he'd responded to any of her texts. When she arrived on campus, she'd texted him, *Here goes nothing/everything.* But he still hadn't texted back. It was so unlike him. He knew she had her audition today. Then again he was working – maybe it was busy at the cupcake shop?

Suddenly, a change in the draft pushed the door to the recital hall open just a bit, and a familiar melody wafted out. Mac blinked for a moment, listening to Claire's precise notes and emotional phrasing. The piece she was playing was familiar, and suddenly she understood why. It was *her* piece. The Tchaikovsky.

Mac leaped to her feet. This couldn't be happening. Claire was supposed to play Popper. Blake had said she was. But did she really have to ask why she'd switched all of a sudden? Only, how did she know what piece Mac had chosen? The only people she'd told were her parents – and *they* wouldn't say anything – and Blake.

Blake. Mac's heart stopped. She looked at her phone again. Still no text back. *No*, she told herself. It couldn't be. Blake wouldn't betray her like that. Claire had found out another way.

'Miss Wright?' An iron-haired woman in a tailored suit stood in the doorway with a clipboard, peering over the top of her glasses. 'Are you ready?'

Mackenzie felt as if her cello weighed five hundred pounds as she carried it into the recital hall. The stage was brightly lit, and she could barely make out the five panelists a few rows back. The Juilliard accompanist, a balding, dark-skinned man wearing a button-down shirt and tie, sat at the grand piano on the stage with her. Otherwise the hall was empty. She started to unpack her instrument and set up her things, her hands trembling violently.

'My name is Mackenzie Wright. Thank you for your consideration,' she said, her voice wavering. But then something

214

came over her. *Forget Claire*, a voice said. *Forget everyone. Think about your talents. Think about how much you want this.*

She took a deep breath and started to play.

There was no applause after each piece, but it didn't matter. She knew she was acing it. She didn't miss a note of the Elgar or the Beethoven, and her rendition of 'The Swan' soared elegantly from her fingers. Before the final song, she swallowed. 'Excuse me,' she said to the accompanist. 'I'd like to change my last selection, if you wouldn't mind.'

He looked surprised but smiled. Mac took a deep breath. It was now or never – and she wasn't going down without a fight. She looked at the judges. 'I know I put on my form that I'd be playing Tchaikovsky's *Pezzo capriccioso*, but instead I will be playing Popper's *Spinning Song* for you.'

She raised her bow, holding absolutely still for a long moment. Then, nodding at the pianist, she launched into one of the most difficult pieces in the cello repertoire.

The song started with a frenzied succession of high-pitched notes. It was deadly fast and sent the cellist's hands flying up and down the neck of the instrument at roller-coaster speeds. Mackenzie had always thought the song was kind of annoying, but it was one of the best songs to show off with, and now, as she played, a strange thing happened. For the first time, she found the playfulness of the piece. Instead of sounding strained and manic and frantic to her, it sounded *fun*. Flippant, and careless, and energetic. She almost laughed out loud as she played. For just a moment, nothing could touch her.

When she was finished, she sat still, almost breathless. She didn't know if it would be enough to get her in, but she knew one thing: she'd just had the best audition of her life.

'Thank you, Miss Wright. That was beautiful,' said a voice from the panelists. 'You'll be hearing from us soon.'

Mac almost skipped out of the recital hall. 'Yes,' she said, pumping her fist in the hallway. She looked at her phone again, but still no text from Blake.

She barely remembered driving to the cupcake store. She parked out front and was about to push through the door and call his name. But when she saw Blake behind the counter, she froze on the sidewalk.

Another girl's arms were wrapped around him. A girl with short, curly hair, dressed from head to foot in concert black. *Claire.*

'It was perfect,' Claire said, gazing up into Blake's eyes. There were two open windows at the front of the shop; Mac could hear every word. 'I totally nailed it. And I saw her go in, too. She was super pale. Probably freaked that I'd done the Tchaikovsky.'

Mackenzie's blood curdled. She turned away, her hands on the door handle, when Claire's voice rang out.

'Oh, hey, *Macks.'* Her voice oozed sarcasm. 'How was your audition? You weren't unprepared or anything, were you?'

Mackenzie turned to see Claire's ugly smile. Then she peeked at Blake. His eyes were lowered. He'd turned pale. All thoughts in her brain froze.

But then she blurted, 'I thought you guys broke up.'

Claire unwound herself from Blake and stepped out from the back of the counter. 'I knew you'd fall for it,' she sneered at Mac.

216

Mac blinked. 'F-fall for what?'

'I told Blake to hang out with you, schedule a few extra band rehearsals.' Claire grinned. 'I knew you'd drop everything. Even practicing for your audition.'

'You . . . what?' She glanced at Blake, but he still wouldn't look at her. None of this was making any sense.

'I wanted him to distract you before the audition.' She smirked. 'And he did. Oh, and all your confessions to Blake? He told me everything. Including that you were playing Tchaikovsky.' She reached across the counter and clutched his hand. 'And we aren't broken up. We're stronger than ever.'

Mac stared at Blake, her heart pounding fast. 'Is that true?'

But Blake still had his eyes lowered. He didn't answer Mac, but he didn't stand up for Claire, either. He looked trapped and humiliated. 'I . . .' he started, then looked away.

'Yes,' Claire spoke for him. 'Every single word is true.'

Mac could feel the tears forming in her eyes. But then she realized: she could give Claire exactly what she wanted and bawl her eyes out right now, or she could beat Claire at the only game either of them had ever really cared about. She placed her hands on her hips and glared at her ex-friend. 'Well, maybe Blake doesn't want me,' she heard herself say. 'But I'm pretty sure Juilliard does. Good luck at Oberlin,' she said with a sniff for good measure.

Before Claire could get another word in, Mackenzie turned on her heel and pushed out the door.

CHAPTER TWENTY-EIGHT

Friday evening, Julie studied the miniature windmill in front of her, biting her lip. She and Carson were at the Beacon Heights mini golf course, where they were playing a girls-versus-boys tournament with a bunch of kids from school. She'd have to time this shot just right to get the ball through the moving slats of the windmill and to the other side, where a tiny white flag fluttered on the Astroturf, marking the end of the putt-putt hole.

She stepped forward, squared her shoulders, and pulled back the putter to swing.

'Don't miss,' Carson teased just as the golf club made contact.

Julie's neon-pink ball went wildly off course and landed in the water hazard on the far right. 'Hey!' she cried. 'That's not fair.' But the words died in her throat as she came face-to-face with Carson's wry smile.

'Oh, I'm sorry, we're playing fair now?' he teased, reaching up to brush a strand of hair behind her ear. Julie shivered and closed her eyes. It felt *so* good.

'Come on, Wells, it's your turn,' James Wong called out from behind them. Julie stepped aside, feeling lighter than normal.

She knew why: Ashley wasn't here.

She glanced over at Carson, her eyes drifting to where the hem of his pale blue T-shirt grazed the top of his Bonobos cargo shorts, revealing a thin strip of stomach. Carson caught her staring and winked. For a moment, nothing else mattered.

It was Carson's turn next. He gripped his putter and took an expert swing, sending the ball easily into the hole in just one shot. 'Yes!' Carson exclaimed. The other boys fist-pumped him in victory.

As everyone started toward the next hole, Carson fell into step next to Julie, reaching for her hand and giving it a squeeze. Her heart raced at the contact.

'I'm sorry for playing dirty,' Carson said, his voice low. 'What if I make it up to you? I could help you on this hole, show you the proper technique.'

'Oh you will, will you?' Julie crooned, liking the sound of that. Then she looked up . . . and froze. Standing underneath the bright red-and-white umbrella of the snack stand was Ashley. She stared hard at Julie and Carson, her eyes blazing.

Julie dropped Carson's hand. 'Um, you know what?' she stammered. 'I actually need to go change out my putter.' It was a stupid excuse – all the putters were the same. 'I'll be right back.'

'Um, okay?' Carson said, confused. But Julie was already halfway down the sidewalk, anger coursing through her veins.

'What do *you* want?' she snapped at Ashley, who was lounging at a metal picnic table drinking lemonade. Julie noticed that Ashley was wearing the Alice + Olivia turquoise jeans that Julie hadn't been able to afford, and a billowy white top almost

219

the same as her own, except that Ashley's was too low-cut and had some kind of stain on the shoulder.

Ashley smiled. 'Can't a girl come say hi to her friend? You know, Julie, I just think you're the *cat's pajamas*.'

'Please, Ashley.' Julie hated the tremor in her voice. It sounded like weakness. She tried to stand up a little straighter. 'Please don't tell anyone about what you know. What can I do to change your mind?'

Ashley's eyes flashed. 'That's not how this works. Unlike the rest of your little army of minions, I don't blindly follow orders.' She nodded in the direction of the group, then broke out into a smile. 'I just wanted to see you in your natural habitat one last time. Enjoy your final moments of freedom.'

'Ashley –'

'Save your breath for someone who cares.' Ashley threw her lemonade in the trash and walked out.

Julie stood there, watching Ashley's retreating form, stunned. Surely she wouldn't really reveal her secret. But what if she did? What would happen if everyone found out – if *Carson* found out? Suddenly, all Julie could think about was her last school, after word of her secret got out. No one would talk to her. She ate lunch alone in the bathroom. People cleared a wide path for her in the halls, worried they would catch a disease from her, her house was so dirty.

The worst part was, she'd known better. She'd been distracted with Carson, and she hadn't noticed Ashley following her home that day. Normally, she was so vigilant and protective of her secret – it was how she'd maintained her status for so long. This was why she had rules not to date. Not only because

220

she couldn't let anyone in, but also because she ran the risk of losing her head. And now she *had*.

She turned back to the rest of the group, pasting a smile on her face. *Enjoy your final moments of freedom*. Whatever Ashley was going to do, she was going to do it soon.

And then everything would come crashing down around her. *Again*.

CHAPTER TWENTY-NINE

Friday night, Alex and Ava stood beneath the glowing marquee of the Majestic Theater, out on their first dinner-and-a-movie date in far too long. Raindrops glittered in the multicolored lights. A small crowd of moviegoers milled around beneath the overhang, most of them college kids dressed in thrift-store sweaters and chunky scarves. They talked in animated voices and passed around clove cigarettes.

'You've been awfully quiet all night,' Alex said, taking Ava's hand.

Ava looked up at him, her heart humming in her chest. He was wearing a soft flannel shirt and dark-wash jeans. Tonight, his unkempt curls and five o'clock shadow didn't look scruffy so much as . . . arty. She noticed some of the college girls glancing their way enviously, and smiled.

'Oh, I'm just thinking about the movie,' she said. They'd just gotten out of a showing of *Wings of Desire*. Ava had never seen anything like it. It didn't have much of a plot, but it was about angels following people around Berlin, listening to the humans' thoughts. She wasn't sure she'd understood it, but it was weird and sad and beautiful, and it made her miss her mother.

Alex fumbled with his umbrella and held it high over her head as they walked toward his car. 'Isn't it cool? I saw it for the first time in German class and it blew my mind. I wish Granger showed us more foreign stuff like that. All the old Hollywood movies he shows are great, but they're all kind of the same, you know?' His lips twisted into a slightly arrogant smirk. 'Of course, I don't think he's smart enough to teach anything really challenging.'

An icicle formed in her gut at the mention of Granger. 'He's smarter than you think,' she murmured. *Maybe even smart enough to get away with murder.*

Alex glanced at her sidelong. 'Why are you defending him?'

'I'm not,' Ava snapped. 'You know I don't like him. I just don't think that because he's an asshole, he's dumb. He's clearly smart, to get away with what he's been doing.'

'Okay, okay.' Alex raised his hands, palms up, and looked apologetic. 'It's just that that guy gets creepier all the time. Yesterday morning he was up at six AM digging in the backyard.'

Ava felt a chill crawl up her spine. 'Did you get a video of him or anything? Something to send to the cops?'

Alex looked chagrined. 'I ran to grab my phone, but by that time, he'd gone back inside. Still. It seemed really sketchy. Wonder what he's hiding back there.'

Ava tapped her fingers against her Hermès cuff bracelet. Obviously Granger wasn't burying Nolan . . . but what else could he be doing? She suddenly wished she could tell Alex everything. She hated having these secrets.

They drove home in a companionable silence, the swishy sound of the windshield wipers lulling Ava into a dreamy sort of calm. The rain blurred the scenery, the car was warm, and her favorite National song crooned softly from the stereo. After about ten minutes, Alex pulled into her circular gravel driveway. The lights in the front hall were on. It wasn't even ten yet – her father would still be awake, watching the nightly news in the den. She bit her lip, feeling reckless. Would Leslie really say anything if she brought Alex in just for a little bit?

'Do you want to come in?' she asked, turning to face him.

A shy smile broke across his face. 'That sounds nice.'

'It won't be, honestly.' She gave a nervous laugh. 'I mean, Leslie will be a bitch. She'll be pissed off that I'm disobeying her strict orders.' She rolled her eyes.

'I've handled her before, and I can handle her again.' Alex cradled her cheek in his hand and leaned in to kiss her. But before their lips touched, the world erupted in sound and light.

Four police cars were speeding up the drive, lights flashing and sirens wailing. Ava jerked upright as cop cars pulled up on either side of them. She jumped out of the car and almost walked into Detective Peters.

'Miss Jalali,' he said, his deep voice serious. 'Good timing.'

'What's going on?' Ava asked, hugging her shawl around her bare arms, eyes wide. Out of the corner of her eye, she noticed her father and stepmother walk onto the porch. They stared at the police car . . . and then at Ava. Alex took her hand and held it tight.

'We've finally got a warrant to search your house,' the detective said smoothly. 'Everyone thinks that the half-dozen witnesses who say the last time they saw Nolan Hotchkiss was when he was following you up the stairs is enough to consider you a person of interest. Between that, and the death threat you sent him . . .'

'I never threatened him!' Her voice was a shrill, desperate shriek.

Detective Peters didn't bat an eye. 'We have you on record telling Nolan you were going to kill him. We also have testimony that you orchestrated a plan to murder Nolan during one of your classes in school.'

Alex dropped her hand. Ava shook her head mutely, sputtering. A testimony of their discussion in film studies class. She knew exactly who'd given it. *Granger.*

'It's not what it seems,' she said with a gasp. And then something caught her eye on the front porch. Leslie stood with her mouth drawn into a line so tight her lips were invisible. Next to her, Ava's father stood with tears rolling down his cheeks. He looked at Ava like he didn't even recognize her. Ava waited for him to do something, tell the cops she was a good girl, someone who would never, *ever* hurt anyone. But he didn't. He just stood there.

The cops waved the warrant to her father, and he stepped aside weakly, his form suddenly small and shrunken. Ava felt Alex's arm slide around her waist, stabilizing her. She sagged against him, a single sob bursting up through her chest.

'Ava,' he pleaded. 'What's he talking about? Did you do something to Nolan?'

Ava blinked hard, tears spilling down her cheeks. She saw her bedroom light snap on upstairs. Dark silhouettes of cops ransacking her room. There wasn't anything incriminating in the house – she was almost certain of it. The girls hadn't left any messages, notes, or texts about their plan to prank Nolan – and she hadn't written in her diary in weeks. But the cops were looking to pin the crime on her now, and that meant the film studies group was running out of time.

She turned to Alex, shivering in the rain. 'I can't explain right now,' she whispered.

He looked down at her for a long moment, a frown creasing his forehead. 'Why not?' he cried. 'Ava, what did you do?'

She shook her head. 'It's not what you think. This is . . . messed up.'

Alex stood with his hand on the car door, a tormented expression on his face as he stared back at her. Her father and Leslie turned away, following another set of officers inside.

'Alex,' she said, her voice flat, 'just go.'

He turned without another word and got into his car. She watched his car roll out the driveway, a hollow ache in her chest. Alex believed in her – even when things looked worse than ever, he was on her side. A part of her wished she could call him back, ask him to stay. But she couldn't. It was up to her to get out of this mess.

She pulled out her phone and dialed Caitlin.

'Get the others,' she whispered. 'We need to get into Granger's house and find that cyanide. We're ending this. Tonight.'

CHAPTER THIRTY

An hour later, Parker sat in the back of Caitlin's car as they neared Granger's neighborhood. Caitlin parked five blocks from his house, and everyone quietly got out and walked as nonchalantly as they could to his little bungalow. A full moon shone down through the purple scraps of clouds, sending distorted shadows across the suburban lawns.

Parker glanced around at the others, taking in their scared but determined expressions. Her head twinged with pain, but she gritted her teeth and ignored it. Julie had tried to talk her out of coming, but she'd insisted.

As they walked, Julie touched her arm. 'Are you okay?'

'Not really,' Parker mumbled.

She'd met up with Julie shortly before Caitlin picked them both up, and she'd filled her in on what had happened with Dr. Fielder yesterday. Julie had been horrified, and she'd demanded to know why Parker hadn't come to her sooner. 'I needed some space today,' Parker had said . . . and it was true.

Now, Julie shook her head. 'Why do you think he had pictures of you?'

Parker shrugged. 'Because he's a stalker.' What sort of person follows a patient around, *spying* on her? She felt so betrayed. So *invaded*. It reminded her of her dad. There had been times when he'd spied on her. Found out about the mischievous things that she did. And when she came home and denied the allegations, he showed her the pictures he'd taken – and smacked her right across her face.

Julie's eyes hardened. 'We have to turn that bastard in. We have to *get* him.'

'I guess that will be next on our agenda after this, huh?' Parker gestured to Granger's house, which they were now in front of. All the lights were off. Wind chimes clanged together on the front porch. WELCOME, FRIENDS, read a plaque on the door. Parker snorted. Only grandmas and losers had plaques like that.

Mac placed her hands on her hips and assessed the property. 'How are we going to get in?' she asked in a hushed voice. 'I don't know if I can pick these locks. And he might have a security system.'

'We won't need them,' Ava answered. 'The one time I was here, his bathroom window was open. Maybe it still is.'

'Let's check it out,' Parker said.

The gate gave a soft squeal as Julie pushed it open. Granger's backyard was overgrown, and blades of grass scratched at Parker's ankles. Sure enough, a double-hung window stood open about three inches. Parker could just make out a shower curtain inside.

Caitlin stepped back and measured the height of the window with her eyes. 'I'm pretty sure I can get in there if someone gives me a boost.'

Julie stood next to the house and bent over. Caitlin took off her shoes and socks to get better purchase. Then she stepped lightly onto Julie's back. Julie gave a soft grunt but held steady as Caitlin slid the window open a few inches higher. Then, without warning, she jumped up and hooked her torso through the open window. For just a moment, her legs wiggled behind her. Then she was in.

'Did she learn that in soccer, or Cirque du Soleil?' Parker muttered. A moment later the back patio door slid open.

'Hurry up,' Caitlin whispered into the darkness.

They filed into the house and stood for a moment in Granger's kitchen. The work light over the stove was on, giving off just enough glow to see by. Dirty dishes soaked in the sink, and crumbs dotted the stove top. On the fridge were a half-dozen take-out menus. Definitely a bachelor pad.

'When I was here last, he'd been sent some photography equipment in a box. Maybe there was cyanide in there. I think he put it in his car, though, so I have no idea if it's still here.'

'I'll check the bedroom,' Caitlin said.

'Mackenzie and I will get the living room,' Ava volunteered. 'That leaves the office.'

Parker looked at Julie. 'Let's do this.'

Julie had a tiny LED flashlight attached to her keychain, and she swept the walls as they made their way down the cramped hallway and into the office. An IKEA desk held his computer, and a small three-drawer file cabinet sat beside it. A bulletin board on the wall behind the desk contained dozens of ticket stubs for concerts and Mariners games, a 'save the date' for a couple named Tony and Mandy, and a copy of his class syllabus.

There was just enough illumination from the streetlight outside to see what they were doing. Julie didn't see the box they were looking for, but it was possible the materials were no longer boxed up. She opened the top drawer of the file cabinet and started flipping through the files. Parker bent over the desk. A bulging folder turned out to have nothing but graded homework in it. Beneath that was a scrap of notebook paper. She squinted to make out the handwriting.

Hey Mister Granger I was wondering if I could get some extra help from you if you know what I mean.
Love, You know who.

The note smelled like someone had sprayed it with Coco Mademoiselle. Parker wrinkled her nose and crumpled it in her hand. *Pathetic.*

Julie gestured toward the computer. 'Get his data off of there.' She pulled a pink flash drive from her pocket.

'Got it,' Parker said, heading to the computer and inserting the drive. Her fingers moved quickly, remembering the days when she and Nolan used to wipe his father's computers clean just to mess with him. Ironic that something she and Nolan used to do together would come in handy in nailing his killer.

Files uploading, said a message on the screen. As Parker waited, she scanned the rest of the desk. The top drawer had nothing but pencils and a stapler inside, but when she jerked open the next drawer, she swallowed a cry of surprise. Right on top was a bulging manila envelope. Scrawled across it, in handwriting she recognized from the chalkboard, was *JULIE REDDING.*

She glanced at Julie, whose back was still to her. Why did he have a file on Julie? Were there transcripts inside? Personal details? Maybe he knew about her mom's, uh . . . quirks. Parker fingered the folder, too afraid to look inside. She picked up the envelope and shoved it into her messenger bag. Julie had protected Parker for years. Now it was Parker's turn to do the same.

Then she spied something else. Under the envelope was a yellow legal pad covered with Granger's handwriting. Parker picked it up and angled it to catch the light from the window. When she made out the first line, she almost dropped it.

Nolan – Cyanide.

'Julie,' she whispered. Julie's head snapped up, and she turned around. Parker gestured wildly for her to come read over her shoulder.

Claire, music rival. Stepmother. Parker's dad. (?)

'It's dated,' Julie breathed. 'October eighth.'

'The day we talked about *And Then There Were None*,' Parker said. A splintering shot of pain went through her forehead. Her whole body flinched, but she tried to keep centered. She had to keep her head.

Julie's eyes scanned the paper. 'Look, it's a transcript of everything we talked about. He *did* hear us.'

Parker swallowed hard. 'We should tell the others.'

They ran to the living room. Ava was combing through Granger's mail while Mackenzie examined his bookshelf.

'Guys!' Julie hissed.

They both looked up. A moment later, Caitlin emerged from the bedroom. 'No box, but I did find his private stash of pictures,' she said.

'Forget that.' Julie held up the notepad. 'He has a transcript. He wrote down everything we said that day in class.'

Mackenzie stood up so fast she hit her head on one of the

shelves. Ava covered her mouth with her hand. Everyone flew over to examine the transcript. A small, guttural sound escaped from the back of Mac's throat.

'Do you think it's enough to incriminate us?' Caitlin asked. 'It's just hearsay.'

'Yeah, but who knows what else he's got on us?' Ava asked, her eyes wide. 'What if he recorded us that day in class?'

'Or what if he has another copy?' Mac asked. 'Like on his computer, maybe.'

'I'm getting all that data off his computer,' Parker said. Then she touched the outside of her messenger bag, thinking of the envelope inside. *What could it say about Julie?* Why did he have it? A cold, clammy feeling seemed to spread over her. The ache in her head throbbed rhythmically, like someone was driving a stake down the middle of her forehead and hammering it in a bit farther with every heartbeat, trying to break her in half.

Julie looked at her. 'Is the data transfer almost done?'

Parker nodded. 'I'll go check on it.' But as she was on her way back to the office, footsteps sounded on the porch. Someone cleared his throat. Keys jingled, then came the metallic sound of the lock catching.

Parker froze. A jolt of terror shot through her body.

Ava turned toward the rest of them, her dark eyes wide and blazing. 'Hide!' she breathed.

Parker's eyes met Julie's. Frantic, Julie thumbed toward the bathroom . . . and the open window. *'Go to the car,'* she mouthed to Parker. Parker nodded swiftly, then darted into the bathroom, hefted herself onto the sill, and tumbled out the window . . . just as Granger opened the front door.

232

CHAPTER THIRTY-ONE

Ava watched as her friends ducked behind curtains and shut themselves in closets. But instead of following them, she stood in the middle of the room and smoothed down her hair. When Granger opened the door, he stared at her, his eyes wide. He was in his running clothes, and his hair and skin glistened with sweat.

'Ava?' he said, looking more confused than angry. 'What are you doing here?'

Ava had done some very quick thinking in the last thirty seconds, and she knew what she had to do. It was the only thing that would save them, the very thing she'd done with Nolan the night he died. She parted her lips pensively, cocking her head to one side and glancing up at him with wide eyes. 'I thought I'd surprise you.'

From the corner of her eye, she could just make out Mackenzie, huddled behind the couch. Ava's stomach felt like she was on a roller coaster swooping up and down, but she forced herself to keep it together. Because if Granger figured out why she was really in his house, there was no telling what he would do.

He set his keys down on a table by the door and turned to look at her. Something vied with the surprise on his face – it took her a moment to recognize it as lust. 'By breaking into my house and standing here in the dark?'

Ava swallowed her fear and took a few slow, slinky steps toward him. His eyes lingered on her hips, then flitted back up to her face. 'Do you want me to go?' she murmured. She put a hand on his chest, willing herself not to grimace. The very thought of touching him was repulsive to her now. But she had to.

'No,' Granger decided. 'Definitely not. Just . . . what made you change your mind?'

Ava put on her best innocent-damsel pout and looked down. 'You're my teacher, Mr. Granger. This is wrong, and I was scared. But I couldn't stay away from you. I wanted this too much.'

Then, bracing herself, she leaned up to kiss him. He pulled her sharply close. Her nostrils filled with his musky smell. He pressed his lips to hers, his arms tight around her. Ava could feel the strength in his muscles. It would be easy for him to hurt her, if he wanted to.

Then he let go of her, a strange smirk on his face. He took a few steps toward the couch. Ava was sure he'd see Mackenzie there behind it. She tensed, not sure whether to flee out the door or to throw herself on him. But then he plopped down on the couch, eyeing her appraisingly.

'I don't know, Ava,' he teased. 'You kind of hurt my feelings. You're going to really have to prove you want to make it up to me.'

'Anything you want,' Ava said.

A naughty smile appeared on Granger's lips. 'Okay, then. Let's start with your shirt.'

She froze. 'What?'

Mr. Granger leaned back against the couch and gave her a nod. 'You heard me. I want to see you take your clothes off. Slowly.'

Her cheeks felt like they were on fire. Ava wasn't sure what she'd been planning – she was wildly improvising, trying to buy them some time to figure out how to escape – but she didn't want to do this.

She looked down at herself. She was still wearing the button-down shirt-dress she'd worn out with Alex that night. She glanced up to see Granger, his head back against the sofa, watching her under hooded eyes. Slowly, she unfastened the top button. And then the second button.

'Like this?' she asked, her voice low and husky.

He sat forward suddenly, his eyes going wide. 'Yes,' he said hoarsely. 'Like that.'

She thought about the other girls watching her do this from the corners and felt sick to her stomach. *This isn't me*, she wanted to say. But she didn't have any choice. One by one, button by button, she unfastened the front of her dress. She slid one shoulder free so it was bare. Mr. Granger had a hungry leer on his face, his eyes glittering in the half-light.

She shrugged off the dress and stood in her bra and panties, feeling utterly humiliated. He stood up and stepped closer to her, resting his hands on her hips. 'You're so beautiful,' he murmured, leaning toward her for a kiss. She put her finger up to block his lips.

'Now can I make a request?' Ava asked, her heart pumping fast again. 'I want you to take a hot, steamy shower and get clean for me,' she asked. 'I want this to be perfect.'

A greedy smile spread across Granger's face. 'Sure. Want to join me?'

'I would,' Ava murmured, looking at him from under her eyelashes. 'But I have something special I need to prepare while you're in the shower.'

His eyes lit up. He looked up and down her body one last time. Then he let go of her and went into the bathroom. Turned on the light. Shut the door.

Ava strained to listen. The moment she heard the water hit tile, she hissed to her friends, 'Get out of here! Hurry!'

Mackenzie popped up from behind the couch. 'Ava, that was . . .'

'Don't,' Ava pleaded, pulling her dress back on and grabbing her shoes. 'I feel so disgusting.'

'I was going to say *amazing*,' Mac said.

The others came out from where they'd been hiding, faces pale and drawn.

'You just saved our asses,' Caitlin whispered.

'Let's get out of here,' Julie said. 'We don't have much time.'

Ava shook her head. 'I'll be right behind you. I have to do one more thing first.'

The girls hurried out the door. Mackenzie stopped at the doorway, looking like she was going to argue, but after a moment she turned and followed the others. Ava hurried into his office, grabbed the flash drive, and then ran through the kitchen and out onto the patio.

He was up at six AM digging in the backyard, Alex had said.

The yard was dark, but the moon was pushing its way through the clouds. It only took her a moment to find the fresh dirt overturned in the corner.

Ava knelt down and started scooping dirt out with her hands. It was moist and rich, and it stuck to her skin as she dug, but she didn't slow down. Just a few feet down, her hands found something hard and rectangular. She brushed off the last bit of dirt and pulled it out.

It was a plain metal box with a latch. Hands trembling, she fumbled at the latch until it sprang open.

Another flash drive.

She stared down at it, her mouth hanging open. Then she realized – it was quiet. Too quiet.

The shower was off.

Ava slipped both flash drives into her pocket and turned to run down Mr. Granger's lawn in her half-buttoned dress. Her bra peeked out with every stride. The hem of the dress flipped up to reveal her underwear. Her bare feet sank in the dewy grass. Caitlin's headlights blazed to life in front of her, and the back door swung open for her to leap in.

'Drive!' Ava screamed as she slammed the door.

It wasn't until the girls were speeding down the street that Ava looked back out the window and saw someone in the street, staring after her. At first she thought it was Granger – that he'd figured it out. But then her throat caught. It wasn't Granger at all.

It was Alex.

CHAPTER THIRTY-TWO

Caitlin drove fast and blind, running up on the curb as she took a quick right. No one seemed to be following them. She could just make out Ava's face, ashen and streaked with mud, in the rearview mirror. She looked as if she was going to throw up.

She peeled out onto a main road and stepped on the gas. 'Slow down,' Julie said in a strangled voice. 'The last thing you need right now is to get a ticket.'

Caitlin relaxed her foot on the pedal a little, but her knuckles were still white on the steering wheel. They'd just *broken into someone's house*. They'd just watched their teacher *practically have sex with Ava*. And the way she'd felt, hiding in the kitchen – well, she never wanted to feel that terrified again.

Once they'd gone through two stoplights, Ava looked around cautiously and held up something between her fingers. It glinted under a streetlight as the car passed it. 'I found this buried in his backyard.'

'What is it?' Mackenzie asked, squinting.

'A second flash drive,' Ava answered.

'Give it here.' Julie grabbed it. Then she rummaged around in the backpack she'd brought and pulled out a laptop. It chimed as she turned it on and waited for it to boot up.

'Did you say he'd *buried* it?' Caitlin asked.

'That's right,' Ava said. 'Alex saw him bury something.' Her face fell when she said Alex's name. 'I found a metal box, and this was the only thing in there.'

'What do you think he has on here?' Caitlin wondered. 'More pictures of girls?'

'It's got to be something bad enough to bury,' Ava posited. She squeezed her eyes shut. 'I'm sure he realizes I just screwed him over. Maybe he even knows the drive is missing. If we can't bust him soon, he'll come after us.'

'You guys.'

They all looked at Julie. Her face shone blue in the light from her computer. 'This isn't Granger's flash drive.' She looked up, her eyes full of terror. 'It's *Nolan's.*'

Everyone gasped. Caitlin clamped her mouth shut, her skin prickling. She pulled into an empty parking lot. A dingy brick building housing a plumbing supply store loomed in the distance. Across the street, the bright lights of a 7-Eleven cast an eerie pallor on the pavement.

'But that's good, right?' Caitlin broke the silence, twisting around and looking at Julie. 'I mean, why would Granger have it buried in his yard? The fact that he had it will be incriminating.'

'It would have been, if we'd left it in his yard.' Julie started opening files, staring down at the screen. 'Now, as far as anyone knows, *we* have it.' She moved her finger on the trackpad. 'His e-mail is on here. The messages are current up to the day he died.'

She turned the screen so that Caitlin and Mackenzie in

the front seat could get a good look. Caitlin watched as she opened the *Sent* folder. Caitlin leaned over to see better, her eyes widening. There were dozens of e-mails to Lucas Granger.

Julie opened the first. The subject line read only *Extra Credit*.

Hey Mr. G – I think that you may have made a mistake when you graded my paper on Jean Cocteau. I'm pretty sure it should have been an A.

Then Julie clicked on an attachment. It was a still shot of Mr. Granger leaning toward Justine Williams. Ava gasped.

Then Julie opened an e-mail that said *Field Trip*. Caitlin squinted at the message.

You're a funny guy, Mr. G. Unfortunately I cannot provide all originals unless we double the amount we previously agreed on. My car got keyed again. Fixing that is expensive, you know?

'Like Nolan needed teacher-salary-level money,' Mackenzie muttered. 'The guy was loaded!'

'Let's try not to feel too sorry for Granger,' Julie snarled.

Caitlin's heart pounded. She reached for her phone in her pocket. 'I'm calling Detective Peters. This is some serious proof that Nolan was blackmailing him.'

'I *told* you,' Ava said.

'Yes, do it,' Julie ordered.

With shaking fingers, Caitlin dialed the station. It rang six times before someone picked up. 'I need to speak with Detective

Peters,' she said after the officer identified himself. 'Please,' she added.

The officer snorted. 'Peters is off duty. Do you want to leave a message?'

She blinked. Since when were detectives off duty? She thought they were like doctors, always on call. 'Is his partner there? Detective Mc . . . McGillicutty?'

'Miss, if you haven't noticed, it's ten PM. Is this urgent?'

'Well, it's really important. It's about the Nolan Hotchkiss case. I've . . . found something. Maybe I could drop it with you?'

The cop paused, almost like he was considering it. Then he said, 'You'll have to speak to Peters. I'll tell him you're coming. What's your name?'

Caitlin froze. Something about telling him her name seemed like a bad idea, but she did it anyway. The cop repeated it back to her, and then said Peters would see her at noon tomorrow. Then the line went dead.

Caitlin turned to the others, her mouth hanging open.

'Well?' Mac asked. 'Are we going?'

She shook her head, explaining what had happened. Julie's shoulders slumped.

'What should we do in the meantime?' Mackenzie asked.

They all went silent for a long moment, thinking. Then Caitlin started her car again. 'I guess we do what we have to do,' she said. 'We get through the night . . . and then we go rat this jerkwad out.'

She dropped off the girls at the parking lot where they'd left their cars. They made a plan to meet the next morning at the police station. Then Caitlin pulled away, her head humming.

241

Even though she knew she should go home and get some rest, she knew she'd be too wired to sleep. She needed to talk to someone.

And suddenly, she realized who that someone was.

* * *

Ten minutes later, she pulled up to the Fridays' curb. Most of the windows were dark, but a single one shone in the basement. Caitlin's heart thudded as she slipped out of the car. Mercifully, Josh's car wasn't in the driveway. He had texted her earlier this evening, asking if she wanted to go out with his buddies to celebrate winning the big game on Thursday – something she'd barely *thought* about since it happened. But he hadn't seemed particularly bummed when she declined. Besides, it wasn't Josh she wanted to see tonight. It was Jeremy.

Caitlin tiptoed around to the back of the house where the basement windows were and peered inside. Her heart lifted. There was Jeremy, sitting on the couch, watching Cartoon Network, looking adorable.

She tapped once on the window. His head immediately snapped up, and his face brightened when he saw it was her. He leaped to his feet and unlocked the basement door. 'What are you doing here?' he asked in a bewildered voice, his cheeks flushed.

'I – I wanted to see you,' Caitlin said, suddenly feeling embarrassed.

'I thought you were out with Josh,' Jeremy said. Then he looked at her carefully. 'You seem . . . frazzled. Is everything okay?'

Caitlin looked away. Of course she wasn't okay, but there was no way she was going to drag him into the Granger nightmare.

'I've just had a confusing and weird couple of days.'

Jeremy cocked his head. 'I thought you'd be on cloud nine. You know, after the soccer victory.'

Caitlin shut her eyes. She *should* be on cloud nine. She'd scored three goals in that game. The UDub recruiter had spoken to her personally afterward, saying there was a spot for her on the university team. Her teammates and her moms had swarmed her, giving her huge hugs, and she'd *wanted* to feel elated and victorious, like she used to when the team had a win. But she felt as if there were a hole in the part of her that used to love soccer. Or maybe everything else she was worried about – thinking about – was taking up all the available space.

'There's more to life than soccer,' she said simply, looking at Jeremy.

'Gotcha,' Jeremy said, nodding. His throat bobbed as he swallowed. 'Um, do you want to come in?'

'Yes,' Caitlin said, surprised at her forwardness. She was even more surprised when she took Jeremy's hand and let him lead her through the door. The basement smelled like popcorn, and the family's dog, Scruffy, lay on his bed in the corner. He noticed Caitlin and wagged his tail, then put his head back down.

'Hey, Scruffs,' she said.

Caitlin and Jeremy sat down on the couch together, their knees touching. Jeremy turned down the sound and stared into her eyes.

'I missed you,' Caitlin blurted.

'I've been thinking so much about you,' Jeremy said at the same time.

They both sat back and awkwardly laughed. Then Caitlin reached out and touched his smooth cheek. Jeremy shuddered. He lifted his gaze to her again and leaned forward. Their lips touched, and tingles shot up Caitlin's spine. Oh, how she wanted this, *needed* this. It immediately washed all her bad feelings away.

She wasn't sure how long they kissed, the light from the anime film flashing against their faces. Finally, Jeremy pulled back, out of breath.

He grabbed her hands. 'Caitlin,' he said softly, 'I want to be with you.'

She pressed her lips together. 'I know.'

He took a deep breath. 'But I get that it's . . . complicated.'

Caitlin bit her lip. It was obvious what he meant. It was weird, too – here she was, in Josh's house, Josh's basement, on a couch where she and Josh had made out hundreds of times. It was so familiar, and yet it was also totally . . . *new*.

'I mean, you and Josh are still together,' Jeremy said carefully. 'But you don't want to be with him, right?'

Caitlin cleared her throat. 'No,' she admitted. 'I don't think so.'

Jeremy's eyes gleamed. 'Are you ready to be with me? To, like, *really* be with me? Not to hide under bleachers. Not to sneak around in my basement. Because I'm ready to be with you.'

It was such a simple question, but it gave Caitlin pause. She thought about what would happen if she broke up with Josh. What the team would think. The parties she probably wouldn't be invited to anymore. How uncomfortable it would be next year at UDub.

But all that she could get past. It was the part about their

244

families that tripped her up. Her parents, Josh's parents – they were so *into* them being together. Would her moms be disappointed in her?

Then Jeremy leaned forward and kissed her again. Suddenly, all of Caitlin's doubts faded away. She slid her hands up his tight abs, breathing in his scent.

'Yes,' she whispered. 'Jeremy, yes. I'm ready.'

His lips moved tenderly across her neck and jawbone, and she closed her eyes, tilting her head back. That was when she saw the slice of yellow light from the door up the stairs. And that was when she saw a figure standing in the doorway, staring at them.

Caitlin shot back as Josh walked down the stairs, but it was too late. His gaze moved from Caitlin and then to his brother. His lip curled, and his nose wrinkled. His hands became tight fists.

'Josh,' Caitlin blurted worriedly, afraid Josh might punch his younger brother. 'It's not his fault.'

Josh stared at her again. 'So it's *yours?*' His nostrils flared. 'He's had a crush on you for *years*, Caitlin. I just never thought you'd fall for it.'

Then the basement door swung open wider. Caitlin turned. Josh and Jeremy's parents appeared down the stairs. Both of them were in bathrobes and socks.

'What's going on here?' Mr. Friday said sleepily. Then he noticed Caitlin. 'Caitlin?' His voice grew stern. 'I didn't realize you were over.'

'Oh, Caitlin wanted a little alone time with Jeremy.' Josh's voice was bitter. 'Isn't that right, Caitlin?'

All eyes turned to her. There were all sorts of words jammed

245

in Caitlin's throat, but she couldn't quite get them out. She felt Jeremy sitting next to her, waiting for her to tell the truth. To say, *It's right. I've chosen Jeremy.*

But somehow, even though it was true, she just couldn't do it.

Instead, she felt herself jump up from the couch and back toward the basement door. 'Um, I have to go,' she blurted, fumbling for the knob. 'I'm sorry.'

The knob turned in her hands, and she fell through the door and into the garage. Just before she shut the door, she turned back and gave everyone a final look. The fury was clear on Josh's face. Mr. and Mrs. Friday looked tired and confused. And then there was Jeremy. His mouth hung open. His eyes turned down at the corners. He looked like Caitlin had just slapped him.

But all she could do was stab the button to open the garage door. It growled to life, and she didn't even wait until it was fully up before slipping outside. No one ran after her as she sprinted to her car. Maybe because no one knew what to make of what had happened.

Or maybe because they did.

CHAPTER THIRTY-THREE

Very late that night, Parker reunited with Julie at Jaime's Big Bite, the only twenty-four-hour restaurant in Kirkland, a town twenty minutes away from Beacon Heights. On the wood-paneled walls, which dated back to the early Eighties, were faded photographs of breakfast food. According to Beacon Heights High lore, an order of Jaime's chicken and waffles with a side of maple bacon would magically soak up all the alcohol from your blood and leave you hangover-free the next morning. Back before everything bad happened, Parker and Julie used to stop there on their way home from a party, Parker stoned or drunk and Julie usually sober, since she was the one driving. They would split a massive order of fries and an Oreo shake and giggle over everything crazy that had happened that night. Looking around the restaurant, Parker saw versions of their younger selves doing that exact thing, girls with wilted hair and smudged make-up laughing at stupid drunk jokes. She felt a familiar pang in the pit of her stomach for what could have been . . . if only.

A waitress sat them under a portrait of French toast, and Julie ordered chili fries for both of them. She and Julie sat on the same side of the table, a habit they'd instituted early on, mostly a tongue-in-cheek parody of all the lovey-dovey high-school couples who couldn't bear to even spend a single meal not holding hands. Tonight, though, they held hands, too. Parker didn't know about Julie, but gripping someone else's palm kept her hand from wildly trembling.

'Thanks for getting me out of there,' Parker mumbled as the waitress placed the fries on the table mere seconds after they ordered.

'Of course,' Julie said, grabbing the ketchup bottle. 'There was no way I was risking you getting caught. I don't think you could have handled it.'

Parker nodded. 'You're probably right.'

They didn't say much else while they ate. Parker's hands continued to tremble as she swiped a cheese-and-chili-powder-covered fry in ketchup. She felt as if she hadn't eaten in days. She'd had no appetite lately, with everything going on. But maybe, finally, the nightmare was almost over.

She looked up, getting an idea. 'Next year, let's go as far away from this shithole as we can,' she suddenly blurted.

Julie blinked, then picked up another fry. 'Where do you want to go?'

Parker shrugged. 'Your Spanish is good. Let's go live in Mexico. Cabo, Cozumel, Cancún. Somewhere on a beach. I bet it's cheap.'

'What about college?'

Parker snorted. 'No one's going to take me with my grades. And besides, there's no way my mom will pay for it.'

Julie looked down at the plate. 'Yeah, I don't know how I'm

going to pay for it, either. I think I'm going to be stuck here – UDub's resident tuition isn't cheap, but if I work, I should be able to manage it.' She saw Parker's face and frowned. 'Wait, are you serious?'

'Yeah,' said Parker challengingly. 'I am.'

They looked at each other for a long moment. Parker's head gave an ominous throb. She suddenly realized that, soon, she and Julie might be apart. She'd always assumed that, no matter what, she and Julie would be together somewhere. If Julie decided to move to Seattle, what would she do? She couldn't stay here any longer. The place held too many bad memories.

Then Julie's gaze focused on a point to the right. Her cheeks paled, and her mouth fell open. 'Oh my god.'

'What?' Parker asked, looking up from the plate of fries. She followed Julie's gaze . . . and her jaw dropped, too. Elliot Fielder was standing at the to-go counter, handing the cashier his credit card. He picked up a Styrofoam box and turned to go.

Then his eyes met Parker's, and he froze. Her heart started to pound. She felt herself shrink into the booth. Then, to her horror, Elliot started walking *toward* them.

'Stay calm,' Julie whispered, grabbing her hand. 'I'm here with you.'

There was a strange expression on Elliot's face as he approached. Parker wanted to jump up and run, but she felt pinned like an insect to a tray.

Julie sat up straighter as he stopped at their table. 'What are you doing here?' she demanded. 'Did you follow us?'

Elliot didn't even look at her; he kept his gaze on Parker. Suddenly, a strange smile flashed across his face. 'You're out together.'

249

'Uh, *duh*,' Julie said defiantly. 'But I asked you a question. *Did you follow us?*'

'No.' He held up his take-out container. 'I just came to get a burger. I promise. I'm not following you.'

'Good. Then go.' Julie made a shooing motion with her hands.

But Elliot still didn't look in her direction. His gaze bored into Parker, as though waiting for her to say something. Parker stared at the table. The sight of him filled her with a hollow, wrenching feeling of despair. Not long ago, he'd made her feel like there was hope for her – that someday, with appropriate help, with work, she could even find some peace. That made his betrayal sting all the worse.

Julie shook her head, her eyes wide. 'I'm not going to let you get away with stalking Parker. You'd better lay off.'

Elliot's dark eyes seemed fathomless. 'I'm not stalking anyone,' he said calmly.

'Oh yeah?' Julie said loudly. A passing waitress gave them a questioning look. 'Then what were all those photos on your computer?'

'Parker shouldn't have found those,' Elliot said. 'Look, I was just trying to find out more about Parker's condition. I think I can help her. I might even be able to help you, Julie. If I can help one of you, I can probably help both of you.'

Julie scoffed. 'I don't think I need your help, but thanks.'

Parker could sense his eyes on her again. 'Parker, I'm sorry I didn't tell you I was watching you. But I did it for important reasons.' He reached into his pocket and pulled out a business card. 'I was just awarded a grant, and I'm moving to Arizona, but if you ever want to talk, I'm here for you.' His voice became urgent. 'Please give me a chance. You can trust me.'

His words hung in the air for a long time. Parker could sense that both Elliot and Julie were waiting for her to finally speak up. She took a deep breath, looking up and meeting Elliot's eyes.

'You know who got chance upon chance upon chance?' she whispered. 'My dad. Lesson learned.'

Elliot's face went pink. He took a step toward her, but Julie stood up and stepped between them, her eyes blazing. When she spoke, her voice was low and controlled, but there was no mistaking the fury underneath.

'Arizona or not, if we catch you following Parker again, we'll report you to the medical board. We'll tell them you seduced her. You'll lose your license. You'll lose everything.'

The therapist's expression changed, the carefully neutral mask slipping to reveal a cold and arrogant smirk. He raised an eyebrow, looking directly at Julie for the first time since he'd come to their table. 'Even if that were true, no one would believe her.'

'Then I'll say it was me.'

He and Julie stared at each other for what felt like forever. Then, slowly, Elliot smiled. 'Fine. You win. I'll never contact either of you again.'

He took a few steps toward the door, then turned back and smiled at them, this time almost gently. 'You know, I'm glad you girls have each other,' he said. 'You help each other survive.' Then he held his hand in a good-bye wave. The bells on the door jingled in his wake.

Parker stared down at the cold fries lying under a blanket of congealed cheese. 'Well,' she muttered. 'That was weird.' Then she grabbed Julie's hand. 'Thanks. For, you know. Everything.'

'No problem,' Julie said softly, hugging Parker tight. 'Thank god he's leaving.'

After that encounter, Parker felt exhausted, drained. But Elliot had been right about one thing: she really *did* need Julie. The very idea of going away from Julie, after all they'd been through together, filled her with panic. Julie was the only person who still loved her. The only person who knew her, who knew what she'd been through and still cared about her.

She looked up and realized Julie was staring at her, too. And, in that way the two of them often had, Parker had a sense Julie was thinking the exact same thing.

'I don't want to leave you,' Julie whispered.

'I know,' Parker said. 'If you want to stay here and go to school, I'll stay, too.'

'Deal,' Julie said. Then she grinned. 'But we've *got* to get our own place. Those cats are cramping our style.'

'We'll get a place up on Capitol Hill,' Parker said wistfully. 'We can decorate it ourselves.'

'I'll get a job at the university pool, and you'll get a job in the bookstore insulting customers' book choices,' Julie daydreamed.

'No one will be able to bother us. We'll be all right on our own.'

Julie took Parker's hand and squeezed it tight. 'All this crap with Nolan will be behind us forever.'

Parker smiled, all at once believing it wholeheartedly. To hell with Elliot Fielder and his bullshit attempts to help. She was with Julie, and that was all that mattered.

CHAPTER THIRTY-FOUR

After a sleepless night, Mackenzie sat up in bed and rubbed her eyes. Even though it was early, she could hear the sounds of breakfast downstairs. Swallowing hard, she threw on her slippers and padded to the kitchen. Her mom and dad were at the counter, both wearing their bathrobes. Sierra was there, too, sipping hot chocolate from a mug that had a treble clef printed on it.

'You guys are up early,' she said blearily.

Her mother jumped off her stool and hurried over to her, hugging her close. 'Well, we were *trying* to wait up for you last night – but you came home too late.'

Mac frowned. Her mom had texted asking where she was, and Mac had lied and said she was at her new friend Julie Redding's house and would be home soon. Was she in trouble? Her heart sped up. Did they somehow know that they'd broken into Granger's?

But then she looked at her dad. He was beaming brightly. Even Sierra looked kind of excited. Mac settled onto a bar stool at the counter. 'What's going on?'

'There's a message on the voice mail,' Mrs. Wright said excitedly. 'You got in!'

Mac blinked. 'In?'

'Into *Juilliard!*' Mrs. Wright leaped across the room to the cordless phone console. 'My friend Darlene called! She hears *everything* that goes on with Juilliard admissions, and . . .'

She pressed play. After a beep, a woman's voice blared through the room. 'Hey, Elise, it's Darlene! So listen, it's not official yet, but the judge was *thrilled* by Mackenzie's performance,' she said excitedly. 'Anticipate a letter in the next week! And tell your girl a big congratulations! She's following in your footsteps and going to Juilliard!'

Mac screamed. She'd done it. *She got in.* It didn't even bother her that her parents had found out first. It was the most amazing news she'd ever heard.

Her little sister inched forward, giving Mac a hug. 'You'll never believe the other news, too,' she said excitedly. 'Tell her, Mom.'

Mrs. Wright beamed. 'Well, Mrs. Coldwell called me last night. They have inside contacts as well, and it looks like Claire's getting in, too!'

Mackenzie froze. A high-pitched wail rang in her ears. 'Wait. What?'

'I know!' Her mother shook her head, marveling. 'What are the odds? But you're both going. Isn't it exciting? You can room together!'

A sour taste filled Mackenzie's mouth. All the excitement of a moment ago twisted inside her, changing shape until she didn't know how she felt. Anger, disappointment, resentment, and anxiety tainted the brief sense of triumph she'd felt. All she'd wanted to do was beat Claire, once and for all.

And now, instead of getting even, she'd be stuck with her for four more years.

'This calls for a celebration!' Her mother bustled to the fridge and pulled out a chocolate cake decorated with musical notes in delicate white icing. Her father started pouring milk into wineglasses. Only Sierra sat with a knowing expression on her face, watching Mackenzie. She'd always seemed to suspect how Mackenzie really felt about her 'best friend.'

'Well? Don't you have anything to say?' asked her mother, handing her a plate.

'Yeah, Juilliard girl, how are you feeling?' her dad said.

Sierra lifted her glass. 'Speech! Speech!'

Mackenzie stared around at her family, holding the slice of cake in her hands. The smell took her back in a sudden rush of memory to the night in Cupcake Kingdom when she and Blake had kissed. Tears burned in her eyes, but she blinked them away so no one could see.

'I've never been so happy,' she said.

Or so miserable.

CHAPTER THIRTY-FIVE

That morning, Julie carefully pulled on a dark blue dress and inspected herself in her full-length mirror. Behind her, Parker snickered. 'That's what you're wearing to the police station? You look like one of the kids in *Harry Potter*.'

Julie frowned. She had been going for *I'm-responsible-and-you-should-take-me-seriously*, but now that she thought about it, the long blue dress did look a little too Hogwarts-chic. She pulled it over her head and changed into a gray-cardigan-and-dark-wash-jeans combo instead.

'Are you sure you don't want to come?' she asked Parker as she put on her fake pearl studs. 'It might be . . . I don't know. Satisfying.'

'No thanks.' Parker shook her head emphatically. 'As long as Elliot is out there, I don't want to leave this house. Anyway, you guys don't really need me, do you? Just to give the cops Nolan's flash drive.'

'You're right,' Julie said, then nervously shook out her hands. She just wanted this *over* with. She couldn't wait till Granger was behind bars, and everything could go back to normal.

As she was selecting a pair of flats, she noticed that the e-mail bubble on her laptop was flashing. She clicked on it, thinking it might be someone asking for a ride. But then she saw the name . . . and the subject. Her heart stopped in her chest.

From: Ashley Ferguson
To: Ashley Ferguson
Bcc: Julie Redding
Subject: Julie Redding's Dirty Little Secret

In the body of the e-mail there was no text, just the link to an article, the one describing how Julie and her mom were evicted from their old house in Oakland. The one Parker had *erased*.

Well, Ashley had somehow resurrected it.

Julie leaned forward and clutched the edge of the desk until her knuckles were white, concentrating on counting. *One, two* – Ashley had BCC'd the recipients; who were they? – *three, four* – Was it the whole school? – *five, six, seven* – Or could it have just been sent to Julie herself, to remind her how much she was in Ashley's power?

'Julie?' Parker asked across the room.

Julie let out a small, wounded sob. Parker kicked off the covers and hurried over. 'What's going on?'

Julie wordlessly stepped aside from the e-mail. Parker's gaze slid over it fast. 'That *bitch*,' she snarled.

'I don't understand,' Julie said weakly. She kept counting. *Twenty-six, twenty-seven.* It wasn't helping at all. 'Why? Why would she do that?'

Parker paced around Julie's room, seeming suddenly on edge, as if the space weren't big enough to contain her. 'She is

257

everything that's wrong with the world. You can't trust anyone except your real friends.'

But Julie was only half listening. She fumbled for her phone, pressing Ashley's number, with shaking hands.

Ashley picked up on the first ring. 'Hey, dirty girl,' she sang. 'Did you like my e-mail?'

'What the *hell*, Ashley?' Julie raged. 'Who did you send it to?'

'Oh, you know. Everyone.'

Julie leaned over, sure she was going to throw up. She thought of everyone, reading that article. Seeing the picture of her. Putting it all together. *Aha!* they would think. This *is why Julie never has anyone over!* 'But, why?' she sobbed into the phone. 'I never did anything to you!'

'Exactly,' Ashley said amiably. 'You never did *anything* to me – or for me. You were happy to just sit there and let your friends make fun of me. And let's be honest – you haven't been exactly nice lately. Well, now it's your turn to feel what it's like on the outside. See you at school!' She paused. 'Oh, and say hi to your mom for me! Maybe, if you're lucky, you'll grow up to be just like her!' And with that, she hung up.

Julie stared at the phone in her hand. Tears streamed down her face. Suddenly, her laptop let out another *ping*. It was another note from Ashley. *This is what Carson thinks of you now*, read the subject line.

The only thing in the message was a photograph. Julie brought her face closer to the laptop. It was a picture of Carson . . . and *Ashley*. They were standing in front of the Rachel the Piggy Bank at the Pike Place Fish Market, and the same sun that shone outside Julie's window beamed over them. Carson had a disgusted look on his face, and he made a thumbs-down gesture with one hand. Ashley was holding his other hand. They were standing very, very close together.

Julie let out a squeak. Well, that settled that.

Parker sat next to her, squeezing her shoulder tight. Julie blinked, trying to imagine the shape the rest of the school year would take, but all she could see was a gaping black hole. Parker really *was* all she had now. No more friends. Definitely no Carson.

No *anything*.

CHAPTER THIRTY-SIX

An hour later, Ava pulled into the parking lot of the police station. She pulled down the mirror and glanced at her reflection: minimal make-up, just a touch of mascara, and clear lip gloss, her hair in a low ponytail. Her men's large Huskies T-shirt hung loose over her Lululemon yoga pants. Her skin was still crawling at the memory of the striptease she'd performed for Mr. Granger – the striptease her friends had seen, that *Alex* had probably even seen. She wanted to look nothing like she had the night before.

She grabbed her phone again and dialed Alex's number again. The phone rang and rang, then went to voice mail. A lump formed in Ava's throat. Was he sitting next to it, staring as her name flashed on the screen? 'Please let me explain,' she said after the voice mail beep. 'It wasn't what you think, okay? I *love* you.'

But all her protests sounded so weak and pathetic. What was Alex supposed to think? She hadn't even buttoned her dress when she came flying out of Granger's house. Was this the price she had to pay to prove her innocence?

Frustrated, she got out of the car and slammed the door

behind her. The sky was dull and gray, the air heavy with rain. Inside, the station was quiet, with just a few officers at their desks. There was no receptionist at the front, and no sign of Ava's friends. She pulled out her phone and sent a group text: *I'm here. Hurry!*

Tense with pent-up energy, she paced around the lobby, examining the bulletin board covered in posters of missing girls and wanted drug dealers, and ads for bondsmen and local lawyers. There was even an ad for a mental health counselor named Elliot Fielder at Beacon Heights Mental Health Outreach. When her phone beeped, she lunged for it, hoping it was Alex. But it was just an e-mail from a junior she'd seen with Julie a few times, a girl named Ashley Ferguson. *Julie Redding's Dirty Little Secret*, it read.

Curious, Ava clicked on it and read the accompanying article. Her heart lurched. Poor Julie. This explained why she was so reserved at times, so closed off. What must it be like to live like that? And no wonder Julie never wanted anyone to meet her at her house.

A few moments later, all the girls hurried in. Ava watched as Julie stumbled inside last, looking exhausted and puffy-eyed. She'd clearly seen the article, too. Ava stepped forward, wanting to say something to her – that Ashley Ferguson was a horrible bitch, maybe, and that karma would get her someday.

Instead, all she could say was, 'I don't care where you live or what your situation is. I'm glad we've become friends.'

Tears filled Julie's eyes. Her mouth wobbled. She ducked her head and stumbled forward into Ava's arms. Ava hugged her tightly, noticing Mac's and Caitlin's sympathetic glances. They must have seen the e-mail, too. Maybe the whole *school* had.

Then Julie pulled away and wiped her eyes. 'So, um, do you have it?' she asked, looking at Caitlin, who had kept the flash drive with her overnight.

Caitlin nodded and patted her canvas bag. 'I checked on it about fifty million times. It's here.'

A junior-looking officer walked past, and Ava cleared her throat. 'Um, we're here to see Detectives Peters and McMinnamin.'

The officer looked at the girls skeptically, but before he had a chance to respond, the two detectives appeared from the back of the precinct. McMinnamin led the way, clearly the senior of the two partners.

'Okay, girls,' Detective McMinnamin intoned, running a hand through his thinning blond hair. 'Follow me.'

Ava took a deep breath and snaked past a series of messy desks piled high with intake folders and cardboard coffee cups. They turned down a long hall, passed a water fountain and doors for the men's and women's bathrooms, and settled into the same interrogation room she'd been brought to earlier that week. It seemed like much longer.

Just as before, the venetian blinds were open, revealing two long mirrors. Ava glanced at them nervously. Was someone on the other side of the window watching them?

'So,' Peters began, lacing his enormous fingers together on the table. 'The officer on duty said you had information about Nolan Hotchkiss. Are you ready to share?'

The girls looked at one another. Julie nodded encouragingly. Then Caitlin pushed the flash drive across the table. Her clammy fingers left sweaty marks on the dark surface.

'It belonged to Nolan,' Julie explained in a halting voice. 'W-we found it at Lucas Granger's house. It *proves* that Nolan knew Granger was hooking up with students.'

'And that he was blackmailing Granger,' Ava jumped in. 'Asking him to give him better grades, write letters of recommendations, pay for things – you name it.'

'Granger did it,' Mackenzie said. 'He killed Nolan . . . and now he's trying to frame us.'

Peters turned to face Ava, his brown eyes unreadable. 'And how did you girls come by this flash drive. Did he just hand it over?' There was a smirk on his face.

Ava blushed. Julie shifted in her seat. Caitlin leaned in, her eyes blazing. 'Well, he tried to seduce Ava. She took it when she escaped from him.'

McMinnamin sighed and rubbed his temples. 'So you . . . *stole* it?'

Ava's mouth dropped open. 'Well, I . . .'

'And what time of night was this, ladies?' Peters asked, his brow furrowed.

Ava glanced at the others. She wasn't sure what that had to do with anything. 'Um, I don't know. Evening, I guess.'

'Eleven? Twelve?'

'Why don't you actually *look* at the content on this drive?' Julie interrupted, sliding it toward them. 'And *then* make your decision. Because I think it proves that Granger is the murderer. And it proves you should arrest him.'

'I don't doubt that Granger was doing something illicit,' McMinnamin said smugly. 'But there's no way we can arrest him.'

Ava blinked, suddenly deflating. 'What? Why?'

The detective's gaze was steady. 'Because he's dead.'

Ava gasped. *'What?'* she asked faintly.

'There was a nine-one-one call to his house last night,' Peters said. 'When the ambulances came, there were signs of a struggle.'

Blood rushed to Ava's head. This wasn't making any sense. And all at once, she understood what the detective was getting at. 'I didn't do anything to him,' she said very slowly.

'Be careful what you say next,' Peters growled. 'Because we have a witness who places you all at the crime scene at ten PM – right around the time of death.'

Ava's heart was beating so furiously she was surprised it hadn't leaped out of her chest. 'Who?' And then, suddenly, it hit her. She remembered the figure on the lawn. The look of betrayal and disgust and horror on his face. Her heart broke into a million pieces.

'Alex Cohen,' Peters said, looking at her. 'He lives on the same block, I understand? And I believe he said you were his *ex*-girlfriend?' Peters smiled grimly. 'I guess he didn't want to be dating a girl who is now under investigation for murder.'

CHAPTER THIRTY-SEVEN

Parker hurried forward to the entrance of the police station, where the other girls were stepping out into the sunshine. They all looked like shit. Julie had been texting her updates the whole time it took Parker to get here on the bus – that the cops were letting the girls go, saying there wasn't enough evidence to charge them with Granger's murder until they'd completely searched his house; that they'd taken their fingerprints and done DNA cheek swabs. They'd even taken their photographs under the harsh fluorescent lights. Parker couldn't imagine Julie took *that* very well. She and Julie exchanged a look, and then Parker ran forward to pull her best friend into a hug.

'Don't try pulling anything stupid,' Detective Peters called out from the front entrance. 'We're watching you – all of you,' he added, looking at Parker and frowning. Parker shivered. Her prints were already in the system, from what had happened with her dad. She was as much a suspect as the other girls.

Parker looked at the others after the cops left. Ava was sobbing. Caitlin clenched her jaw. Mac looked like she was going to throw up. 'My parents are going to murder me,' she whispered.

'I can't believe they called our parents,' Ava said miserably. Julie's mouth twitched, and Parker took her hand, thinking of that horrible message that had gone around just an hour ago. But really, compared with this, did Julie's secret really matter? Did *anything* matter?

Julie hung onto Parker's hand as if it were the only thing keeping her upright. 'They'll realize they made a mistake,' she said in a level voice. 'The police will realize we were framed.'

'Will they?' Ava's eyes were wild. 'We were *there*, Julie. Alex *saw* us. And our fingerprints are all over that house.' Tears streamed down her face. 'I thought this would be *over*. I thought Granger was doing this to us. So now it's someone else?'

Parker shivered. That thought had crossed her mind, too – they didn't have this solved at all. She squeezed her eyes shut and reached far into her brain, trying to put together the pieces from last night. If only she could remember someone lurking outside Granger's property. A mysterious car parked across the street. *Something*. But when she groped for the memory, there was only emptiness. All she could recall was running out of Granger's house, her heart pounding hard. And then a chasm of darkness – she was probably curled in a ball somewhere, shutting down like she always did. And then meeting Julie a little later at the diner, groggy and spotty.

'Who was watching us last night?' Parker whispered.

'And *is* Granger Nolan's killer?' Caitlin asked aloud. 'Or did Nolan's killer kill Granger, too – and make it look like us *again*?'

Ava frowned. 'But why would Nolan's killer need to kill Granger?'

Parker swallowed hard, considering this possibility. 'Maybe Granger knew something about Nolan's murder.'

'So we were looking for the wrong thing at his house all this time?' Ava asked.

'I don't know,' Parker said slowly. She looked around the group. 'But maybe everything we thought we knew isn't true at all.'

Everyone shuddered. Caitlin tipped her head up, her brow furrowing. Julie looked as if her brain had just exploded. But Parker wondered, suddenly, if it could be true. Memory was a tricky thing, but reality was even trickier. Once you made up your mind about something, it was hard to comprehend that the truth could be something else. But what if it *was*? And how could they figure that out?

And what if they were too late?

ACKNOWLEDGEMENTS

I am so pleased at how this book came together. Alfred Hitchcock says, 'Always make an audience suffer as much as possible,' and this series truly does that in the best of ways! I want to thank the brains at Alloy Entertainment for helping to put all the puzzle pieces in the correct places: Josh Bank, Les Morgenstein, Sara Shandler, Lanie Davis, and Katie McGee. Once again, for seemingly the millionth time, you guys are amazing and masterful. Many thanks to Liz Dresner for designing the perfect cover for our perfectionists.

Big thanks also to HarperCollins for green-lighting this book project and going along on our crazy ride, namely Jen Klonsky, Kari Sutherland, and Alice Jerman. Thanks also to the brilliant filmmakers of yore who inspired not only part of the premise for this story, but whose dark, twisted, devious dramas helped to create its ambiance. And a huge, huge, HUGE thank-you to Jen Graham. You are a true talent, and this book wouldn't exist without you!